BEHIND THAT CURTAIN

In San Francisco, former head of Scotland Yard Sir Frederic Bruce pursues the long-cold trail of a murderer. Sixteen years previously, a London solicitor had been killed. The only clue — the Chinese slippers he wore. At the same time there was another mystery: a series of women around the world had vanished — and all were linked to the disappearance of a woman in India, named Eve Durand. But then, at a dinner party attended by important guests, Inspector Bruce is killed — and he had been wearing a pair of Chinese slippers. Now it's left to Chan to solve the case . . .

Books by Earl Derr Biggers
Published by The House of Ulverscroft:

THE HOUSE WITHOUT A KEY
THE CHINESE PARROT
THE BLACK CAMEL

EARL DERR BIGGERS

◆

BEHIND THAT CURTAIN

Complete and Unabridged

ULVERSCROFT
Leicester

First published in
the United States of America in 1928

This Large Print Edition
published 2013

The moral right of the author has been asserted

A catalogue record for this book is available
from the British Library.

ISBN 978–1–4448–1531–3

Published by
F. A. Thorpe (Publishing)
Anstey, Leicestershire

Set by Words & Graphics Ltd.
Anstey, Leicestershire
Printed and bound in Great Britain by
T. J. International Ltd., Padstow, Cornwall

This book is printed on acid-free paper

CONTENTS

1

The Man From Scotland Yard

Bill Rankin sat motionless before his typewriter, grimly seeking a lead for the interview he was about to write. A black shadow shot past his elbow and materialized with a soft thud on his desk. Bill's heart leaped into his throat and choked him.

But it was only Egbert, the office cat. Pretty lonesome round here, seemed to be Egbert's idea. How about a bit of play? Rankin glared at the cat with deep disgust. Absurd to be so upset by a mere Egbert, but when one has been talking with a great man for over an hour and the subject of the talk has been murder, one is apt to be a trifle jumpy.

He reached out and pushed Egbert to the floor. 'Go away,' he said. 'What do you mean, scaring me out of a year's growth? Can't you see I'm busy?'

His dignity offended, Egbert stalked off through the desert of typewriter tables and empty chairs. Bill Rankin watched him disappear at last through the door leading into the hall. The hour was five-thirty; the street ten stories below was filled with home-going throngs, but up here in the city room of the *Globe* a momentary quiet reigned. Alone of all the green-shaded lamps in the room, the one above Rankin's typewriter was alight, shedding a ghastly radiance on the blank sheet of paper in his machine. Even the copy desk was deserted. In his cubby-hole at the rear sat the *Globe's* city editor, the only other human thing in sight. And he was not, if you believed the young men who worked for him, so very human at that.

Bill Rankin turned back to his interview. For a brief moment he sat wrapped in thought; then his long, capable fingers sought the keys. He wrote:

'The flights of genius and miracles of science which solve most of the crimes in detective stories have no real part in detective work. This is the verdict of Sir Frederic Bruce, former head of the Criminal Investigation Department at Scotland Yard.

'Sir Frederic, who is stopping over for two weeks in San Francisco during the course of a trip around the world, is qualified to give an expert opinion. For nearly seventeen years he acted as Deputy-Commissioner at the head of the most famous detective organization in existence, and though he has now retired, his interest in crime detection is as keen as ever. Sir Frederic is a big man, with a kindly twinkle in his grey eyes, but occasionally those eyes have a steely look that made this reporter nervous. If we had killed the old Earl of Featherstone-haugh on his rare Persian rug, we would not care to have Sir Frederic on our trail. For the great detective is that type of Scotsman who is a stranger to defeat. He would never abandon the scent.

''I read a great deal of detective fiction,' Sir Frederic said. 'It amuses me, but there is usually nothing for a detective to learn from it. Except for the fingerprint system and work in the chemical laboratory on stains, scientific research has furnished little assistance to crime detection. Murder mysteries and other difficult criminal cases are solved by intelligence, hard work and luck, with little help from the delicate scientific devices so dear to the authors of — ''

Suddenly Bill Rankin stopped writing and sat erect in his uncomfortable chair. There was a familiar ring to the ideas he was setting down on paper; he had heard them before, and recently. Opinions identical with these,

3

expressed not in the polished English of Sir Frederic, but in a quite different idiom — Ah, yes. He smiled, recalling that pudgy little man he had interviewed three days ago in the lobby of the Stewart Hotel.

The reporter rose from his chair and, lighting a cigarette, began to pace the floor. He spoke aloud: 'Of course — and I never thought of it. A corking feature story staring me right in the face, and I was blind — blind. I must be losing my grip.' He looked anxiously at the clock, tossed aside his cigarette and resumed his chair. Completing the sentence which he had interrupted midway, he continued:

'Sir Frederic was asked what he considered the greatest piece of detective work within his knowledge.

''I cannot answer that because of the important part played by chance,' he replied. 'As I have just said, most criminal cases are solved by varying proportions of hard work, intelligence and luck, and I am sorry I must add that of these three, luck is the greatest by far.

''Hard, methodical work, however, has brought results in many instances. For example, it unravelled the famous Crippen mystery. The first intimation we had of something wrong in that case came when we heard that the woman treasurer of a music-hall — ''

Bill Rankin wrote on, with lightning speed now, for he was eager to finish. The thing he was doing had suddenly become a minor matter. A far better story was running through his head. His fingers flew over the keys; when he paused, at rare intervals, it was to turn an inquiring gaze on the clock.

He ripped the final sheet of paper from his machine, snatched up the story, and hurried towards the city editor's nook. The lone man in charge of the copy desk, just returned from a bitter argument with the composing-room foreman, watched him sourly as he passed, and grimly sharpened a blue pencil.

'Wha's 'at?' inquired the city editor, as Bill Rankin threw the story down before him.

'Interview with Sir Frederic Bruce,' Bill reminded him.

'Oh, you found him, did you?'

'We all found him. The room was full of reporters.'

'Where was he?'

'He's putting up at Barry Kirk's bungalow. Kirk knew his son in London. I tried the hotels until my feet ached.'

The editor snorted. 'The more fool you.

No Englishman ever stops at a hotel if he can wangle board and room from somebody. You've been sent out to find enough lecturing British authors to know that.'

'The interview's blah,' said Rankin. 'Every paper in town will have it. But while I was writing it, an idea for a feature hit me hard. It'll be a humdinger — if I can only put it over on Sir Frederic. I thought I'd go back up there and see what I can do.'

'A feature?' The editor frowned. 'If you happen on a bit of news in the course of your literary work, you'll let me know, won't you? Here I am, trying to get out a newspaper, and all I get from you fellows is an avalanche of pretty little essays. I suspect you're all hoping that some day you'll be tapped for the *Atlantic Monthly*.'

'But this feature's good,' Rankin protested. 'I must hurry along — '

'Just a minute. I'm only your editor, of course. I don't want to pry into your plans — '

Rankin laughed. He was an able man, and privileged. 'I'm sorry, sir, but I can't stop to explain now. Someone may beat me to it yet. Gleason of the *Herald* was up there to-day, and he'll get the same hunch as sure as fate. So if you don't mind — '

The editor shrugged. 'All right — go to it.

Hurry up to the Kirk Building. And don't let this sudden attack of energy die there. Hurry back, too.'

'Yes, sir,' agreed the reporter. 'Of course, I'll need a bit of dinner — '

'*I* never eat,' growled his charming employer.

Bill Rankin sped across the city room. His fellow reporters were drifting in now from their afternoon assignments, and the place was coming to life. Near the door, Egbert, black as the night from pole to pole, crossed Rankin's path with haughty, aloof manner and dignified stride.

Descending to the street, the reporter stood for a moment undecided. The Kirk Building was not far away; he could walk there — but time was precious. Suppose he arrived to be met by the news that Sir Frederic was dressing for dinner. With this famous and correct Englishman, the act would be a sacred rite not to be lightly interrupted by panting pressmen. No, he must reach Sir Frederic before the detective reached for his black pearl studs. He hailed a passing taxi.

As the car drew up to the kerb, a red-cheeked boy, one of the *Globe's* younger reporters, emerged from the crowd and with a deep bow, held open the taxi door.

'To the Royal Opera, my good man,' he

shouted, 'and a nice crisp note for you if we pass the Duke's car on the way.'

Rankin pushed the facetious one aside. 'Don't interfere with your betters, my lad,' he remarked, and added, to the driver: 'The Kirk Building, on California Street.'

The taxi swung out into Market Street, followed the intricate car tracks for a few blocks, and turned off into Montgomery. In another moment they were in the financial district of San Francisco, now wrapped in its accustomed evening calm. The huge buildings of trust companies, investment houses and banks stood solemn and solid in the dusk; across the doorways of many, forbidding bronze gates were already shut. Gilded signs met Rankin's eye — 'The Yokohama Bank'; on another window, 'The Shanghai Trading Company'; one may not forget the Orient in the city by the Gate. Presently the taxi drew up before a twenty-story office building, and Rankin alighted.

The Kirk Building was architecturally perfect, in the excellent taste that had marked the family ever since the first Dawson Kirk had made his millions and gone his way. Now it was the particular hobby of young Barry Kirk, who lived in bachelor splendour in the spacious but breezy bungalow on its roof. Its pure white lobby was immaculate; its elevator girls trim and pretty in neat uniforms; its elevator starter resplendent as an Admiral of the Fleet. At this hour the fever of the day was ended and cleaning women knelt reverently on the marble floor. One elevator was still running, and into this Bill Rankin stepped.

'All the way,' he said to the girl.

He alighted at the twentieth floor, the final stop. A narrow stair led to Barry Kirk's bungalow, and the reporter ascended two steps at a time. Pausing before an imposing door, he rang. The door opened and Paradise, Kirk's English butler, stood like a bishop barring Rankin's path.

'Ah — er — I'm back,' panted Rankin.

'So I see, sir.' Very like a bishop indeed, with that great shock of snow-white hair. His manner was not cordial. Earlier that day he had admitted many reporters, but with misgivings.

'I must see Sir Frederic at once. Is he in?'

'Sir Frederic is in the offices, on the floor below. I fancy he is busy, but I will announce you — '

'No — please don't trouble,' said Rankin quickly. Running down to the twentieth floor, he noted a door with Barry Kirk's name on the frosted glass. As he moved towards it, it opened suddenly, and a young woman came out.

Rankin stopped in his tracks. A remarkably

pretty young woman — that much was obvious even in the dim light on the twentieth floor. One of those greatly preferred blondes, with a slender figure trim in a green dress of some knitted material. Not precisely tall, but —

What was this? The young woman was weeping. Silently, without fuss, but indubitably weeping. Tears not alone of grief, but, if Rankin was any judge, of anger and exasperation, too. With a startled glance at the reporter, she hastily crossed the hall and disappeared through a door that bore the sign 'Calcutta Importers, Inc.'

Bill Rankin pushed on into Barry Kirk's office. He entered a sort of reception-room, but a door beyond stood open, and the newspaper man went confidently forward. In the second room, Sir Frederic Bruce, former head of the C.I.D., sat at a big, flat-topped desk. He swung around, and his grey eyes were stern and dangerous.

'Oh,' he said. 'It's you.'

'I must apologize for intruding on you again, Sir Frederic,' Bill Rankin began. 'But — I — er — may I sit down?'

'Certainly.' The great detective slowly gathered up some papers on the desk.

'The fact is — ' Rankin's confidence was ebbing. An inner voice told him that this was not the genial gentleman of the afternoon interview in the bungalow upstairs. Not the gracious visitor to San Francisco, but Sir Frederic Bruce of Scotland Yard, unbending, cold and awe-inspiring. 'The fact is,' continued the reporter lamely, 'an idea has struck me.'

'Really?' Those eyes — they looked right through you.

'What you told us this afternoon, Sir Frederic — Your opinion of the value of scientific devices in the detection of crime, as against luck and hard work — ' Rankin paused. He seemed unable to finish his sentences. 'I was reminded, when I came to write my story, that oddly enough I had heard that same opinion only a few days ago.'

'Yes? Well, I made no claim to originality.' Sir Frederic threw his papers into a drawer.

'Oh, I haven't come to complain about it,' smiled Rankin, regaining a trace of his jaunty spirit. 'Under ordinary conditions, it wouldn't mean anything, but I heard your ideas from the lips of a rather unusual man, Sir Frederic. A humble worker in your own field, a detective who has evolved his theories far from Scotland Yard. I heard them from Detective-Sergeant Charlie Chan, of the Honolulu police.'

Sir Frederic's bushy eyebrows rose. 'Really?

Then I must applaud the judgment of Sergeant Chan — whoever he may be.'

'Chan is a detective who has done some good work in the Islands. He happens to be in San Francisco at the moment, on his way home. Came to the mainland on a simple errand, which developed into quite a case before he had finished with it. I believe he acquitted himself with credit. He's not very impressive to look at, but — '

Sir Frederic interrupted. 'A Chinese, I take it?'

'Yes, sir.'

The great man nodded. 'And why not? A Chinese should make an excellent detective. The patience of the East, you know.'

'Precisely,' agreed Bill Rankin. 'He's got that. And modesty — '

Sir Frederic shook his head. 'Not such a valuable asset, modesty. Self-assurance, a deep faith in one's self — they help. But Sergeant Chan is modest?'

'Is he? 'Falling hurts least those who fly low' — that's the way he put it to me. And Sergeant Chan flies so low he skims the daisies.'

Sir Frederic rose and stepped to the window. He gazed down at the spatter of lights flung like a handful of stars over the darkening town. For a moment he said nothing. Then he turned to the reporter.

'A modest detective,' he said, with a grim smile. 'That's a novelty at any rate. I should like very much to meet this Sergeant Chan.'

Bill Rankin sighed with relief. His task was unbelievably easy, after all.

'That's exactly what I came here to suggest,' he said briskly. 'I'd like to bring you and Charlie Chan together — hear you go over your methods and experiences — you know, just a real good talk. I was wondering if you would do us the great honour to join Mr. Chan and me at lunch tomorrow?'

The former head of the C.I.D. hesitated. 'Thank you very much. But I am more or less in Mr. Kirk's hands. He is giving a dinner to-morrow night, and I believe he said something about luncheon to-morrow, too. Much as I should like to accept at once, decidedly we must consult Mr. Kirk.'

'Well, let's find him. Where is he?' Bill Rankin was all business.

'I fancy he is up in the bungalow.' Sir Frederic turned and, swinging shut the door of a big wall safe, swiftly twirled the knob.

'You did that just like an American business man, Sir Frederic,' Rankin smiled.

The detective nodded. 'Mr. Kirk has kindly allowed me to use his office while I am his guest.'

'Ah — then you're not altogether on a pleasure trip,' said Bill Rankin quickly.

The grey eyes hardened. 'Absolutely — a pleasure trip. But there are certain matters — private business — I am writing my *Memoirs* — '

'Ah, yes — of course,' apologized the reporter.

The door opened, and a cleaning woman entered. Sir Frederic turned to her. 'Good evening,' he said. 'You understand that no papers on this desk — or in it — are to be interfered with in any way?'

'Oh, yes, sir,' the woman answered.

'Very good. Now, Mr. — er — Mr. — '

'Rankin, Sir Frederic.'

'Of course. There are stairs in this rear room leading up to the bungalow. If you will come with me — '

They entered the third and last room of the office suite, and Bill Rankin followed the huge figure of the Englishman aloft. The stairs ended in a dark passage-way on the floor above. Throwing open the nearest door, Sir Frederic flooded the place with light, and Bill Rankin stepped into the great living-room of the bungalow. Paradise was alone in the room; he received the reporter with cold disdain. Barry Kirk, it appeared, was dressing for dinner, and the butler went reluctantly to

14

inform him of the newspaper man's unseemly presence.

Kirk appeared at once, in his shirt-sleeves and with the ends of a white tie dangling about his neck. He was a handsome, lean young man in the late twenties, whose manner spoke of sophistication, and spoke true. For he had travelled to the far corners of the earth seeking to discover what the Kirk fortune would purchase there, and life held no surprises for him any more.

'Ah, yes — Mr. Rankin of the *Globe*,' he said pleasantly. 'What can I do for you?'

Paradise hastened forward to officiate with the tie, and over the servant's shoulder Bill Rankin explained his mission. Kirk nodded.

'A bully idea,' he remarked. 'I have a lot of friends in Honolulu, and I've heard about Charlie Chan. I'd like to meet him myself.'

'Very happy to have you join us,' said the reporter.

'Can't be done. You must join me.'

'But — the suggestion of the lunch was mine — ' began Rankin uncomfortably.

Kirk waved a hand in the airy manner of the rich in such a situation. 'My dear fellow — I've already arranged a luncheon for to-morrow. Some chap in the district attorney's office wrote me a letter. He's interested in criminology and wants to meet

15

Sir Frederic. As I explained to Sir Frederic, I couldn't very well ignore it. We never know when we'll need a friend in the district attorney's office these days.'

'One of the deputies?' inquired Rankin.

'Yes, A fellow named Morrow — J. V. Morrow. Perhaps you know him?'

Rankin nodded. 'I do,' he said.

'Well, that's the scenario,' went on Kirk. 'We're to meet this lad at the St. Francis to-morrow at one. The topic of the day will be murder, and I'm sure your friend from Honolulu will fit in admirably. You must pick up Mr. Chan and join us.'

'Thank you very much,' said Rankin. 'You're extremely kind. We'll be there. I — I won't keep you any longer.'

Paradise came forward with alacrity to let him out. At the foot of the stairs on the twentieth floor he met his old rival, Gleason of the *Herald*. He chuckled with delight.

'Turn right around,' he said. 'You're too late. I thought of it first.'

'Thought of what?' asked Gleason, with assumed innocence.

'I'm getting Sir Frederic and Charlie Chan together, and the idea's copyrighted. Lay off.'

Gloomily Mr. Gleason turned about, and accompanied Bill Rankin to the elevators. As they waited for the car, the girl in the green dress emerged from the office of the Calcutta Importers and joined them. They rode down together. The girl's tears had vanished, and had happily left no trace. Blue eyes — that completed the picture. A charming picture. Mr. Gleason was also showing signs of interest.

In the street Gleason spoke. 'I never thought of it until dinner,' he said sourly.

'With me, my career comes first,' Rankin responded. 'Did you finish your dinner?'

'I did, worse luck. Well, I hope you get a whale of a story — a knock-out, a classic.'

'Thanks, old man.'

'And I hope you can't print one damn word of it.'

Rankin did not reply as his friend hurried off into the dusk. He was watching the girl in the green dress disappear up California Street. Why had she left the presence of Sir Frederick Bruce to weep outside that office door? What had Sir Frederic said to her? Might ask Sir Frederic about it tomorrow. He laughed mirthlessly. He saw himself — or any other man — prying into the private affairs of Sir Frederic Bruce.

2

What Happened to Eve Durand?

The next day at one, Sir Frederic Bruce stood in the lobby of the St. Francis, a commanding figure in a grey tweed suit. By his side, as immaculate as his guest, stood Barry Kirk, looking out on the busy scene with the amused tolerance befitting a young man of vast leisure and not a care in the world. Kirk hung his stick on his arm, and took a letter from his pocket.

'By the way, I had this note from J. V. Morrow in the morning's mail,' he said. 'Thanks me very politely for my invitation, and says that I'll know him when he shows up because he'll be wearing a green hat. One of those green plush hats, I suppose. Hardly the sort of thing I'd put on my head if I were a deputy district attorney.'

Sir Frederic did not reply. He was watching Bill Rankin approach rapidly across the floor. At the reporter's side walked, surprisingly light of step, an unimpressive little man with a bulging waistband and a very earnest expression on his chubby face.

18

'Here we are,' Rankin said. 'Sir Frederic Bruce — may I present Detective-Sergeant Chan, of the Honolulu police?'

Charlie Chan bent quickly like a jack-knife. 'The honour,' he said, 'is unbelievably immense. In Sir Frederic's reflected glory I am happy to bask. The tiger has condescended to the fly.'

Somewhat at a loss, the Englishman caressed his moustache and smiled down on the detective from Hawaii. As a keen judge of men, already he saw something in those black restless eyes that held his attention.

'I'm happy to know you, Sergeant Chan,' he said. 'It seems we think alike on certain important points. We should get on well together.'

Rankin introduced Chan to the host, who greeted the little Chinese with obvious approval. 'Good of you to come,' he said.

'A four-horse chariot could not have dragged me in an opposite direction,' Chan assured him.

Kirk looked at his watch. 'All here but J. V. Morrow,' he remarked. 'He wrote me this morning that he's coming in at the Post Street entrance. If you'll excuse me, I'll have a look around.'

He strolled down the corridor towards Post Street. Near the door, on a velvet davenport, sat a strikingly attractive young woman. No other seat was available, and with an interested glance at the girl Kirk also dropped down on the davenport. 'If you don't mind — ' he murmured.

'Not at all,' she replied, in a voice that somehow suited her.

They sat in silence. Presently Kirk was aware that she was looking at him. He glanced up, to meet her smile.

'People are always late,' he ventured.

'Aren't they?'

'No reason for it, usually. Just too inefficient to make the grade. Nothing annoys me more.'

'I feel the same way,' the girl nodded.

Another silence. The girl was still smiling at him.

'Go out of your way to invite somebody you don't know to lunch,' Kirk continued, 'and he isn't even courteous enough to arrive on time.'

'Abominable,' she agreed. 'You have all my sympathy — Mr. Kirk.'

He started. 'Oh — you know me?'

She nodded. 'Somebody once pointed you out to me — at a charity bazaar,' she explained.

'Well,' he sighed, 'their charity didn't extend to me. Nobody pointed you out.' He looked at his watch.

'This person you're expecting — ' began the girl.

'A lawyer,' he answered. 'I hate all lawyers. They're always telling you something you'd rather not know.'

'Yes — aren't they?'

'Messing around with other people's troubles. What a life.'

'Frightful.' Another silence. 'You say you don't know this lawyer?' A rather unkempt young man came in and hurried past. 'How do you expect to recognize him?'

'He wrote me he'd be wearing a green hat. Imagine! Why not a rose behind his ear?'

'A green hat.' The girl's smile grew even brighter. Charming, thought Kirk. Suddenly he stared at her in amazement. 'Good lord — you're wearing a green hat!' he cried.

'I'm afraid I am.'

'Don't tell me — '

'Yes — it's true. I'm the lawyer. And you hate all lawyers. What a pity.'

'But I didn't dream — '

'J. V. Morrow,' she went on. 'The first name is June.'

'And I thought it was Jim,' he cried. 'Please forgive me.'

'You'd never have invited me if you'd known — would you?'

'On the contrary — I wouldn't have invited

21

anybody else. But come along. There are a lot of murder experts in the lobby dying to meet you.'

They rose, and walked rapidly down the corridor. 'You're interested in murder?' Kirk inquired.

'Among other things,' she smiled.

'Must take it up myself,' Kirk murmured.

Men turned to look at her a second time, he noticed. There was an alertness in her dark eyes that resembled the look in Chan's, her manner was brisk and businesslike, but for all that she was feminine, alluring.

He introduced her to the surprised Sir Frederic, then to Charlie Chan. The expression on the face of the little Chinese did not alter. He bowed low.

'The moment has charm,' he remarked.

Kirk turned to Rankin. 'And all the time,' he accused, 'you knew who J. V. Morrow was.'

The reporter shrugged. 'I thought I'd let you find it out for yourself. Life holds so few pleasant surprises.'

'It never held a pleasanter one for me,' Kirk answered. They went in to the table he had engaged, which stood in a secluded corner.

When they were seated, the girl turned to her host. 'This was so good of you. And of Sir Frederic, too. I know how busy he must be.'

The Englishman bowed. 'A fortunate

moment for me,' he smiled, 'when I decided I was not too busy to meet J. V. Morrow. I had heard that in the States young women were emancipated — '

'Of course, you don't approve,' she said.

'Oh — but I do,' he murmured.

'And Mr. Chan. I'm sure Mr. Chan disapproves of me.'

Chan regarded her blankly. 'Does the elephant disapprove of the butterfly? And who cares?'

'No answer at all,' smiled the girl. 'You are returning to Honolulu soon, Mr. Chan?'

A delighted expression appeared on the blank face. 'Tomorrow at noon the *Maui* receives my humble person. We churn over to Hawaii together.'

'I see you are eager to go,' said the girl.

'The brightest eyes are sometimes blind,' replied Chan. 'Not true in your case. It is now three weeks since I arrived on the mainland, thinking to taste the joys of holiday. Before I am aware events engulf me, and like the postman who has day of rest I foolishly set out on long, tiresome walk. Happy to say that walk are ended now. With beating heart I turn towards little home on Punchbowl Hill.'

'I know how you feel,' said Miss Morrow.

'Humbly begging pardon to mention it, you do not. I have hesitation in adding to your ear that one thing calls me home with unbearable force. I am soon to be happy father.'

'For the first time?' asked Barry Kirk.

'The eleventh occasion of the kind,' Chan answered.

'Must be sort of an old story by now,' Bill Rankin suggested.

'That is one story which does not get aged,' Chan replied. 'You will learn. But my trivial affairs have no place here. We are met to honour a distinguished guest.' He looked towards Sir Frederic.

Bill Rankin thought of his coming story. 'I was moved to get you two together,' he said, 'because I found you think alike. Sir Frederic is also scornful of science as an aid to crime detection.'

'I have formed that view from my experience,' remarked Sir Frederic.

'A great pleasure,' Chan beamed, 'to hear that huge mind like Sir Frederic's moves in same groove as my poor head-piece. Intricate mechanics good in books, in real life not so much so. My experience tell me to think deep about human people. Human passions. Back of murder what, always? Hate, greed, revenge, need to make silent the slain one. Study human people at all times.'

'Precisely,' agreed Sir Frederic. 'The

human element — that is what counts. I have had no luck with scientific devices. Take the dictaphone — it has been a complete washout at the Yard.' He talked on, while the luncheon progressed. Finally, he turned to Chan. 'And what have your methods gained you, Sergeant? You have been successful, I hear.'

Chan shrugged. 'Luck — always happy luck.'

'You're too modest,' said Rankin. 'That won't get you anywhere.'

'The question now arises — where do I want to go?'

'But surely you're ambitious?' Miss Morrow suggested.

Chan turned to her gravely. 'Coarse food to eat, water to drink, and the bended arm for a pillow — that is an old definition of happiness in my country. What is ambition? A canker that eats at the heart of the white man, denying him the joys of contentment. Is it also attacking the heart of white woman? I hope not,' The girl looked away. 'I fear I am victim of crude philosophy from Orient. Man — what is he? Merely one link in a great chain binding the past with the future. All times I remember I am link. Unsignificant link joining those ancestors whose bones repose on far distant hillsides with the ten children — it may now be eleven — my house on Punchbowl Hill.'

'A comforting creed,' Barry Kirk commented.

'So, waiting the end, I do my duty as it rises. I tread the path that opens.' He turned to Sir Frederic. 'On one point, from my reading, I am curious. In your work at Scotland Yard, you follow only one clue. What you call the essential clue.'

Sir Frederic nodded. 'Such is usually our custom. When we fail, our critics ascribe it to that. They say, for example, that our obsession over the essential clue is the reason why we never solved the famous Ely Place murder.'

They all sat up with interest. Bill Rankin beamed. Now things were getting somewhere. 'I'm afraid we never heard of the Ely Place murder, Sir Frederic,' he hinted.

'I sincerely wish I never had,' the Englishman replied. 'It was the first serious case that came to me when I took charge of the C.I.D. over sixteen years ago. I am chagrined to say I have never been able to fathom it.'

He finished his salad, and pushed away the plate. 'Since I have gone so far, I perceive I must go farther. Hilary Galt was the senior partner in the firm of Pennock and Galt, solicitors, with offices in Ely Place, Holborn. The business this firm carried on for more than a generation was unique of its kind.

Troubled people in the highest ranks of society went to them for shrewd professional advice and Mr. Hilary Galt and his father-in-law, Pennock, who died some twenty years ago, were entrusted with more numerous and romantic secrets than any other firm of solicitors in London. They knew the hidden history of every rascal in Europe, and they rescued many persons from the clutches of blackmailers. It was their boast that they never kept records of any sort.'

Dessert was brought, and after this interruption, Sir Frederic continued.

'One foggy January night sixteen years ago, a caretaker entered Mr. Hilary Galt's private office, presumably deserted for the day. The gas lights were ablaze, the windows shut and locked; there was no sign of any disturbance. But on the floor lay Hilary Galt, with a bullet in his brain.

'There was just one clue, and over that we puzzled for many weary months at the Yard. Hilary Galt was a meticulous dresser, his attire was perfect, always. It was perfect on this occasion — with one striking exception. His highly polished boots — I presume you call them shoes over here — were removed and standing on a pile of papers on top of his desk. And on his feet he wore a pair of velvet slippers, embellished with a curious design.

'These, of course, seemed to the Yard the essential clue, and we set to work. We traced those slippers to the Chinese Legation in Portland Place. Mr. Galt had been of some trifling service to the Chinese minister, and early on the day of his murder the slippers had arrived as a gift from that gentleman. Galt had shown them to his office staff, and they were last seen wrapped loosely in their covering near his hat and stick. That was as far as we got.

'For sixteen years I have puzzled over those slippers. Why did Mr. Hilary Galt remove his boots, don the slippers, and prepare himself as though for some extraordinary adventure? I don't know to this day. The slippers still haunt me. When I resigned from the Yard, I rescued them from the Black Museum and took them with me as a souvenir of my first case — an unhappy souvenir of failure. I should like to show them to you, Miss Morrow.'

'Thrilling,' said the girl.

'Annoying,' corrected Sir Frederic grimly.

Bill Rankin looked at Charlie Chan. 'What's your reaction to that case, Sergeant?' he inquired.

Chan's eyes narrowed in thought. 'Humbly begging pardon to inquire,' he said, 'have you the custom, Sir Frederic, to put yourself in place of murderer?'

'It's a good idea,' the Englishman answered, 'if you can do it. You mean — '

'A man who has killed — a very clever man — he knows that Scotland Yard has fiercely fixed idea about essential clue. His wits accompany him. He furnishes gladly one essential clue which has no meaning and leads no place at all.'

Sir Frederic regarded him keenly. 'Excellent,' he remarked. 'And it has one great virtue — from your point of view. It completely exonerates your countrymen at the Chinese Legation.'

'It might do more than that,' suggested Barry Kirk.

Sir Frederic thoughtfully ate his dessert. No one spoke for some moments. But Bill Rankin was eager for more material.

'A very interesting case, Sir Frederic,' he remarked.

'You must have a lot like it up your sleeve. Murders that ended more successfully for Scotland Yard — '

'Hundreds,' nodded the detective. 'But none that still holds its interest for me like the crime in Ely Place. As a matter of fact, I have never found murder so fascinating as some other things. The murder case came and went and, with a rare exception such as this I have mentioned, was quickly forgotten. But there is one mystery that to me has always been the most exciting in the world.'

'And what is that?' asked Rankin, while they waited with deep interest.

'The mystery of the missing,' Sir Frederic replied. 'The man or woman who steps quietly out of the picture and is never seen again. Hilary Galt, dead in his office, presents a puzzle, of course; still, there is something to get hold of, something tangible, a body on the floor. But if Hilary Galt had disappeared into the fog that gloomy night, leaving no trace — that would have been another story.

'For years I have been enthralled by the stories of the missing,' the detective went on. 'Even when they were outside my province, I followed many of them. Often the solution was simple, or sordid, but that could never detract from the thrill of the ones that remained unsolved. And of all those unsolved cases, there is one that I have never ceased to think about. Sometimes in the night I wake up and ask myself — what happened to Eve Durand?'

'Eve Durand,' repeated Rankin eagerly.

'That was her name. As a matter of fact, I had nothing to do with the case. It happened outside my bailiwick — very far outside. But I followed it with intense interest from the first.

There are others, too, who have never forgotten — just before I left England I clipped from a British weekly paper a brief reference to the matter — I have it here.' He removed a bit of paper from his purse. 'Miss Morrow — will you be kind enough to read this aloud?'

The girl took the clipping. She began to read, in a low, clear voice:

★　★　★

'A gay crowd of Anglo-Indians gathered one night fifteen years ago on a hill outside Peshawar to watch the moon rise over that isolated frontier town. Among the company were Captain Eric Durand and his wife, just out 'from home.' Eve Durand was young, pretty and wellborn — a Miss Mannering, of Devonshire. Someone proposed a game of hide-and-seek before the ride back to Peshawar. The game was never finished. They are still looking for Eve Durand. Eventually all India was enlisted in the game. Jungle and bazaar, walled city and teak forest, were fine-combed for her. Through all the subterranean channels of that no-white-man's land of native life the search was carried by the famous secret service. After five years her husband retired to a life of seclusion in England, and Eve Durand

31

became a legend — a horror tale to be told by ayahs to naughty children, along with the ghost stories of that north country.'

★   ★   ★

The girl ceased reading, and looked at Sir Frederic, wide-eyed. There followed a moment of tense silence.

Bill Rankin broke the spell. 'Some little game of hide-and-seek,' he said.

'Can you wonder,' asked Sir Frederic, 'that for fifteen years the disappearance of Eve Durand, like Hilary Galt's slippers, has haunted me? A notably beautiful woman — a child, really — she was but eighteen that mysterious night at Peshawar. A blonde, blue-eyed, help-less child, lost in the dark of those dangerous hills. Where did she go? What became of her? Was she murdered? What happened to Eve Durand?'

'I'd rather like to know myself,' remarked Barry Kirk softly.

'All India, as the clipping says, was enlisted in the game. By telegraph and by messenger, inquiries went forward. Her heart-broken, frantic husband was given leave, and at the risk of his life he scoured that wild country. The secret service did its utmost. Nothing happened. No word ever came back to Peshawar.

32

'It was like looking for a needle in a haystack, and in time, for most people, the game lost its thrill. The hue and cry died down. All save a few forgot.

'When I retired from the Yard and set out on this trip around the world, India was of course on my itinerary. Though it was far off my track, I resolved to visit Peshawar. I went down to Ripple Court in Devonshire and had a chat with Sir George Mannering, the uncle of Eve Durand. Poor man, he is old before his time. He gave me what information he could — it was pitifully meagre. I promised I would try to take up the threads of this old mystery when I reached India.'

'And you did?' Rankin inquired.

'I tried — but, my dear fellow, have you ever seen Peshawar? When I reached there the hopelessness of my quest struck me, as Mr. Chan might say, with an unbearable force. The Paris of the Pathans, they call it, and its filthy alleys teem with every race in the East. It isn't a city, it's a caravanserai, and its population is constantly shifting. The English garrison is changed frequently, and I could find scarcely anyone who was there in the time of Eve Durand.

'As I say, Peshawar appalled me. Anything could happen there. A wicked town — its sins are the sins of opium and hemp and jealousy

33

and intrigue, of battle, murder and sudden death, of gambling and strange intoxications, the lust of revenge. Who can explain the devilry that gets into men's blood in certain latitudes? I walked the Street of the Story Tellers and wondered in vain over the story of Eve Durand. What a place to bring a woman like that, delicately reared, young, inexperienced.'

'You learned nothing?' inquired Barry Kirk.

'What could you expect?' Sir Frederic dropped a small lump of sugar into his coffee. 'Fifteen years since that little picnic party rode back to Peshawar, back to the compound of the lonely garrison, leading behind them the riderless pony of Eve Durand. And fifteen years, I may tell you, make a very heavy curtain on India's frontier.'

Again Bill Rankin turned to Charlie Chan. 'What do you say, Sergeant?' he asked.

Chan considered. 'The town named Peshawar stands with great proximity to the Khyber Pass, leading into wilds of Afghanistan,' he said.

Sir Frederic nodded. 'It does. But every foot of the pass is guarded night and day by British troops, and no European is permitted to leave by that route, save under very special conditions. No, Eve Durand could never have left India by way of the Khyber Pass. The thing would have been impossible. Grant the impossible, and she could not have lived a day among the wild hillmen over the border.'

Chan gravely regarded the man from Scotland Yard. 'It is not to be amazed at,' he said, 'that you have felt such deep interest. Speaking humbly for myself, I desire with unlimited yearning to look behind that curtain of which you speak.'

'That is the curse of our business, Sergeant,' Sir Frederic replied. 'No matter what our record of successes, there must always remain those curtains behind which we long with unlimited yearning to look — and never do.'

Barry Kirk paid the check, and they rose from the table. In the lobby, during the course of the good-byes, the party broke up momentarily into two groups. Rankin, Kirk and the girl went to the door, and after a hurried expression of thanks, the reporter dashed out to the street.

'Mr. Kirk — it was wonderful,' Miss Morrow said. 'Why are all Englishmen so fascinating? Tell me that.'

'Oh — are they?' He shrugged. 'You tell me. You girls always fall for them, I notice.'

'Well — they have an air about them. An atmosphere. They're not provincial, like a Rotarian who wants to tell you about the water-works. He took us travelling, didn't he? London and Peshawar — I could listen to him for hours. Sorry I have to run.'

'Wait. You can do something for me.'

'After what you've done for me,' she smiled, 'anything you ask.'

'Good. This Chinese — Chan — he strikes me as a gentleman, and a mighty interesting one. I believe he would go big at my dinner to-night. I'd like to ask him, but that would throw my table out of gear. I need another woman. How about it? Will old man Blackstone let you off for the evening?'

'He might.'

'Just a small party — my grandmother, and some people Sir Frederic has asked me to invite. And since you find Englishmen so fascinating, there'll be Colonel John Beetham, the famous Asiatic explorer. He's going to show us some movies he took in Tibet — which is the first intimation I've had that anything ever moved in Tibet.'

'That will be splendid. I've seen Colonel Beetham's picture in the papers.'

'I know — the women are all crazy about him, too. Even poor grandmother — she's thinking of putting up money for his next expedition to the Gobi Desert. You'll come then? Seven-thirty.'

'I'd love to — but it does seem

36

presumptuous. After what you said about lawyers — '

'Yes — that was careless of me. I'll have to live it down. Give me a chance. My bungalow — you know where it is — '

She laughed. 'Thanks. I'll come. Good-bye — until to-night.'

Meanwhile, Sir Frederic Bruce had led Charlie Chan to a sofa in the lobby. 'I was eager to meet you, Sergeant,' he said, 'for many reasons. Tell me, are you familiar with San Francisco's Chinatown?'

'I have slight acquaintance with same,' Chan admitted. 'My cousin, Chan Kee Lim, is an honoured resident of Waverly Place.'

'Have you, by any chance, heard of a Chinese down there — a stranger, a tourist — named Li Gung?'

'No doubt there are many so named. I do not know the one you bring up.'

'This man is a guest of relatives on Jackson Street. You could do me a great service, Sergeant.'

'It would remain,' said Chan, 'a golden item on the scroll of memory.'

'Li Gung has certain information and I want it. I have tried to interview him myself, but naturally with no success.'

'Light begins to dawn.'

'If you could strike up an acquaintance

with him — get into his confidence — '

'Humbly asking pardon, I do not spy on my own race with no good reason.'

'The reasons in this case are excellent.'

'Only a fool could doubt it. But what you hint would demand a considerable interval of time. My humble affairs have rightly no interest for you, so you have properly overlooked my situation. To-morrow at noon I hasten to my home.'

'You could stay over a week. I would make it greatly worth your while.'

A stubborn look came into the little eyes. 'One path only is worth my while now. The path to my home on Punchbowl Hill.'

'I mean I would pay — '

'Again asking pardon — I have food, I have clothes which cover even the vast area I possess. Beyond that, what is money?'

'Very good. It was only a suggestion.'

'I am desolated by acute pain,' replied Chan. 'But I must refuse.'

Barry Kirk joined them. 'Mr. Chan, I'm going to ask you to do something for me,' he began.

Chan sought to keep concern from his face, and succeeded. But what next, he wondered. 'I am eagerly at attention,' he said. 'You are my host.'

'I've just invited Miss Morrow to dinner

38

to-night, and I need another man. Will you come?'

'Your requests are high honours, which only an ungrate would refuse. But I am now already in your debt. More is going to embarrass me.'

'Never mind that. I'll expect you at seven-thirty — my bungalow on the Kirk Building.'

'Splendid,' said Sir Frederic. 'We'll have another talk, then, Sergeant. My requests are not precisely honours, but I may yet persuade you.'

'Chinese funny people,' remarked Chan. 'They say no, no is what they mean. They say yes, and they are glued to same. With regard to dinner, I say yes, greatly pleased.'

'Good,' said Barry Kirk.

'Where's that reporter?' Sir Frederic asked.

'He hurried away,' Kirk explained. 'Anxious to get to his story, I imagine.'

'What story?' asked the Englishman blankly.

'Why — the story of our luncheon. Your meeting with Sergeant Chan.'

A startled expression crossed the detective's face. 'Good lord — you don't mean he's going to put that into print?'

'Why naturally. I supposed you knew — '

'I'm afraid I'm woefully ignorant of American customs. I thought that was merely a social function. I didn't dream — '

'You mean you don't want him to print it?' asked Barry Kirk, surprised.

Sir Frederic turned quickly to Charlie. 'Good-bye, Sergeant. This has been a real pleasure. I shall see you to-night — '

He hastily shook hands with Chan, and dragged the dazed Barry Kirk to the street. There he motioned for a taxi. 'What paper was that young scoundrel representing?' he inquired.

'The *Globe*,' Kirk told him.

'The *Globe* office — and quickly, please,' Sir Frederic ordered.

The two got in, and for a moment rode in silence.

'You are curious, perhaps,' said Sir Frederic at last.

'I hope you won't think it's unnatural of me,' smiled Kirk.

'I know I can rely on your discretion, my boy. I told only a small part of the story of Eve Durand at luncheon, but even that must not reach print just yet. Not here — not now — '

'Great Scott. Do you mean — '

'I mean I am near the end of a long trail. Eve Durand was not murdered in India. She ran away. I know why she ran away. I even suspect the peculiar method of her going.

40

More than that — '

'Yes?' cried Kirk eagerly.

'More than that I cannot tell you at present.' The journey was continued in silence, and presently they drew up before the office of the *Globe*.

In the city editor's cubby-hole, Bill Rankin was talking exultantly to his chief. 'It's going to be a corking good feature — ' he was saying, when he felt a grip of steel on his arm. Turning, he looked into the face of Sir Frederic Bruce. 'Why — why — hello,' he stammered.

'There has been a slight mistake,' said the detective.

'Let me explain,' suggested Barry Kirk. He shook hands with the editor and introduced Sir Frederic, who merely nodded, not relaxing his grip on the reporter's paralysed arm. 'Rankin, this is unfortunate,' Kirk continued, 'but it can't be helped. Sir Frederic is unfamiliar with the ways of the American press, and he did not understand that you were gathering a story at lunch. He thought it a purely social affair. So we have come to ask that you print nothing of the conversation you heard this noon.'

Rankin's face fell. 'Not print it? Oh — I say — '

'We appeal to you both,' added Kirk to the editor.

'My answer must depend on your reason for making the request,' said that gentleman.

'My reason would be respected in England,' Sir Frederic told him. 'Here, I don't know your custom. But I may tell you that if you print any of that conversation, you will seriously impede the course of justice.'

The editor bowed. 'Very well. We shall print nothing without your permission, Sir Frederic,' he said.

'Thank you,' replied the detective, releasing Rankin's arm. 'That concludes our business here, I fancy.' And wheeling, he went out. Having added his own thanks, Kirk followed.

'Well, of all the rotten luck,' cried Rankin, sinking into a chair.

Sir Frederic strode on across the city room. A cat may look at a king, and Egbert stood staring with interest at the former head of the C.I.D. Just in front of the door, the Englishman paused. It was either that or a collision with Egbert, moving slowly like a dark shadow across his path.

3

The Bungalow in the Sky

Barry Kirk stepped from his living-room through french windows leading into the tiny garden that graced his bungalow in the sky — 'my front yard,' he called it. He moved over to the rail and stood looking out on a view such as few front yards have ever offered. Twenty stories below lay the alternate glare and gloom of the city; far in the distance the lights of the ferry-boats plodded across the harbour like weary fireflies.

The stars were bright and clear and amazingly close above his head, but he heard the tolling of the fog bell over by Belvedere, and he knew that the sea mist was drifting in through the Gate. By midnight it would whirl and eddy about his lofty home, shutting him off from the world like a veil of filmy tulle. He loved the fog. Heavy with the scent of distant gardens, salt with the breath of the Pacific, it was the trade-mark of his town.

He went back inside, closing the window carefully behind him. For a moment he stood looking about his living-room, which wealth and good taste had combined to furnish charmingly. A huge, deep sofa, many comfortable chairs, a half-dozen floor lamps shedding their warm yellow glow, a brisk fire crackling on a wide hearth — no matter how loudly the wind rattled at the casements, here were comfort and good cheer.

Kirk went on into his dining-room. Paradise was lighting the candles on the big table. The flowers, the snowy linen, the old silver, made a perfect picture, forecasting a perfect dinner. Kirk inspected the ten place cards. He smiled.

'Everything seems to be O.K.,' he said. 'It's got to be, to-night. Grandmother's coming, and you know what she thinks about a man who lives alone. To hear her tell it, every home needs a woman's touch.'

'We shall disillusion her once again, sir,' Paradise remarked.

'Such is my aim. Not that it will do any good. When she's made up her mind, that's that.'

The door-bell rang, and Paradise moved off with slow, majestic step to answer it. Entering the living-room, Barry Kirk stood for a moment fascinated by the picture he saw there. The deputy district attorney had paused just inside the door leading from the hall; she wore a simple, orange-coloured dinner gown, her dark eyes were smiling.

'Miss Morrow,' Kirk came forward eagerly. 'If you don't mind my saying so, you don't look much like a lawyer to-night.'

'I presume that's intended for a compliment,' she answered. Chan appeared at her back. 'Here's Mr. Chan. We rode up together in the elevator. Heavens — don't tell me we're the first.'

'When I was a boy,' smiled Kirk, 'I always started in by eating the frosting off my cake. Which is just to tell you that with me, the best is always first. Good evening, Mr. Chan.'

Chan bowed. 'I am deeply touched by your kindness. One grand item is added to my mainland memories tonight.' He wore a somewhat rusty dinner coat, but his linen gleamed and his manners shone.

Paradise followed with their outdoor gear on his arm, and disappeared through a distant doorway. Another door opened. Sir Frederic Bruce stood on the threshold.

'Good evening, Miss Morrow,' he said. 'My word — you look charming. And Mr. Chan. This is luck — you're the first. You know I promised to show you a souvenir of my dark past.'

He turned and re-entered his room. Kirk led his guests over to the blazing fire.

'Sit down — do,' he said. 'People are always

asking how I can endure the famous San Francisco zephyrs up here.' He waved a hand towards the fireplace. 'This is one of my answers.'

Sir Frederic rejoined them, a distinguished figure in his evening clothes. He carried a pair of slippers. Their tops were of cut velvet, dark red like old Burgundy, and each bore as decoration a Chinese character surrounded by a design of pomegranate blossoms. He handed one to the girl, and the other to Charlie Chan.

'Beautiful,' cried Miss Morrow. 'And what a history! The essential clue.'

'Not any too essential, as it turned out,' shrugged the great detective.

'You know, I venture to presume, the meaning of the character inscribed on velvet?' Chan inquired.

'Yes,' said Sir Frederic. 'Not any too appropriate in this case, I believe. I was told it signifies 'Long life and happiness.''

'Precisely.' Chan turned the slipper slowly in his hand. 'There exist one hundred and one varieties of this character — one hundred for the people, one reserved for the Emperor. A charming gift. The footwear of a mandarin, fitting only for one high-placed and wealthy.'

'Well, they were on Hilary Galt's feet when we found him, murdered on the floor,' Sir

46

Frederic said. ' "Walk softly, my best of friends" — that was what the Chinese minister wrote in the letter he sent with them. Hilary Galt was walking softly that night — but he never walked again.' The Englishman took the slippers. 'By the way — I hesitate to ask it — but I'd rather you didn't mention this matter tonight at dinner.'

'Why, of course,' remarked the girl, surprised.

'And that affair of Eve Durand. Ah — er — I fear I was a little indiscreet this noon. Now that I'm no longer at the Yard, I allow myself too much rope. You understand, Sergeant?'

Chan's little eyes were on him with a keenness that made Sir Frederic slightly uncomfortable. 'Getting immodest for a minute,' the Chinese said, 'I am A1 honour student in school of discretion.'

'I'm sure of that,' the great man smiled.

'No impulse to mention these matters would assail me, I am certain,' Chan went on. 'You bright man, Sir Frederic — you know Chinese are psychic people.'

'Really?'

'Undubitably. Something has told me — '

'Ah, yes — we needn't go into that,' Sir Frederic put in hastily. 'I have a moment's business in the offices below. If you will excuse me — '

47

He disappeared with the slippers into his room. Miss Morrow turned in amazement to Kirk.

'What in the world did he mean? Surely Eve Durand — '

'Mr. Chan is psychic,' Kirk suggested. 'Maybe he can explain it.'

Chan grinned. 'Sometimes psychic feelings lead positively nowhere,' he remarked.

Paradise escorted two more guests through the outer hall into the living-room. A little, bird-like woman was on tiptoe, kissing Barry Kirk.

'Barry, you bad boy. I haven't seen you for ages. Don't tell me you've forgotten your poor old grandmother.'

'I couldn't do that,' he laughed.

'Not while I have my health and strength,' she returned. She came towards the fireplace. 'How cosy you are — '

'Grandmother — this is Miss Morrow,' Kirk said. 'Mrs. Dawson Kirk.'

The old lady took both the girl's hands. 'My dear, I'm happy to know you — '

'Miss Morrow is a lawyer,' Kirk added.

'Lawyer fiddlesticks,' his grandmother cried. 'She couldn't be — and look like this.'

'Just what I said,' nodded Kirk.

The old lady regarded the girl for a brief moment. 'Youth and beauty,' she remarked.

'If I had those, my child, I wouldn't waste time over musty law books.' She turned towards Chan. 'And this is — '

'Sergeant Chan, of the Honolulu police,' Kirk told her.

The old lady gave Charlie a surprisingly warm handclasp. 'Know all about you,' she said. 'I like you very much.'

'Flattered and overwhelmed,' gasped Chan.

'Needn't be,' she answered.

The woman who had accompanied Mrs. Kirk stood rather neglected in the background. Kirk hurried forward to present her. She was, it seemed, Mrs. Tupper-Brock, Mrs. Kirk's secretary and companion. Her manner was cold and distant. Chan gave her a penetrating look and then bowed low before her.

'Paradise will show you into one of the guest rooms,' said Kirk to the women. 'You'll find a pair of military brushes and every book on football Walter Camp ever wrote. If there's anything else you want, try and get it.'

They followed the butler out. The bell rang, and going to the door himself, Kirk admitted another couple. Mr. Carrick Enderby, who was employed in the San Francisco office of Thomas Cook and Sons, was a big, slow, blond man with a monocle and nothing much behind it. All the family brilliance seemed to be monopolized by his wife, Eileen, a dark, dashing woman of thirty-five or so, who came in breezily. She joined the women, and the three men stood in the ill-at-ease silence that marks a dinner party in its initial stages.

'We're in for a bit of fog, I fancy,' Enderby drawled.

'No doubt of it,' Kirk answered.

When the women reappeared, Mrs. Dawson Kirk came at once to Chan's side.

'Sally Jordan of Honolulu is an old friend of mine,' she told him. 'A very good friend. We're both living beyond our time, and there's nothing cements friendship like that. I believe you were once — er — attached — '

Chan bowed. 'One of the great honours of my poor life. I was her house-boy, and memories of her kindness will survive while life hangs out.'

'Well, she told me how you repaid that kindness recently. A thousandfold, she put it.'

Chan shrugged. 'My old employer has only one weakness. She exaggerates stupendously.'

'Oh, don't be modest,' said Mrs. Kirk. 'Gone out of fashion, long ago. These young people will accuse you of something terrible if you try that tune. However, I like you for it.'

A diversion at the door interrupted her. Colonel John Beetham entered the living-room. John Beetham the explorer, whose feet had stood in many dark and lonely places, who knew Tibet and Turkestan, Tsaidam and southern Mongolia. He had lived a year in a house-boat on the largest river in the heart of Asia, had survived two heart-breaking, death-strewn retreats across the snowy plateau of Tibet, had walked amid the ruins of ancient desert cities that had flourished long before Christ was born.

For once, here was a man who looked the part. Lean, tall, bronzed, there was a living flame in his grey eyes. But like Charlie Chan, he came of a modest race, and his manner was shy and aloof as he acknowledged the introductions.

'So glad,' he muttered. 'So glad.' A mere formula.

Suddenly Sir Frederic Bruce was again in the room. He seized Colonel Beetham's hand.

'I met you several years ago,' he said. 'You wouldn't recall it. You were the lion of the hour, and I a humble spectator. I was present at the dinner of the Royal Geographical Society in London when they gave you that enormous gold doodad — the Founders Medal — wasn't that it?'

'Ah, yes — of course. To be sure,' murmured Colonel Beetham.

His eyes bright as buttons in the subdued light, Charlie Chan watched Sir Frederic being presented to the ladies — to Mrs.

Tupper-Brock and Eileen Enderby. Paradise arrived with something on a tray.

'All here except Miss Garland,' Kirk announced. 'We'll wait just a moment.' The bell rang, and he motioned to his servant that he would go.

When Kirk returned, he was accompanied by a handsome woman whose face was flushed and who carried some burden in her jewelled hands. She hurried to a table, and deposited there a number of loose pearls.

'I had the most ridiculous accident on the stairs,' she explained. 'The string of my necklace broke, and I simply shed pearls right and left. I do hope I haven't lost any.'

One of the pearls rolled to the floor, and Kirk retrieved it. The woman began counting them off into a gold mesh handbag. Finally she stopped.

'Got them all?' Barry Kirk inquired.

'I — I think so. I never can remember the number. And now — you really must forgive my silly entrance. It would be rather effective on the stage, I fancy, but I'm not on the stage now. In real life, I'm afraid it was rather rude.'

Paradise took her cloak, and Kirk introduced her. Charlie Chan studied her long and carefully. She was no longer young, but her beauty was still triumphant. It would have to be, for her profession was the stage, and she was well-beloved in the Australian theatres.

At the table, Charlie found himself at Mrs. Kirk's right, with June Morrow on his other side. If he was a bit awed by the company in which he had landed, he gave no sign. He listened to several anecdotes of Sally Jordan's past from Mrs. Kirk, then turned to the girl beside him. Her eyes were shining.

'I'm thrilled to the depths,' she whispered. 'Sir Frederic and that marvellous Beetham man all in one evening — and you, too.'

Chan smiled, 'I am pretty lonely fly in this menagerie of lions,' he admitted.

'Tell me — that about being psychic. You don't really think Sir Frederic has found Eve Durand?'

Chan shrugged. 'For one word a man may be adjudged wise, and for one word he may be adjudged foolish.'

'Oh, please don't be so Oriental. Just think — Eve Durand may be at this table to-night.'

'Strange events permit themselves the luxury of occurring,' Chan conceded. His eyes travelled slowly about the board, they rested on Mrs. Tupper-Brock, silent and aloof, on the vivacious Eileen Enderby, longest of all on the handsome Gloria Garland, now completely recovered from her excitement over the scattered pearls.

'Tell me, Sir Frederic,' remarked Mrs. Kirk.

'How are you making out here in Barry's womanless Eden?'

'Splendidly,' smiled the detective. 'Mr. Kirk has been very kind. I not only have the run of this charming bungalow, but he has also installed me in the offices below.' He looked at Kirk. 'Which reminds me — I'm afraid I quite forgot to close the safe downstairs.'

'Paradise can attend to it,' suggested Kirk.

'Oh, no,' said Sir Frederic. 'Please don't trouble. It doesn't matter — as far as I am concerned.'

Carrick Enderby spoke in a loud booming voice. 'I say, Colonel Beetham. I've just read your book, you know.'

'Ah, yes — er — which one?' inquired Beetham blandly.

'Don't be a fool, Carry,' said Eileen Enderby rather warmly. 'Colonel Beetham has written many books. And he's not going to be impressed by the fact that, knowing you were to meet him here to-night, you hastily ran through one of them.'

'But it wasn't hastily,' protested Enderby. 'I gave it my best attention. The *Life*, I mean, you know. All your adventures — and by Jove, they were thrilling. Of course, I can't understand you, sir. For me, the cheery old whisky and soda in the comfortable chair by the warm fire. But you — how you do yearn

54

for the desolate places, my word.'

Beetham smiled. 'It's the white spots — the white spots on the map. They call to me. I — I long to walk there, where no man has walked before. It is an odd idea, isn't it?'

'Well, of course, getting home must be exciting,' Enderby admitted. 'The Kings and the Presidents pinning decorations on you, and the great dinners, and the eulogies — '

'Quite the most terrible part of it, I assure you,' said Beetham.

'Nevertheless, I'd take it in preference to your jolly old deserts,' continued Enderby. 'That time you were lost on the — er — the — '

'The desert of Takla-makan,' finished Beetham. 'I was in a bit of a jam, wasn't I? But I wasn't lost, my dear fellow. I had simply embarked on the crossing with insufficient water and supplies.'

Mrs. Kirk spoke. 'I was enthralled by that entry you quoted from your diary. What you thought was the last entry you would ever make. I know it by heart. 'Halted on a high dune, where the camels fell exhausted. We examined the East through the field-glasses; mountains of sand in all directions; not a straw, no life. All, men as well as camels, are extremely weak, God help us.''

'But it wasn't my last entry, you know,'

Beetham reminded her. 'The next night, in a dying condition, I crept along on my hands and knees until I reached a forest, the bed of a dry river — a pool. Water. I came out much better than I deserved.'

'Pardon me if I make slight inquiry,' said Charlie Chan. 'What of old superstition, Colonel? Mention was made of it by Marco Polo six hundred years ago. When a traveller is moving across desert by night, he hears strange voices calling his name. In bewitched state, he follows ghostly voices to his early doom.'

'It is quite obvious,' returned Beetham, 'that I followed no voices. In fact, I heard none.'

Eileen Enderby shuddered. 'Well, I never could do it,' she said. 'I'm frightfully afraid of the dark. It drives me almost insane with fear.'

Sir Frederic Bruce looked at her keenly. For the first time in some moments he spoke. 'I fancy many women are like that,' he said. He turned suddenly to Mrs. Kirk's companion. 'What has been your experience, Mrs. Tupper-Brock?'

'I do not mind the dark,' said that lady, in a cool, even tone.

'Miss Garland?' His piercing eyes turned on the actress.

She seemed a little embarrassed. 'Why — I — really, I much prefer the spotlight. No,

56

I can't say I fancy darkness.'

'Nonsense,' said Mrs. Dawson Kirk. 'Things are the same in the dark as in the light. I never minded it.'

Beetham spoke slowly. 'Why not ask the gentlemen, Sir Frederic? Fear of the dark is not alone a woman's weakness. Were you to ask me, I should have to make a confession.'

Sir Frederic turned on him in amazement. 'You, Colonel?'

Beetham nodded. 'When I was a little shaver, my life was made miserable by my horror of the dark. Every evening, when I was left alone in my room, I died a thousand deaths.'

'By Jove,' cried Enderby. 'And yet you grew up to spend your life in the dark places of the world.'

'You conquered that early fear, no doubt?' Sir Frederic suggested.

Beetham shrugged. 'Does one ever quite conquer a thing like that? But really — there is too much about me. Mr. Kirk has asked me to let you see, after dinner, some pictures I took last year in Tibet. I fear I shall bore you by becoming as you Americans say, the whole show.'

Again they chatted by two and two. Miss Morrow leaned over to Chan.

'Imagine,' she said, 'that picture of the great explorer, as a little boy, frightened of the dark. It's quite the most charming and human thing I ever heard.'

He nodded gravely, his eyes on Eileen Enderby. 'The dark drives me almost insane with fear,' she had said. How dark it must have been that night in the hills outside Peshawar.

After he had served coffee in the living-room, Paradise appeared with a white, glittering screen which, under the Colonel's direction, he stood on a low table against a Flemish tapestry. Barry Kirk helped Beetham carry in from the hall a heavy motion-picture projector and several boxes of films.

'Lucky we didn't overlook this,' the young man laughed. 'A rather embarrassing thing for you if you had to go home without being invited to perform. Like the man who tried to slip away from an evening party with a harp that he hadn't been asked to play.'

The machine was finally ready, and the company took their places in comfortable chairs facing the screen.

'We shall want, of course, complete darkness,' Beetham said. 'Mr. Kirk, if you will be so kind — '

'Surely. Barry Kirk turned off the lights, and drew thick curtains over doors and windows. 'Is it all right now?'

'The light in the hall,' Beetham suggested.

Kirk also extinguished that. There was a moment of tense silence.

'Heavens — this is creepy,' spoke Eileen Enderby out of the blackness. There was a slight note of hysteria in her voice.

Beetham was placing a roll of film in the machine. 'On the expedition I am about to describe,' he began, 'we set out from Darjeeling. As you no doubt know, Darjeeling is a little hill station on the extreme northern frontier of India — '

Sir Frederic interrupted. 'You have been in India a great deal, Colonel?'

'Frequently — between journeys — '

'Ah, yes — pardon me for breaking in — '

'Not at all.' The film began to unwind. 'These first pictures are of Darjeeling, where I engaged my men, rounded up supplies, and — ' The Colonel was off on his interesting but rather lengthy story.

Time passed, and his voice droned on in the intense darkness. The air was thick with the smoke of cigarettes; now and then there was the stir of someone moving, walking about in the rear, occasionally a curtain parted at a window. But Colonel Beetham gave no heed. He was living again on the high plateau of Tibet; the old fervour to go on had returned; he trekked through snowy passes, leaving men and mules dead in the

59

wasteland, fighting like a fanatic on towards his goal.

A weird feeling of oppression settled down over Charlie Chan, a feeling he attributed to the thick atmosphere of the room. He rose and dodged guiltily out into the roof-top garden. Barry Kirk was standing there, a dim figure in the mist, smoking a cigarette. For it was misty now, the fog bell was tolling its warning, and the roof was wrapped in clouds.

'Hello,' said Kirk, in a low voice. 'Want a bit of air, too, eh? I hope he's not boring my poor guests to death. Exploring's a big business now, and he's trying to persuade grandmother to put up a lot of money for a little picnic he's planning. An interesting man, isn't he?'

'Most interesting,' Chan admitted.

'But a hard one,' added Kirk. 'He leaves the dead behind with never so much as a look over his shoulder. I suppose that's the scientific type of mind — what's a few dead men when you're wiping out one of those white spots on the map? However, it's not my style. That's my silly American sentimentality.'

'It is undubitably the style of Colonel Beetham,' Chan returned. 'I read same in his eyes.'

He went back into the big living-room, and

walked about in the rear. A slight sound in the hall interested him, and he went out there. A man had just entered by the door that led to the floor below. Before he closed it the light outside fell on the blond hair of Carrick Enderby.

'Just having a cigarette on the stairs,' he explained in a hoarse whisper. 'Didn't want to add any more smoke to the air in there. A bit thick, what?'

He stole back into the living-room, and Chan, following, found a chair. A clatter of dishes sounded from the distant pantry, competing with the noise of the unwinding film and the steady stream of Beetham's story. The tireless man was starting on a new reel.

'Voice is getting a bit weary,' the Colonel admitted. 'I'll just run this one off without comment. It requires none.' He fell back from the dim light by the machine, into the shadows.

In ten minutes the reel had unwound its length, and the indomitable Beetham was on hand. He was preparing to start on what he announced as the final reel, when the curtains over one of the french windows parted suddenly, and the white figure of a woman came into the room. She stood there like a wraith in the misty light at her back.

'Oh, stop it!' she cried. 'Stop it and turn up the lights. Quickly! Quickly — please!' There was a real hysteria in Eileen Enderby's voice now.

Barry Kirk leaped to the light switch, and flooded the room. Mrs. Enderby stood, pale and swaying slightly, clutching at her throat. 'What is it?' Kirk asked. 'What's the trouble?'

'A man,' she panted. 'I couldn't stand the dark — it was driving me mad — I stepped out into the garden. I was standing close to the railing when I saw a man leap from a lighted window on the floor below, out on to the fire-escape. He ran down it into the fog.'

'My offices are below,' Kirk said quietly. 'We had better look into this. Sir Frederic — ' His eyes turned from one to the other. 'Why — where is Sir Frederic?' he asked.

Paradise had entered from the pantry. 'I beg your pardon, sir,' he said. 'Sir Frederic went down to the office some ten minutes ago.'

'Down to the offices? Why?'

'The burglar alarm by your bed was buzzing, sir. The one connected up downstairs. Just as I discovered it, Sir Frederic entered your room. 'I will investigate this, Paradise,' he said. 'Don't disturb the others.''

Kirk turned to Charlie Chan. 'Sergeant, will you come with me, please?'

Silently, Charlie followed him to the stairs, and together they went below. The offices were ablaze with light. The rear room, into which the stairs led, was quite empty. They advanced into the middle room.

A window was open as far as it would go, and in the mist outside Chan noted the iron gratings of a fire-escape. This room too seemed empty. But beyond the desk Barry Kirk, in advance, gave a little cry and dropped to his knees.

Chan stepped around the desk. He was not surprised by what he saw, but he was genuinely sorry. Sir Frederic Bruce lay on the floor, shot cleanly through the heart. By his side lay a thin little volume, bound in bright yellow cloth.

Kirk stood up, dazed. 'In my office,' he said slowly, as though that were important. 'It's — it's horrible. Good God — look!'

He pointed to Sir Frederic. On the detective's feet were black silk stockings — and nothing else. He wore no shoes.

Paradise had followed. He stood for a moment staring at the dead man on the floor, and then turned to Barry Kirk.

'When Sir Frederic came downstairs,' he said, 'he was wearing a pair of velvet slippers. Sort of heathen-looking slippers they were, sir.'

4

The Reckoning of Heaven

Barry Kirk stood looking about his office; he found it difficult to believe that into this commonplace, familiar room, tragedy had found its way. Yet there was that silent figure on the floor, a few moments before so full of life and energy.

'Poor Sir Frederic,' he said. 'Only to-day he told me he was near the end of a long trail. Nearer than he dreamed, it appears.' He stopped. 'A long trail, Sergeant — only a few of us know how far back into the past this thing must reach.'

Chan nodded. He had been consulting a huge gold watch; now he snapped shut the case and restored it to his pocket. 'Death is the reckoning of heaven,' he remarked. 'On this occasion, a most complicated reckoning.'

'Well, what shall we do?' Kirk asked helplessly. 'The police, I suppose. But good lord — this is a case beyond any policeman I ever met. Any uniformed man, I mean.' He paused, and a grim smile flashed across his face. 'It looks very much to me, Mr. Chan, as though

64

you would have to take charge and — '

A stubborn light leaped into the little black eyes. 'Miss Morrow is above,' said Chan. 'What a happy chance, since she is from the district attorney's office. If I may humbly suggest — '

'Oh, I never thought of that.' Kirk turned to his servant. 'Paradise, ask Miss Morrow to come here. Make my excuses to my guests, and ask them to wait.'

'Very good, sir,' replied Paradise, and departed.

Kirk walked slowly about the room. The drawers of the big desk were open and their contents jumbled. 'Somebody's been on a frantic search here,' he said. He paused before the safe; its door was slightly ajar.

'Safe stands open,' suggested Chan.

'Odd about that,' said Kirk. 'This afternoon Sir Frederic asked me to take out anything of value and move it upstairs. I did so. He didn't explain.'

'Of course,' nodded Chan. 'And at the dinner table he makes uncalled-for reference to fact that he has not locked safe. The matter struck me at the time. One thing becomes clear — Sir Frederic desired to set a trap. A safe unlocked to tempt marauders.' He nodded to the small volume that lay at the dead man's side. 'We must disturb nothing.

Do not touch, but kindly regard book and tell me where last reposing.'

Kirk leaned over. 'That? Why, it's the year book of the Cosmopolitan Club. It was usually in that revolving case on which the telephone stands. It can't mean anything.'

'Maybe not. Maybe' — Chan's little eyes narrowed — 'a hint from beyond the unknown.'

'I wonder,' mused Kirk.

'Sir Frederic was guest of Cosmopolitan Club?'

'Yes — I gave him a two weeks' card. He wrote a lot of his letters there. But — but — I can't see — '

'He was clever man. Even in moment of passing, his dying hand would seek to leave behind essential clue.'

'Speaking of that,' said Kirk, 'how about those velvet slippers? Where are they?'

Chan shrugged. 'Slippers were essential clue in one case, long ago. What did they lead to? Positively nothing. If I am suiting my own taste, this time I look elsewhere.'

Miss Morrow entered the room. Her face was usually full of colour — an authentic colour that is the gift of the fog to San Francisco's daughters. Now it was deathly pale. Without speaking, she stepped beyond the desk and looked down. For a moment she swayed, and Barry Kirk leaped forward.

'No, no,' cried the girl.

'But I thought — ' he began.

'You thought I was going to faint. Absurd. This is my work — it has come to me and I shall do it. You believe I can't — '

'Not at all,' protested Kirk.

'Oh, yes you do. Everybody will. I'll show them. You've called the police, of course.'

'Not yet,' Kirk answered.

She sat down resolutely at the desk, and took up the telephone. 'Davenport 20,' she said. 'The Hall of Justice? . . . Captain Flannery, please . . . Hello — Captain? Miss Morrow of the district attorney's office speaking. There has been a murder in Mr. Kirk's office on the top floor of the Kirk Building. You had better come yourself . . . Thank you . . . Yes — I'll attend to that.'

She got up, and, going round the desk, bent over Sir Frederic. She noted the book, and her eyes strayed wonderingly to the stockinged feet. Inquiringly she turned to Chan.

'The slippers of Hilary Galt,' he nodded. 'Souvenir of that unhappy case, they adorned his feet when he came down. Here is Paradise — he will explain to you.'

The butler had returned, and Miss Morrow faced him. 'Tell us what you know, please,' she said.

67

'I was busy in the pantry,' Paradise said. 'I thought I heard the buzz of the burglar alarm by Mr. Kirk's bed — the one connected with the windows and safe in this room. I hastened to make sure, but Sir Frederic was just behind. It was almost as though he had been expecting it. I don't know how I got that impression — I'm odd that way — '

'Go on,' said the girl. 'Sir Frederic followed you into Mr. Kirk's room?'

'Yes, Miss. 'There's someone below, sir,' I said. 'Someone who doesn't belong there.' Sir Frederic looked back into the pitch-dark living-room. 'I fancy so, Paradise,' he said. He was smiling. 'I will attend to it. No need to disturb Mr. Kirk or his guests.' I followed him into his room. He tossed off his patent leather pumps. 'The stairs are a bit soiled, I fear, sir,' I reminded him. He laughed. 'Ah, yes,' he said. 'But I have the very thing.' The velvet slippers were lying near his bed. He put them on. 'I shall walk softly in these, Paradise,' he told me. At the head of the stairs, I stopped him. A sort of fear was in my heart — I am given to that — to having premonitions — '

'You stopped him,' Kirk cut in.

'I did, sir. Respectfully, of course. 'Are you armed, Sir Frederic?' I made bold to inquire. He shook his head. 'No need, Paradise,' he answered. 'I fancy our visitor is of the weaker

68

sex.' And then he went down, sir — to his death.'

They were silent for a moment, pondering the servant's story.

'We had better go,' said the girl, 'and tell the others. Someone must stay here. If it's not asking too much, Mr. Chan — '

'I am torn with grief to disagree,' Chan answered. 'Please pardon me. But for myself, I have keen eagerness to note how this news is taken in the room above.'

'Ah, yes. Naturally.'

'I shall be glad to stay, Miss,' Paradise said.

'Very well,' the girl answered. 'Please let me know as soon as Captain Flannery arrives.' She led the way above, and Kirk and the little detective from Honolulu followed.

Barry Kirk's guests were seated, silent and expectant, in the now brightly lighted living-room. They looked up inquiringly as the three from below entered. Kirk faced them, at a loss how to begin.

'I have dreadful news for you,' he said. 'An accident — a terrible accident.' Chan's eyes moved rapidly about the group and, making their choice, rested finally on the white, drawn face of Eileen Enderby. 'Sir Frederic Bruce has been murdered in my office,' Kirk finished.

There was a moment's breathless silence,

and then Mrs. Enderby got to her feet. 'It's the dark,' she cried in a harsh, shrill voice. 'I knew it. I knew something would happen when the lights were turned off. I knew it, I tell you — '

Her husband stepped to her side to quieten her, and Chan stood staring not at her, but at Colonel John Beetham. For one brief instant he thought the mask had dropped from those weary, disillusioned eyes. For one instant only.

They all began to speak at once. Gradually Miss Morrow made herself heard above the din. 'We must take this coolly,' she said, and Barry Kirk admired her composure.

'Naturally, we are all under suspicion. We — '

'What? I like that!' Mrs. Dawson Kirk was speaking.

'Under suspicion, indeed — '

'The room was in complete darkness,' Miss Morrow went on. 'There was considerable moving about. I don't like to stress my official position here, but perhaps you would prefer my methods to those of a police captain. How many of you left this room during the showing of Colonel Beetham's pictures?'

An embarrassed silence fell. Mrs. Kirk broke it. 'I thought the pictures intensely interesting,' she said. 'True, I did step into the kitchen for a moment — '

'Just to keep an eye on my domestic arrangements,' suggested Barry Kirk.

'Nothing of the sort. My throat was dry. I wanted a glass of water.'

'You saw nothing wrong?' inquired Miss Morrow.

'Aside from the very wasteful methods that seemed to be in vogue in the kitchen — nothing,' replied Mrs. Kirk firmly.

'Mrs. Tupper-Brock?' said Miss Morrow.

'I was on the sofa with Miss Garland,' replied that lady. 'Neither of us moved from there at any time.' Her voice was cool and steady.

'That's quite true,' the actress added.

Another silence. Kirk spoke up. 'I'm sure none of us intended a discourtesy to the Colonel,' he said. 'The entertainment he gave us was delightful, and it was gracious of him to honour us. I myself — er — I was in the room constantly — except for one brief moment in the garden. I saw no one there — save — '

Chan stepped forward. 'Speaking for myself, I found huge delight in the pictures. A moment I wish to be alone, in order that I may digest great events flashed before me on silvery screen. So I also invade the garden, and meet Mr. Kirk. For a time we marvel at the distinguished Colonel Beetham — his indomitable courage, his deep resource, his service to humanity. Then we rush back, that we may miss no more.' He paused. 'Before I again recline in sitting posture, noise in hall offend me. I hurry out there in shushing mood, and behold — '

'Ah — er — the pictures were marvellous,' said Carrick Enderby. 'I enjoyed them immensely. True enough, I stepped out on the stairs for a cigarette — '

'Carry, you fool,' his wife cried. 'You would do that.'

'But I say — why not? I saw nothing. There was nothing to see. The floor below was quite deserted.' He turned to Miss Morrow. 'Whoever did this horrible thing left by way of the fire-escape. You've already learned that — '

'Ah, yes,' cut in Chan. 'We have learned it, indeed — from your wife.' He glanced at Miss Morrow and their eyes met.

'From my wife — yes,' repeated Enderby. 'Look here — what do you mean by that? I — '

'No matter,' put in Miss Morrow. 'Colonel Beetham — you were occupied at the picture machine. Except for one interval of about ten minutes, when you allowed it to run itself.'

'Ah, yes,' said the Colonel evenly. 'I did not

72

leave the room, Miss Morrow.'

Eileen Enderby rose. 'Mr. Kirk — we really must be going. Your dinner was charming — how terrible to have it end in such a tragic way. I — '

'Just a moment,' said June Morrow. 'I cannot let you go until the captain of police releases you.'

'What's that?' the woman cried. 'Outrageous. You mean we are prisoners here — '

'Oh — but, Eileen — ' protested her husband.

'I'm very sorry,' said the girl. 'I shall protect you as much as possible from the annoyance of further questioning. But you really must wait.'

Mrs. Enderby flung angrily away, and a filmy scarf she was wearing dropped from one shoulder and trailed after her. Chan reached out to rescue it. The woman took another step, and he stood with the scarf in his hand. She swung about. The detective's little eyes, she noticed, were fixed with keen interest on the front of her pale blue gown, and following his gaze, she looked down.

'So sorry,' said Chan. 'So very sorry. I trust your beautiful garment is not a complete ruin.'

'Give me that scarf,' she cried, and snatched it rudely from him.

Paradise appeared in the doorway. 'Miss

73

Morrow, please,' he said. 'Captain Flannery is below.'

'You will kindly wait here,' said the girl. 'All of you. I shall arrange for your release at the earliest possible moment.'

With Kirk and Charlie Chan, she returned to the twentieth floor. In the central room they found Captain Flannery, a grey-haired, energetic policeman of about fifty. With him were two patrolmen and a police doctor.

'Hello, Miss Morrow,' said the Captain. 'This is a he — I mean, a terrible thing. Sir Frederic Bruce of Scotland Yard — we're up against it now. If we don't make good quick we'll have the whole Yard on our necks.'

'I'm afraid we shall,' admitted Miss Morrow. 'Captain Flannery — this is Mr. Kirk. And this — Detective-Sergeant Charlie Chan, of Honolulu.'

The Captain looked his fellow detective over slowly. 'How are you, Sergeant? I've been reading about you in the paper. You got on this job mighty quick.'

Chan shrugged. 'Not my job, thank you,' he replied. 'All yours, and very welcome. I am here in society rôle, as guest of kind Mr. Kirk.'

'Is that so?' The Captain appeared relieved. 'Now, Miss Morrow, what have you found out?'

'Very little. Mr. Kirk was giving a dinner upstairs.' She ran over the list of guests, the showing of the pictures in the dark, and the butler's story of Sir Frederic's descent to the floor below, wearing the velvet slippers. 'There are other aspects of the affair that I will take up with you later,' she added.

'All right. I guess the D.A. will want to get busy on this himself.'

The girl flushed. 'Perhaps. He is out of town to-night. I hope he will leave the matter in my hands — '

'Great Scott, Miss Morrow — this is important,' said the Captain, oblivious of his rudeness. 'You're holding those people upstairs?'

'Naturally.'

'Good. I'll look 'em over later. I ordered the night-watchman to lock the front door and bring everybody in the building here. Now, we better fix the time of this. How long's he been dead, Doctor?'

'Not more than half an hour,' replied the doctor.

'Humbly begging pardon to intrude,' said Chan. 'The homicide occurred presumably at ten twenty.'

'Sure of that?'

'I have not the habit of light speaking. At ten twenty-five we find body, just five minutes after lady on floor above rush in with news of man escaping from this room by fire-escape.'

'Huh. The room seems to have been searched.' Flannery turned to Barry Kirk. 'Anything missing?'

'I haven't had time to investigate,' said Kirk. 'If anything has been taken, I fancy it was Sir Frederic's property.'

'This is your office, isn't it?'

'Yes. But I had made room here for Sir Frederic. He had various papers and that sort of thing.'

'Papers? What was he doing? I thought he'd retired.'

'It seems he was still interested in certain cases, Captain,' Miss Morrow said. 'That is one of the points I shall take up with you later.'

'Again interfering with regret,' remarked Chan, 'if we do not know what was taken, all same we know what was hunted.'

'You don't say.' Flannery looked at Chan coldly. 'What was that?'

'Sir Frederic English detective, and great one. All English detectives make exhausting records of every case. No question that records of certain case, in which murderer was hotly interested, were sought here.'

'Maybe,' admitted the Captain. 'We'll go over the room later.' He turned to the patrolmen. 'You boys take a look at the fire-escape.' They climbed out into the fog. At that moment the door leading from the reception-room into the hall opened, and an odd little group came in. A stout, middle-aged man led the procession; he was Mr. Cuttle, the night-watchman.

'Here they are, Captain,' he said. 'I've rounded up everybody in the building, except a few cleaning women who have nothing to do with this floor. You can see 'em later, if you like. This is Mrs. Dyke, who takes care of the top floors.'

Mrs. Dyke, very frightened, said that she had finished with Kirk's office at seven and gone out, leaving the burglar alarm in working order, as was her custom. She had not been back since. She had seen no one about the building whom she did not recognize.

'And who is this?' inquired the Captain, turning to a pale, sandy-haired young man who appeared extremely nervous.

'I am employed by Brace and Davis, Certified Public Accountants, on the second floor,' said the young man. 'My name is Samuel Smith. I was working to-night to catch up — I have been ill — when Mr. Cuttle informed me I was wanted up here. I know nothing of this horrible affair.'

Flannery turned to the fourth and last

member of the party, a young woman whose uniform marked her as an operator of one of the elevators. 'What's your name?' he asked.

'Grace Lane, sir,' she told him.

'Run the elevator, eh?'

'Yes, sir. Mr. Kirk had sent word that one of us must work overtime to-night. On account of the party.'

'How many people have you brought up since the close of business?'

'I didn't keep count. Quite a few — ladies and gentlemen — Mr. Kirk's guests, of course.'

'Don't remember anybody who looked like an outsider?'

'No, sir.'

'This is a big building,' said Flannery. 'There must have been others working here to-night besides this fellow Smith. Remember anybody?'

The girl hesitated. 'There — there was one other, sir.'

'Yes? Who was that?'

'A girl who is employed in the office of the Calcutta Importers, on this floor. Her name is Miss Lila Barr.'

'Working here to-night, eh? On this floor. She's not here now?'

'No, sir. She left some time ago.'

'How long ago?'

'I can't say exactly, sir. Half an hour

— perhaps a little more than that.'

'Humph.' The Captain took down their names and addresses, and dismissed them. As they went out, the two patrolmen entered from the fire-escape, and, leaving them in charge, Flannery asked to be directed upstairs.

The dinner guests were sitting with rather weary patience in a semi-circle in the living-room. Into their midst strode the Captain, with an air of confidence he was far from feeling. He stood looking them over.

'I guess you know what I'm doing here,' he said. 'Miss Morrow tells me she's had a talk with you, and I won't double back over her tracks. However, I want the name and address of every one of you.' He turned to Mrs. Kirk. 'I'll start with you.'

She stiffened at his tone. 'You're very flattering, I'm sure. I am Mrs. Dawson Kirk.' She added her address.

'You.' Flannery turned to the explorer.

'Colonel John Beetham. I am a visitor in the city, stopping at the Fairmont.'

Flannery went on down the list. When he had finished, he added:

'Anyone got any light to throw on this affair? If you have, better give it to me now. Things'll be a lot pleasanter all round than if I dig it up for myself later.' No one spoke. 'Some lady saw a man running down the fire-escape,' he prompted.

'Oh — I did,' said Eileen Enderby. 'I've been all over that with Miss Morrow. I had gone out into the garden — ' Again she related her experience.

'What'd this man look like?' demanded Flannery.

'I couldn't say. A very dim figure in the fog.'

'All right. You can all go now. I may want to see some of you later.' Flannery strode past them into the garden.

One by one they said their strained farewells and departed — Mrs. Kirk and her companion, Miss Gloria Garland, then the Enderby's, and finally the explorer. Charlie Chan also got his hat and coat, while Miss Morrow watched him inquiringly.

'Until dark deed shaded the feast,' said Chan, 'the evening was an unquestioned joy. Mr. Kirk — '

'Oh, but you're not leaving,' cried Miss Morrow. 'Please. I want to have a talk with you.'

'To-morrow I am sea-going man,' Chan reminded her. 'The experience weakens me considerably. I have need of sleep, and relaxing — '

'I'll keep you only a moment,' she pleaded, and Chan nodded.

Captain Flannery appeared from the garden. 'Dark out there,' he announced. 'But if I'm not mistaken, anyone could have reached the floor below by way of the fire-escape. Is that right?'

'Undoubtedly,' replied Kirk.

'An important discovery,' approved Chan. 'On the gown of one of the lady guests were iron rust stains, which might have been suffered by — But who am I to speak thus to keen man like the Captain? You made note of the fact, of course?'

Flannery reddened. 'I — I can't say I did. Which lady?'

'That Mrs. Enderby, who witnessed fleeing man. Do not mention it, sir. So happy to be of slightest service.'

'Let's go back downstairs,' growled Flannery. On the floor below, he stood for a long moment, looking about. 'Well, I got to get busy here.'

'I will say farewell,' remarked Chan.

'Going, eh?' said Flannery, with marked enthusiasm.

'Going far,' smiled Chan. 'To-morrow I am directed towards Honolulu. I leave you to the largest problem of your life, Captain. I suffer no envy for you.'

'Oh, I'll pull through,' replied Flannery.

'Only the witless could doubt it. But you

will travel a long road. Consider. Who is great man silent now on couch? A famous detective with a glorious record. The meaning of that? A thousand victories — and a thousand enemies. All over broad world are scattered men who would do him into death with happy hearts. A long road for you, Captain. You have my warmest wishes for bright outcome. May you emerge in the shining garments of success.'

'Thanks,' said Flannery.

'One last point. You will pardon me if I put in final oar.' He took up from the table a little yellow book, and held it out. 'Same was at the dead man's elbow when he fell.'

Flannery nodded. 'I know. The Cosmopolitan Club book. It can't mean a damn thing.'

'Maybe. I am stupid Chinese from tiny island. I know nothing. But if this was my case I would think about book, Captain Flannery. I would arouse in the night to think about it. Good-bye, and all good wishes already mentioned.'

He made a deep bow, and went through the reception-room into the hall. Kirk and the girl followed swiftly. The latter put her hand on Chan's arm.

'Sergeant — you mustn't,' she cried despairingly. 'You can't desert me now. I need you.'

'You rip my heart to fragments,' he replied. 'However, plans are set.'

'But poor Captain Flannery — all this is far beyond him. You know more about the case than he does. Stay, and I'll see that you're given every facility — '

'That's what I say,' put in Barry Kirk. 'Surely you can't go now. Good lord, man, have you no curiosity?'

'The bluest hills are those farthest away,' Chan said. 'Bluest of all is Punchbowl Hill, where my little family is gathered, waiting for me — '

'But I was depending on you,' pleaded the girl. 'I must succeed — I simply must. If you would stay — '

Chan drew away from her. 'I am so sorry. Postman on his holiday, they tell me, takes long walk. I have taken same, and I am weary. So very sorry — but I return to Honolulu to-morrow.' The elevator door was open. Chan bowed low. 'The happiest pleasure to know you both. May we meet again. Good-bye.'

Like a grim, relentless Buddha he disappeared below. Kirk and the girl re-entered the office, where Captain Flannery was eagerly on the hunt.

Chan walked briskly through the fog to the Stewart Hotel. At the desk the clerk handed him a cable, which he read with beaming face. He was still smiling when, in his room, the telephone rang. It was Kirk.

'Look here,' Kirk said. 'We made the most astonishing discovery in the office after you left.'

'Pleased to hear it,' Chan replied.

'Under the desk — a pearl from Gloria Garland's necklace!'

'Opening up,' said Chan, 'a new field of wonderment. Hearty congratulations.'

'But see here,' Kirk cried, 'aren't you interested? Won't you stay and help us get at the bottom of this?'

Again that stubborn look in Charlie's eyes. 'Not possible. Only a few minutes back I have a cable that calls me home with unbearable force. Nothing holds me on the mainland now.'

'A cable? From whom?'

'From my wife. Glorious news. We are now in receipt of our eleventh child — a boy.'

5

The Voice in the Next Room

Charlie Chan rose at eight the next morning, and as he scraped the stubble of black beard from his cheeks, he grinned happily at his reflection in the glass. He was thinking of the small, helpless boy-child who no doubt at this moment lay in the battered old crib on Punchbowl Hill. In a few days, the detective promised himself, he would stand beside that crib, and the latest Chan would look up to see, at last, his father's welcoming smile.

He watched a beetle-browed porter wheel his inexpensive little trunk off on the first leg of its journey to the Matson docks, and then neatly placed his toilet articles in his suitcase. With jaunty step he went down to breakfast.

The first page of the morning paper carried the tragic tale of Sir Frederic's passing, and for a moment Chan's eyes narrowed. A complicated mystery, to be sure. Interesting to go to the bottom of it — but that was the difficult task of others. Had it been his duty, he would have approached it gallantly, but, from his point of view, the thing did not concern him. Home — that alone concerned him now.

He laid the paper down, and his thoughts flew back to the little boy in Honolulu. An American citizen, a future boy scout under the American flag, he should have an American name. Chan had felt himself greatly attracted to his genial host of the night before. Barry Chan — what was the matter with that?

As he was finishing his tea, he saw in the dining-room door the thin, nervous figure of Bill Rankin, the reporter. He signed his check, left a generous tip, and joined Rankin in the lobby.

'Hello,' said the reporter. 'Well, that was some little affair up at the Kirk Building last night.'

'Most distressing,' Chan replied. They sat down on a broad sofa, and Rankin lighted a cigarette.

'I've got a bit of information I believe you should have,' the newspaper man continued.

'Begging pardon, I think you labour under natural delusion,' Chan said.

'Why — what do you mean?'

'I am not concerned with case,' Chan calmly informed him.

'You don't mean to say — '

'In three hours I exit through Golden Gate.'

Rankin gasped. 'Good lord. I knew you'd planned to go, of course, but I supposed — Why, man alive, this is the biggest thing that's broke round here since the fire. Sir Frederic Bruce — it's an international catastrophe. I should think you'd leap at it.'

'I am not,' smiled Charlie, 'a leaping kind of man. Personal affairs call me to Hawaii. The postman refuses to take another walk. Very interesting case, but as I have heard my slanging cousin Willie say, I am not taking any of it.'

'I know,' said Rankin. 'The calm, cool Oriental. Never been excited in your life, I suppose?'

'What could I have gained by that? I have watched the American citizen. His temples throb. His heart pounds. The fibres of his body vibrate. With what result? A year subtracted from his life.'

'Well, you're beyond me,' said Rankin, leaning back and seeking to relax a bit himself. 'I hope I won't be boring you if I go on talking about Sir Frederic. I've been all over our luncheon at the St. Francis in my mind, and do you know what I think?'

'I should be pleased to learn,' returned Chan.

'Fifteen years make a very heavy curtain on the Indian frontier, Sir Frederic said. If you

87

ask me, I'd say that in order to solve the mystery of his murder last night, we must look behind that curtain.'

'Easy said, but hard to do,' suggested Chan.

'Very hard, and that's why you — Oh, well, go on and take your boat ride. But the disappearance of Eve Durand is mixed up in this somehow. So, perhaps, is the murder of Hilary Galt.'

'You have reason for thinking this?'

'I certainly have. Just as I was about to sit down and write a nice feature story about that luncheon, Sir Frederic rushed into the *Globe* office and demanded I hush it all up. Why should he do that? I ask you.'

'And I pause for your reply.'

'You'll get it. Sir Frederic was still working on one, or maybe both of those cases. More than that, he was getting somewhere. That visit to Peshawar may not have been as lacking in results as he made out. Eve Durand may be in San Francisco now. Someone connected with one of those cases is certainly here — someone who pulled that trigger last night. For myself, I would *cherchez la femme*. That's French — '

'I know,' nodded Chan. 'You would hunt the woman. Excellent plan. So would I.'

'Aha — I knew it. And that's why this information I have is vital. The other night I went up to the Kirk Building to see Sir Frederic. Paradise told me he was in the office. Just as I was approaching the office door, it opened, and a young woman — '

'One moment,' Chan cut in. 'Begging pardon to interrupt, you should go at once with your story to Miss June Morrow. I am not connected.'

Rankin stood up. 'All right. But you're certainly beyond me. The man of stone. I wish you a pleasant journey. And if this case is ever solved, I hope you never hear about it.'

Chan grinned broadly. 'Your kind wishes greatly appreciated. Good-bye, and all luck possible.'

He watched the reporter as he dashed from the lobby into the street, then going above, he completed his packing. A glance at his watch told him he had plenty of time, so he went to say good-bye to his relative in Chinatown. When he returned to the hotel to get his bags, Miss Morrow was waiting for him.

'What happy luck,' he said. 'Once again I am rewarded by a sight of your most interesting face.'

'You certainly are,' she replied. 'I simply had to see you again. The district attorney has put this whole affair in my hands, and it's my big chance. You are still determined to go home?'

'More than usual.' He led her to a sofa. 'Last night I have joyous cable — '

'I know. I was there when Mr. Kirk telephoned you. A boy, I think he said.'

'Heaven's finest gift,' nodded Chan.

Miss Morrow sighed. 'If it had only been a girl,' she said.

'Good luck,' Chan told her, 'dogs me in such matters. Of eleven opportunities, I am disappointed but three times.'

'You're to be congratulated. However, girls are a necessary evil.'

'You are unduly harsh. Necessary, of course. In your case, no evil whatever.'

Barry Kirk came into the lobby and joined them. 'Good morning, father,' he smiled. 'Well, we're all here to speed the parting guest.'

Chan consulted his watch. Miss Morrow smiled. 'You've quite a lot of time,' she said. 'At least give me the benefit of your advice before you leave.'

'Happy to do so,' agreed Chan. 'It is worthless, but you are welcome.'

'Captain Flannery is completely stumped, though of course he won't admit it. I told him all about Hilary Galt and Eve Durand, and he just opened his mouth and forgot to close it.'

'Better men than the Captain might also pause in yawning doubt.'

90

'Yes — I admit that.' Miss Morrow's white forehead wrinkled in perplexity. 'It's all so scattered — San Francisco and London and Peshawar — it almost looks as though whoever solved it must make a trip around the world.'

Chan shook his head. 'Many strings reach back, but solution will lie in San Francisco. Accept my advice, and take heart bravely.'

The girl still puzzled. 'We know that Hilary Galt was killed sixteen years ago. A long time, but Sir Frederic was the sort who would never abandon a trail. We also know that Sir Frederic was keenly interested in the disappearance of Eve Durand from Peshawar. That might have been a natural curiosity — but if it was, why should he rush to the newspaper office and demand that nothing be printed about it? No — it was more than curiosity. He was on the trail of something.'

'And near the end of it,' put in Kirk. 'He told me that much.'

Miss Morrow nodded. 'Near the end — what did that mean? Had he found Eve Durand? Was he on the point of exposing her identity? And was there someone — Eve Durand or someone else — who was determined he should never do so? So determined, in fact, that he — or she — would not stop short of murder to silence him?'

'All expressed most clearly,' approved Chan.

'Oh — but it isn't clear at all. Was Hilary Galt's murder connected somehow with the disappearance of that young girl from Peshawar? The velvet slippers — where are they now? Did the murderer of Sir Frederic take them? And if so — why?'

'Many questions arise,' admitted Chan. 'All in good time you get the answers.'

'We'll never get them,' sighed the girl, 'without your help.'

Chan smiled. 'How sweet your flattery sounds.' He considered. 'I make no search of the office last night. But Captain Flannery did. What was found? Records? A casebook?'

'Nothing,' said Kirk, 'that had any bearing on the matter. Nothing that mentioned Hilary Galt or Eve Durand.'

Chan frowned. 'Yet without question of doubt, Sir Frederic kept records. Were those records the prize for which the killer made frantic search? Doubtless so. Did he — or she — then, find them? That would seem to be true, unless — '

'Unless what?' asked the girl quickly.

'Unless Sir Frederic had removed same to safe and distant place. On face of things, he expected marauder. He may have baited trap with pointless paper. You have hunted his personal effects, in bedroom?'

92

'Everything,' Kirk assured him. 'Nothing was found. In the desk downstairs were some newspaper clippings — accounts of the disappearance of other women who walked off into the night. Sir Frederic evidently made such cases his hobby.'

'Other women?' Chan was thoughtful.

'Yes. But Flannery thought those clippings meant nothing, and I believe he was right.'

'And the cutting about Eve Durand remained in Sir Frederic's purse?' continued Chan.

'By gad!' Kirk looked at the girl. 'I never thought of that. The clipping was gone!'

Miss Morrow's dark eyes were filled with dismay. 'Oh — how stupid,' she cried. 'It was gone, and the fact made no impression on me at all. I'm afraid I'm just a poor, weak woman.'

'Calm your distress,' said Chan soothingly. 'It is a matter to note, that is all. It proves that the quest of Eve Durand held important place in murderer's mind. You must, then, *cherchez la femme*. You understand?'

'Hunt the woman,' said Miss Morrow.

'You have it. And in such an event, a huntress will be far better than a hunter. Let us think of guests at party. Mr. Kirk, you have said a portion of these people are there because Sir Frederic requested their presence. Which?'

'The Enderby's,' replied Kirk promptly. 'I didn't know them. But Sir Frederic wanted them to come.'

'That has deep interest. The Enderbys. Mrs. Enderby approached state of hysteria all evening. Fear of dark might mean fear of something else. Is it beyond belief that Eve Durand, with new name, marries again into bigamy?'

'But Eve Durand was a blonde,' Miss Morrow reminded him.

'Ah, yes. And Eileen Enderby has hair like night. It is, I am told, a matter that is easily arranged. Colour of hair may be altered, but colour of eyes — that is different. And Mrs. Enderby's eyes are blue, matching oddly raven locks.'

'Never miss a trick, do you?' smiled Kirk.

'Mrs. Enderby goes to garden, sees man on fire-escape. So she informs us. But does she? Or does she know her husband, smoking cigarette on stairs, has not been so idly occupied? Is man on fire-escape a myth of her invention, to protect her husband? Why are stains on her gown? From leaning with too much hot excitement against garden rail, damp with the fog of night? Or from climbing herself on to fire-escape — you apprehend my drift? What other guests did Sir Frederic request?'

Kirk thought. 'He asked me to invite Gloria

Garland,' the young man announced.

Chan nodded. 'I expected it. Gloria Garland — such is not a name likely to fall to human lot. Sounds like a manufacture. And Australia is so placed on map it might be appropriate end of journey from Peshawar. Blonde, blue-eyed, she breaks necklace on the stair. Yet you discover a pearl beneath the office desk.'

Miss Morrow nodded. 'Yes — Miss Garland certainly is a possibility.'

'There remains,' continued Chan, 'Mrs. Tupper-Brock. A somewhat dark lady — but who knows? Sir Frederic did not ask her presence?'

'No — I don't think he knew she existed,' said Kirk.

'Yes? But it is wise in our work, Miss Morrow, that even the smallest improbabilities be studied. Men stumble over pebbles, never over mountains. Tell me, Mr. Kirk — was Colonel John Beetham the idea of Sir Frederic too?'

'Not at all. And now that I remember, Sir Frederic seemed a bit taken back when he heard Beetham was coming. But he said nothing.'

'We have now traversed the ground. You have, Miss Morrow, three ladies to receive your most attentive study — Mrs. Enderby,

Miss Garland, Mrs. Tupper-Brock. All of proper age, so near as a humble man can guess it in this day of beauty rooms with their appalling tricks. These only of the dinner party — '

'And one outside the dinner party,' added the girl, to Chan's surprise.

'Ah — on that point I have only ignorance,' he said blankly.

'You remember the elevator operator spoke of a girl employed by the Calcutta Importers, on the twentieth floor? A Miss Lila Barr. She was at work in her office there last night.'

'Ah, yes,' nodded Chan.

'Well, a newspaper man, Rankin of the *Globe*, came to see me a few minutes ago. He said that the other evening — night before last — he went to call on Sir Frederic in Mr. Kirk's office, rather late. Just as he approached the door, a girl came out. She was crying. Rankin saw her dab at her eyes and disappear into the room of the Calcutta Importers. A blonde girl, he said.'

Chan's face was grave. 'A fourth lady to require your kind attention. The matter broadens. So much to be done — and you in the midst of it all, like a pearl in a muddy pool.' He stood up. 'I am sorry. But the *Maui* must even now be straining at her moorings — '

'One other thing,' put in the girl. 'You made quite a point of that Cosmopolitan Club year book lying beside Sir Frederic. You thought it important?'

Chan shrugged. 'I fear I was in teasing mood. I believed it hardest puzzle of the lot. Therefore I am mean enough to press it on Captain Flannery's mind. What it meant, I cannot guess. Poor Captain Flannery will never do so.'

He looked at his watch. The girl rose. 'I won't keep you longer,' she sighed. 'I'm very busy, but somehow I can't let you go. I'm trailing along to the dock with you, if you don't mind. Perhaps I'll think of something else on the way.'

'Who am I,' smiled Chan, 'to win such overwhelming honour. You behold me speechless with delight. Mr. Kirk — '

'Oh, I'm going along,' said Kirk. 'Always like to see a boat pull out. The Lord meant me for a travelling salesman.'

Chan got his bag, paid his bill, and the three of them entered Kirk's car, parked round the corner.

'Now that the moment arrives,' said Chan, 'I withdraw from this teeming mainland with some regret. Fates have been in smiling mood with me here.'

'Why go?' suggested Kirk.

'Long experience,' replied Chan, 'whispers not to strain fates too far. Their smile might fade.'

'Want to stop anywhere on the way?' Kirk asked. 'You've got thirty minutes to sailing time.'

'I am grateful, but all my farewells are said. Only this morning I have visited Chinatown — ' He stopped. 'So fortunate you still hang on,' he added to the girl. 'I was forgetting most important information for you. Still another path down which you must travel.'

'Oh, dear,' she sighed. 'I'm dizzy now. What next?'

'You must at once inflict this information on Captain Flannery. He is to find a Chinese, a stranger here, stopping with relatives on Jackson Street. The name, Li Gung.'

'Who is Li Gung?' asked Miss Morrow.

'Yesterday, when delicious lunch was ended, I hear of Li Gung from Sir Frederic.' He repeated his conversation with the great man. 'Li Gung had information much wanted by Sir Frederic. That alone I can say. Captain Flannery must extract this information from Li.'

'He'll never get it,' replied the girl pessimistically. 'Now you, Sergeant — '

Chan drew a deep breath. 'I am quite overcome,' he remarked, 'by the bright loveliness of this morning on which I say farewell to the mainland.'

They rode on in silence, while the girl thought hard. If only she could find some way of reaching this stolid man by her side, some appeal that would not roll off like water from a duck's back. She hastily went over in her mind all she had ever read of the Chinese character.

Kirk drove his smart roadster on to the pier, a few feet from the *Maui's* gangplank. The big white ship was gay with the colour of women's hats and frocks. Taxis were sweeping up, travellers were alighting, white-jacketed stewards stood in a bored line ready for another sailing. Good-byes and final admonitions filled the air.

A steward stepped forward and took Chan's bag. 'Hello, Sergeant,' he said. 'Going home, eh? What room, please?'

Chan told him, then turned to the young people at his side. 'At thought of your kindness,' he remarked, 'I am choking. Words escape me. I can only say — good-bye.'

'Give my regards to the youngest Chan,' said Kirk. 'Perhaps I'll see him some day.'

'Reminding me,' returned Chan, 'that only this morning I scour my brain to name him. With your kind permission, I will denote him Barry Chan.'

'I'm very much flattered,' Kirk answered gravely. 'Wish to heaven I had something to send him — er — a mug — or a what-you-may-call-it. You'll hear from me later.'

'I only trust,' Chan said, 'he grows up worthy of his name. Miss Morrow — I am leaving on this dock my heartiest good wishes — '

She looked at him oddly. 'Thank you,' she remarked in a cool voice. 'I wish you could have stayed, Mr. Chan. But of course I realize your point of view. The case was too difficult. For once, Charlie Chan is running away. I'm afraid the famous Sergeant of the Honolulu police has lost face today.'

A startled expression crossed that usually bland countenance. For a long moment Chan looked at her with serious eyes, then he bowed, very stiffly. 'I wish you good-bye,' he said, and walked with offended dignity up the gangplank.

Kirk was staring at the girl in amazement. 'Don't look at me like that,' she cried ruefully. 'It was cruel, but it was my last chance. I'd tried everything else. Well, it didn't work. Shall we go?'

'Oh — let's wait,' pleaded Kirk. 'They're sailing in a minute. I always get a thrill out of it. Look — up there on the top deck.' He nodded towards a pretty girl in grey, with a cluster of orchids pinned to her shoulder. 'A bride, if you ask me. And I suppose that vacant-faced idiot at her side is the lucky man.'

Miss Morrow looked, without interest.

'A great place for a honeymoon, Hawaii,' went on Kirk. 'I've often thought — I hope I'm not boring you?'

'Not much,' she said.

'I know. Brides leave you cold. I suppose divorce is more in your line. You and Blackstone. Well, you shan't blast my romantic young nature.' He took out a handkerchief and waved it towards the girl on the top deck. 'So long, my dear,' he called. 'All the luck in the world.'

'I don't see Mr. Chan,' said the young woman from the district attorney's office.

Mr. Chan was sitting thoughtfully on the edge of the berth in his stateroom, far below. The great happiness of his long-anticipated departure for home had received a rude jolt. Running away — was that it? Afraid of a difficult case? Did Miss Morrow really think that? If she did, then he had lost face indeed.

His gloomy reflections were interrupted by a voice in the next stateroom — a voice he had heard before. His heart stood still as he listened.

'I fancy that's all, Li,' said the familiar voice. 'You have your passport, your money. You are simply to wait for me in Honolulu.

Better lie low there.'

'I will do so,' replied a high-pitched, sing-song voice.

'And if anyone asks any questions, you know nothing. Understand?'

'Yes-s-s. I am silent. I understand.'

'Very good. You're a wonderful servant, Li Gung. I don't like to flatter you, you grinning beggar, but I couldn't do without you. Good-bye — and a pleasant journey.'

Chan was on his feet now, peering out into the dim passageway along which opened the rooms on the lowest deck. In that faint light he saw a familiar figure emerge from the room next door, and disappear in the distance.

The detective stood for a moment, undecided. Of all the guests at Barry Kirk's party one had interested him beyond all others — almost to the exclusion of the others. The tall, grim, silent man who had made his camps throughout the wastelands of the world, who had left a trail of the dead but who had always moved on, relentlessly, towards his goal. Colonel John Beetham, whom he had just seen emerging from the stateroom next to his with a last word of farewell to Li Gung.

Chan looked at his watch. It was never his habit to hurry, but he must hurry now. He sighed a great sigh that rattled the glasses in their rings, and snatched up his bag. On the saloon deck he met the purser.

'Homeward bound, Charlie?' inquired that gentleman breezily.

'So I thought,' replied Chan, 'but it seems I was mistaken. At the last moment, I am rudely wrenched ashore. Yet I have ticket good only on this boat.'

'Oh, they'll fix that up for you at the office. They all know you, Charlie.'

'Thanks for the suggestion. My trunk is already loaded. Will you kindly deliver same to my oldest son, who will call for it when you have docked at Honolulu?'

'Sure.' The 'visitors ashore' call was sounding for the last time. 'Don't you linger too long on this wicked mainland, Charlie,' the purser admonished.

'One week only,' called Chan over his shoulder. 'Until the next boat. I swear it.'

On the dock, Miss Morrow seized Kirk's arm. 'Look. Coming down the gangplank. Colonel Beetham. What's he doing here?'

'Beetham — sure enough,' said Kirk. 'Shall I offer him a lift? No — he's got a taxi. Let him go. He's a cold proposition — I like him not.' He watched the Colonel enter a cab and ride off.

When he turned back to the *Maui*, two husky sailors were about to draw up the plank. Suddenly between them appeared a chubby little figure, one hand clutching a suit-case. Miss Morrow gave a cry of delight.

'It's Chan,' Kirk said. 'He's coming ashore.'

And ashore Charlie came, while they lifted the plank at his heels. He stood before the two young people, ill at ease.

'Moment of gentle embarrassment for me,' he said. 'The traveller who said good-bye is back before he goes.'

'Mr. Chan,' the girl cried, 'you dear! You're going to help us, after all.'

Chan nodded. 'To the extent of my very slight ability, I am with you to finish, bitter or sweet.'

On the top deck of the *Maui* the band began to play — *Aloha,* that most touching of farewells. Long streamers of bright-coloured paper filled the air. The last good-byes, the final admonitions — a loud voice calling: 'Don't forget to write.' Charlie Chan watched, a mist before his eyes. Slowly the boat drew away from the pier. The crowd ran along beside it, waving frantically. Charlie's frame shook with another ponderous sigh.

'Poor little Barry Chan,' he said. 'He would have been happy to see me. Captain Flannery will not be so happy. Let us ride away into the face of our problems.'

6

The Guest Detective

Barry Kirk tossed Chan's suit-case into the luggage compartment of his roadster, and the trio crowded again on to its single seat. The car swung about in the piershed and emerged into the bright sunlight of the Embarcadero.

'You are partially consumed with wonder at my return?' suggested Chan.

The girl shrugged. 'You're back. That's enough for me.'

'All the same, I will confess my shame. It seems I have circulated so long with mainland Americans I have now, by contagion, acquired one of their worst faults. I too suffer curiosity. Event comes off on boat which reveals, like heavenly flash, my hidden weakness.'

'Something happened on the boat?' Miss Morrow inquired.

'You may believe it did. On my supposed farewell ride through city, I inform you of Li Gung. I tell you he must be questioned. He cannot be questioned now.'

'No? Why not?'

'Because he is on *Maui*, churning away. It is not unprobable that shortly he will experience a feeling of acute disfavour in that seat of all wisdom, the stomach.'

'Li Gung on the *Maui*?' repeated the girl. Her eyes were wide. 'What can that mean?'

'A question,' admitted Chan, 'which causes the mind to itch. Not only is Li Gung on *Maui*, but he was warmly encouraged away from here by a friend of ours.' He repeated the brief conversation he had overheard in the adjoining cabin.

Barry Kirk was the first to speak. 'Colonel Beetham, eh?' he said. 'Well, I'm not surprised.'

'Nonsense,' cried Miss Morrow warmly. 'Surely he isn't involved? A fine man like that — '

'A fine man,' Chan conceded, 'and a hard one. Look in his eyes and behold; they are cold and gleaming, like the tiger's. Nothing stands in the way when such eyes are fixed on the goal of large success — stands there long — alive.'

The girl did not seem to be convinced. 'I won't believe it. But shouldn't we have taken Li Gung off the boat?'

Chan shrugged. 'Too late. The opportunity wore rapid wings.'

'Then we'll have him questioned in

106

Honolulu,' Miss Morrow said.

Chan shook his head. 'Pardon me if I say, not that. Chinese character too well known to me. Questioning would yield no result — save one. It would serve to advise Colonel Beetham that we look on him with icy eye. I shudder at the thought — this Colonel clever man. Difficult enough to shadow if he does not suspect. Impossible if he leaps on guard.'

'Then what do you suggest?' asked the girl.

'Let Li Gung, unknowing, be watched. If he seeks to proceed beyond Honolulu, rough hands will restrain him. Otherwise we permit him to lie, like winter overcoat in closet during heated term.' Chan turned to Barry Kirk. 'You are taking me back to hotel?'

'I am not,' smiled Kirk. 'No more hotel for you. If you're going to look into this little puzzle, the place for you is the Kirk Building, where the matter originated. Don't you say so, Miss Morrow?'

'That's awfully kind of you,' said the girl.

'Not at all. It's painfully lonesome up where the fog begins without at least one guest. I'm out of all visitors at the moment — er — ah — I mean Mr. Chan will be doing me a real favour.' He turned to Charlie. 'You shall have Sir Frederic's room,' he added.

Chan shrugged. 'I can never repay such goodness. Why attempt it?'

'Let's go to my office, first of all,' Miss Morrow said. 'I want the district attorney to meet Mr. Chan. We must all be friends — at the start, anyhow.'

'Anywhere you say,' Kirk agreed, and headed the car up Market Street, to Kearny. He remained in the roadster, while the girl and Charlie went up to the district attorney's offices. When then entered that gentleman's private room, they found Captain Flannery already on the scene.

'Mr. Trant — I've good news for you,' the girl began. 'Oh — good morning, Captain.'

Flannery's Irish eyes were not precisely smiling as they rested on Charlie Chan. 'What's this, Sergeant?' he growled. 'I thought you were off for Honolulu at twelve?'

Chan grinned. 'You will be delighted to learn that my plans are changed. Miss Morrow has persuaded me to remain here and add my minute brain power to your famous capacity in same line.'

'Is that so?' mumbled Flannery.

'Yes — isn't it splendid?' cried the girl. 'Mr. Chan is going to help us.' She turned to her chief. 'You must give him a temporary appointment as a sort of guest detective connected with this office.'

Trant smiled. 'Wouldn't that be a bit irregular?' he asked.

108

'Impossible,' said Flannery firmly.

'Not at all,' persisted the girl. 'It's a very difficult case, and we shall need all the help we can get. Sergeant Chan will not interfere with you, Captain — '

'I'll say he won't,' Flannery replied warmly.

'He can act in a sort of advisory capacity. You're a big enough man to take advice, I know.'

'When it's any good,' the Captain added. The girl looked appealingly at Trant.

'You are on leave of absence from the Honolulu force, Sergeant?' inquired the district attorney.

'One which stretches out like an elastic,' nodded Chan.

'Very well. Since Miss Morrow wishes it, I see no reason why you shouldn't lend her your no doubt very useful aid. Remembering, of course, that neither one of you is to interfere with Captain Flannery in any way.'

'Better say that again,' Flannery told him. He turned to Chan. 'That means you're not to butt in and spoil things.'

Chan shrugged. 'It was the wise K'ung-fu-tsze who said, 'he who is out of office should not meddle with the government.' The labour is all yours. I will merely haunt the back ground, thinking tensely.'

'That suits me,' Flannery agreed. 'I'll make

109

all the inquiries.' He turned to the district attorney. 'I'm going to get after that Garland woman right away. The pearl she dropped under Sir Frederic's desk — I want to know all about it.'

'Please don't think I'm interfering,' Miss Morrow said sweetly. 'But as regards the women involved in this case, I feel that perhaps I can get more out of them than you can. Being a woman myself, you know. Will you let me have Miss Garland, please?'

'I can't see it,' said Flannery stubbornly.

'I can,' remarked Trant, decisively. 'Miss Morrow is a clever girl, Captain. Leave the women to her. You take the men.'

'What men?' protested Flannery. 'It's all women, in this affair.'

'Thank you so much,' smiled Miss Morrow, assuming his unproffered consent. 'I will look up Miss Garland, then. There's another woman who must be questioned at once — a Miss Lila Barr. I shall have a talk with her at the first possible moment. Of course, I'll keep you advised of all I do.'

Flannery threw up his hands. 'All right — tell me about it — after it's over. I'm nobody.'

'Quite incorrect,' said Chan soothingly. 'You are everybody. When the moment of triumph comes, who will snatch all credit?

110

And rightly so. Captain Flannery, in charge of the case. Others will fade like fog in local sun.'

The girl stood up. 'We must go along. I'll be in to see you later, Captain. Come, Sergeant Chan — '

Chan rose. He seemed a bit uncomfortable. 'The Captain must pardon me. I fear I afflict him like sore thumb. Natural, too. I would feel the same.'

'That's all right,' returned Flannery. 'You're going to stick in the background, thinking tensely. You've promised. Think all you like — I can't stop that.' His face brightened. 'Think about that Cosmopolitan Club book. I'll turn the heavy thinking on that over to you. Me, I'll be busy elsewhere. One thing I insist on — you're not to question any of these people under suspicion.'

Chan bowed. 'I am disciple of famous philosopher, Captain,' he remarked. 'Old man in China who said, 'The fool questions others, the wise man questions himself.' We shall meet again. Good-bye.' He followed the girl out.

Flannery, his face brick red, turned to the district attorney. 'Fine business,' he cried. 'The toughest case I ever had, and what sort of help do I draw? A doll-faced girl and a

111

Chinaman! Bah — I — I —' He trailed off into profanity.

Trant was smiling. 'Who knows?' he replied. 'You may get more help from them than you expect.'

'If I get any at all, I'll be surprised.' Flannery stood up. 'A woman and a Chinaman. Hell, I'll be the joke of the force.'

The two whom Captain Flannery was disparaging found Barry Kirk waiting impatiently in his car. 'An inner craving,' he announced, 'tells me it's lunch-time. You're both lunching with me at the bungalow. Step lively, please.'

Atop the Kirk Building, Paradise was ordered to lay two more places, and Kirk showed Chan to his room. He left the detective there to unpack, and returned to Miss Morrow.

'You seem the perpetual host,' she smiled, as he joined her.

'Oh, I'm going to get a lot of fun out of Charlie,' he answered. 'He's a good scout, and I like him. But by way of confession, I had other reasons for inviting him here. You and he are going to work together, and that means — what?'

'It means, I hope, that I'm going to learn a lot.'

'From associating with Chan?'

'Precisely.'

'And if you associate with my guest, you'll be bound to stumble over me occasionally. I'm a wise lad. I saw it coming.'

'I don't understand. Why should you want me to stumble over you?'

'Because every time you do I'll leap up and look at you, and that will be another red-letter day in my life.'

She shook her head. 'I'm afraid you're terribly frivolous. If I see much of you, you'll drag me down and down until I lose my job.'

'Look on the other side, lady,' he pleaded. 'You might drag me up and up. It could be done, you know.'

'I doubt it,' she told him.

Chan came into the room, and Paradise, unperturbed by the impromptu guests, served a noble luncheon. Towards its close, Kirk spoke seriously.

'I've been thinking about this Barr girl downstairs,' he said. 'I don't know that I've told you the circumstances under which Sir Frederic came to stay with me. His son happens to be an acquaintance of mine — not a friend, I know him only slightly — and he wrote me his father was to be in San Francisco. I called on Sir Frederic at his hotel. From the start he appeared keenly interested in the Kirk Building. I couldn't quite figure it out. He asked me a lot of questions, and when he learned that I lived on the roof, I must say he practically invited himself to stop with me. Not that I wasn't delighted to have him, you understand — but somehow there was an undercurrent in the talk — well, I just sensed his eagerness. It was odd, wasn't it?'

'Very,' said the girl.

'Well, after he'd been here a couple of days he began to ask questions about the Calcutta Importers, and finally these all seemed to centre on Miss Lila Barr. I knew nothing about the firm or about Miss Barr — I'd never even heard of her. Later he found that my secretary, Kinsey, knew the girl, and the questions were all turned in that direction — though I fancied they grew more discreet. One day in the office I heard Kinsey ask Sir Frederic if he'd like to meet Miss Barr, and I also heard Sir Frederic's answer.'

'What did he say?' Miss Morrow inquired.

'He said simply: 'Later, perhaps,' with what I thought an assumed carelessness. I don't know whether all this is important or not?'

'In view of the fact that Miss Lila Barr once left Sir Frederic's presence in tears, I should say it is very important,' Miss Morrow returned. 'Don't you agree, Mr. Chan?'

Chan nodded. 'Miss Barr has fiercely

interesting sound,' he agreed. 'I long with deep fervour to hear you question her.'

The girl rose from the table. 'I'll call the office of the Calcutta Importers and ask her to step up here,' she announced, and went to the telephone.

Five minutes later Miss Lila Barr entered the living-room under the impeccable chaperonage of Paradise. She stood for a second regarding the three people who awaited her. They noted that she was an extremely pretty girl, slightly under middle height, an authentic blonde, with a sort of startled innocence in her blue eyes.

'Thank you for coming.' The deputy district attorney rose and smiled at the girl in kindly fashion. 'I am Miss Morrow, and this is Mr. Charles Chan. And Mr. Barry Kirk.'

'How do you do,' said the girl, in a low voice.

'I wanted to talk with you — I'm from the district attorney's office,' Miss Morrow added.

The girl stared at her, an even more startled expression in her eyes. 'Ye — es,' she said uncertainly.

'Sit down, please.' Kirk drew up a chair.

'You know, of course, of the murder that took place on your floor of the building last night?' Miss Morrow went on.

'Of course,' replied the girl, her voice barely audible.

'You were working last night in your office?'

'Yes — it's the first of the month, you know. I always have extra work at this time.'

'At what hour did you leave the building?'

'I think it was about ten fifteen. I'm not sure. But I went away without knowing anything of — of this — terrible affair.'

'Yes. Did you see any strangers about the building last night?'

'No one. No one at all.' Her voice was suddenly louder.

'Tell me' — Miss Morrow looked at her keenly — 'had you ever met Sir Frederic Bruce?'

'No — I had never met him.'

'You had never met him. Please think what you are saying. You didn't meet him night before last — when you visited him in his office?'

The girl started. 'Oh — I saw him then, of course. I thought you meant — had I been introduced to him.'

'Then you did go into his office night before last?'

'I went into Mr. Kirk's office. There was a big man, with a moustache, sitting in the second room. I presume it was Sir Frederic Bruce.'

'You presume?'

'Well — of course I know now it was. I saw his picture in this morning's paper.'

'He was alone in the office when you went in?'

'Yes.'

'Was he the person you went there to see?'

'No, he was not.'

'When you left the office, you burst into tears.' Again the girl started, and her face flushed. 'Was it seeing Sir Frederic made you do that?'

'Oh, no,' cried Miss Barr, with more spirit.

'Then what was it made you cry?'

'It was — a purely personal matter. Surely I needn't go into it?'

'I'm afraid you must,' Miss Morrow told her. 'This is a serious affair, you know.'

The girl hesitated. 'Well — I — '

'Tell me all that happened night before last.'

'Well — it wasn't seeing Sir Frederic made me cry,' the girl began. 'It was — not seeing someone else.'

'Not seeing someone else? Please explain that.'

'Very well.' The girl moved impulsively towards Miss Morrow. 'I can tell you. I'm sure you will understand. Mr. Kinsey, Mr. Kirk's secretary, and I — we are — well

117

— sort of engaged. Every night Mr. Kinsey waits for me, and we have dinner. Then he takes me home. Day before yesterday we had a little quarrel — just over some silly thing — you know how it is — '

'I can imagine,' said Miss Morrow solemnly.

'It was about nothing, really. I waited a long time that evening, and he didn't come for me. So I thought maybe I had been in the wrong. I swallowed my pride and went to look for him. I opened the door of Mr. Kirk's office and went in. Of course I thought Mr. Kinsey would be there. Sir Frederic was alone in the office — Mr. Kinsey had gone. I muttered some apology — Sir Frederic didn't say anything, he just looked at me. I hurried out again and — perhaps you know the feeling, Miss Morrow — '

'You burst into tears, because Mr. Kinsey hadn't waited?'

'I'm afraid I did. It was silly of me, wasn't it?'

'Well, that doesn't matter.' Miss Morrow was silent for a moment. 'The company you work for — it imports from India, I believe?'

'Yes — silk and cotton, mostly.'

'Have you ever been in India, Miss Barr?'

The girl hesitated. 'When I was quite young — I lived there for some years — with my mother and father.'

'Where in India?'

'Calcutta, mostly.'

'Other places, too?' The girl nodded. 'In Peshawar, perhaps?'

'No,' answered Miss Barr. 'I was never in Peshawar.' Chan coughed rather loudly, and, catching his eye, Miss Morrow dropped the matter of India. 'You had never heard of Sir Frederic before he came here?' she asked.

'Oh, no, indeed.'

'And you saw him just that once, when he said nothing at all?'

'Only that once.'

Miss Morrow rose. 'Thank you very much. That is all for the present. I trust Mr. Kinsey has apologized?'

The girl smiled. 'Oh, yes — that's all right now. Thank you for asking.' She went out quickly.

Barry Kirk had disappeared from the room, and now he returned. 'Kinseys's on his way up,' he announced. 'Grab him quick before they can compare notes — that was my idea. Getting to be some little detective myself.'

'Excellent,' nodded Miss Morrow approvingly. A tall, dark young man, very well dressed, came in.

'You wanted to see me, Mr. Kirk?' he inquired.

'Yes. Sorry to butt into your private affairs,

Kinsey, but I hear you are sort of engaged to a Miss Lila Barr, who works in one of the offices. Did you know about it?'

Kinsey smiled. 'Of course, Mr. Kirk. I have been meaning to mention the matter to you, but the opportunity hasn't offered.'

'Day before yesterday you had a bit of a quarrel with her?'

'Oh, it was nothing, sir.' Kinsey's dark face clouded. 'It's all fixed up now.'

'That's good. But on that evening, contrary to your custom, you didn't wait to take her home? You walked out on her?'

'I — I'm afraid I did. I was somewhat annoyed — '

'And you wanted to teach her a lesson. What I call the proper spirit. That's all — and please pardon these personal questions.'

'Quite all right, sir.' Kinsey turned to go, but hesitated. 'Mr. Kirk — '

'Yes, Kinsey?'

'Nothing, sir,' said Kinsey, and disappeared.

Kirk turned to Miss Morrow. 'There you are. The story of Miss Lila Barr, duly authenticated.'

'Such a reasonable story, too,' sighed the girl. 'But it gets us nowhere. I must say I'm disappointed. Mr. Chan — you thought I went too far — on India?'

Chan shrugged. 'In this game, better if the

opponent does not know what we are thinking. Assume great innocence is always my aim. Sometimes what I assume is exactly what I've got. Others — I am flying at a low altitude.'

'I'm afraid I should have flown at a lower altitude than I did,' the girl reflected frowning. 'Her story was perfectly plausible, and yet — I don't know — '

'Well, one thing's certain,' remarked Kirk. 'She's not Eve Durand.'

'How do you know that?' asked Miss Morrow.

'Why — her age. She's a mere kid.'

Miss Morrow laughed. 'Lucky a woman is in on this,' she said. 'You men are so painfully blind where a blonde is concerned.'

'What do you mean?'

'I mean there are certain artifices which fool a man, but never fool a woman. Miss Barr is thirty — at the very least.'

Kirk whistled. 'I must be more careful,' he said. 'I thought her sweet and twenty.'

He turned to find Paradise at his elbow. The butler had entered noiselessly, and was holding out a silver tray in the manner of one offering rich treasure.

'What shall I do with these, sir?' he inquired.

'Do with what?' Kirk asked.

'Letters addressed to Sir Frederic Bruce, sir. They have just been delivered by the local office of Thomas Cook and Sons.'

Miss Morrow came eagerly forward. 'I'll take charge of them,' she said. Paradise bowed, and went out. The girl's eyes sparkled. 'We never thought of this, Sergeant. Sir Frederic's mail — it may prove a gold mine.' She held up a letter. 'Here — the first thing — one from London. The Metropolitan Police, Scotland Yard — '

Quickly she ripped open the envelope and withdrawing a single sheet of paper, spread it out. She gave a little cry of dismay.

Kirk and Charlie Chan came nearer. They stared at the sheet of paper that had arrived in the envelope from Scotland Yard. It was just that — a sheet of paper — completely blank.

7

Muddy Water

Miss Morrow stood, her brows contracted in bewilderment, looking down at the unexpected enclosure she had found in the envelope with the London postmark.

'Oh, dear,' she sighed. 'There's just one trouble with this detective business. It's so full of mystery.'

Chan smiled. 'Humbly begging pardon to mention it, I would suggest you iron out countenance. Wrinkles might grow there, which would be a heart-breaking pity. Occasional amazing occurrence keeps life spicy. Accept that opinion from one who knows it.'

'But what in the world does this mean?' she asked. 'One thing I am certain it does not mean,' Chan replied. 'Scotland Yard in sudden playful mood does not post empty paper over six thousand miles of land and water. No, some queer business has blossomed up near at hand, which it is our duty to unveil.' The girl began to smooth the blank sheet. Chan stretched out a warning hand. Despite his girth, the hand was thin and narrow, with long, tapering fingers. 'I beg of you, do not touch further,' he cried. 'A great mistake. For although we cannot see, there is something on that paper.'

'What?' she inquired.

'Finger-prints,' he answered. Gingerly by one corner he removed the paper from her hand. 'The finger-prints, dainty and firm, you have made. The finger-prints, also, perhaps not so dainty of the person who folded it and put it in envelope.'

'Oh, of course,' said Miss Morrow.

'I am no vast admirer of science in this work,' Chan went on. 'But finger-prints tell pretty much truth. Happy to say I have made half-hearted study of the art. In Honolulu, where I am faced by little competition, I rejoice in mouth-filling title of finger-print expert. Mr. Kirk, have you a drawer with heavy lock, to which you alone hold key?'

'Surely,' replied Kirk. He unlocked a compartment in a handsome Spanish desk, and Chan deposited the paper inside. Kirk turned the key, and removing it from the ring, handed it to Charlie.

'Later,' remarked Chan, 'with lamp-black and camel's hair brush, I perform like the expert I have been pronounced. Maybe we discover who has been opening Sir Frederic's mail.' He picked up the empty envelope.

124

'Behold — steam has been applied. The marks unquestionable.'

'Steam,' cried Barry Kirk. 'But who in the world — oh, I say. Sir Frederic's mail came through the local office of Thomas Cook and Sons.'

'Precisely,' grinned Chan.

'And Mr. Carrick Enderby is employed there.'

Chan shrugged. 'You are bright young man. It is not beyond possibility that the mark of Mr. Enderby's large thumb is on that paper. However, speculation is idle thing. Facts must be upearthed. Miss Morrow — may I rudely suggest — the remainder of Sir Frederic's mail?'

'Yes, of course,' said the girl. 'I feel rather guilty about this, but when duty calls, you know — '

She sat down and went through the other letters. Obviously her search was without any interesting result.

'Well,' she said finally, 'that's that. I leave the matter of the blank sheet of paper to you, Sergeant. For myself, I am going to turn my attention to Miss Gloria Garland. What was that pearl from her necklace doing under the desk beside which Sir Frederic was killed?'

'A wise question,' nodded Chan. 'Miss Garland should now be invited to converse.

125

May she prove more pointed talker than Miss Lila Barr.'

'Let me call her up and ask her over here,' suggested Kirk. 'I'll tell her I want to have a talk with her in my office about last night's affair. She may arrive a bit less prepared with an explanation than if she knows it's the police who want to see her.'

'Splendid,' approved Miss Morrow. 'But I'm afraid we're cutting in most frightfully on your business, Mr. Kirk. You must say so if we are.'

'What business?' he inquired airily. 'Like Sergeant Chan, I am now attached to your office. And I'm likely to grow more attached all the time. If you'll pardon me for a moment — '

He went to the telephone and reached Miss Garland at her apartment. The actress agreed to come at once. As Kirk came away from the telephone, the doorbell rang and Paradise admitted a visitor. Captain Flannery strode into the room.

'Hello,' he said. 'You're all here, ain't you? I'd like to look round a bit — if I'm not butting in.'

'Surely no one could be more warmly welcome,' Chan told him.

'Thanks, Sergeant. You solved this problem yet?'

'Not up to date of present speaking,' grinned Chan.

'Well, you're a little slow, ain't you?' Captain Flannery was worried, and not in the best of humour. 'I thought from what I've read about you, you'd have the guilty man locked up in a closet for me, by this time.'

Chan's eyes narrowed. 'Challenge is accepted,' he answered with spirit. 'I have already obliged mainland policemen by filling a few closets with guilty men they could not catch. From my reading in newspapers, there still remains vast amount of work to do in same line.'

'Is that so?' Flannery responded. He turned to Miss Morrow. 'Did you talk with the Barr woman?'

'I did,' said the girl. She repeated Lila Barr's story. Flannery heard her out in silence.

'Well,' he remarked when she had finished, 'you didn't get much, did you?'

'I'll have to admit I didn't,' she replied.

'Maybe not as much as I could have got — and me not a woman, either. I'm going down now and have a talk with her myself. She don't look good to me. Cried because her fellow went and left her? Perhaps. But if you ask me, it takes more than that to make a woman cry nowadays.'

'You may be right,' Miss Morrow agreed.

'I know I'm right. And let me tell you something else — I'm going to be on hand when you talk with Gloria Garland. Make up your mind to that right now.'

'I shall be glad to have you. Miss Garland is on her way here to meet us in the office downstairs.'

'Fine. I'll go and take a look at this weepy dame. If the Garland woman comes before I'm back, you let me know. I've been in this game thirty years, young woman, and no district attorney's office can breeze me out. When I conduct an investigation, I conduct it.'

He strode from the room. Chan looked after him without enthusiasm. 'How loud is the thunder, how little it rains,' he murmured beneath his breath.

'We'd better go to the office,' suggested Kirk. 'Miss Garland is likely to arrive at any moment.'

They went below. The sun was blazing brightly in the middle room; the events of the foggy night now passed seemed like a bad dream. Kirk sat down at his desk, opened a drawer, and handed Chan a couple of press clippings.

'Want to look at those?' he inquired. 'As I told you this morning, it appears that Sir

Frederic was interested, not only in Eve Durand, but in other missing women as well.'

Chan read the clippings thoughtfully, and laid them on the desk. He sighed ponderously. 'A far-reaching case,' he remarked, and was silent for a long time.

'A puzzler, even to you,' Kirk said at length.

Chan came to himself with a start. 'Pardon, please? What did you say?'

'I said that even the famous Sergeant Chan is up against it this time.'

'Oh, yes. Yes, indeed. But I was not thinking of Sir Frederic. A smaller, less important person occupied my mind. Without fail I must go to little Barry Chan on next Wednesday's boat.'

'I hope you can,' smiled Miss Morrow. 'Not many men are as devoted to their families nowadays as you are.'

'Ah — you do not understand,' said Chan. 'You mainland people — I observe what home is to you. An unprivate apartment, a pigeonhole to dive into when the dance or the automobile ride is ended. We Chinese are different. Love, marriage, home, still we cling to unfashionable things like that. Home is a sanctuary into which we retire, the father is high priest, the altar fires burn bright.'

'Sounds rather pleasant,' remarked Barry

Kirk. 'Especially that about the father. By the way, I must send my namesake a cablegram and wish him luck.'

Miss Gloria Garland appeared in the outer office, and Kinsey escorted her into the middle room. She was not quite so effective in the revealing light of day as she had been at a candle-lighted dinner-table. There were lines about her eyes, and age was peering from beneath the heavy make-up.

'Well, here I am, Mr. Kirk,' she said. 'Oh — Miss Morrow — and Mr. Chan. I'm a wreck, I know. That thing last night upset me terribly — such a charming man, Sir Frederic. Has — has anything been unearthed — any clue?'

'Nothing much,' replied Kirk, 'as yet. Please sit down.'

'Just a moment,' said Miss Morrow. 'I must get Captain Flannery.'

'I will go, please,' Chan told her, and hurried out.

He pushed open the door of the office occupied by the Calcutta Importers. Captain Flannery was standing, red-faced and angry, and before him sat Lila Barr, again in tears. The Captain swung about. 'Yes?' he snapped.

'You are wanted, Captain,' Chan said. 'Miss Garland is here.'

'All right.' He turned to the weeping girl.

'I'll see you again, young woman.' She did not reply. He followed Chan to the hall.

'You, too, have some success as a tear-starter,' suggested Chan.

'Yeah — she's the easiest crier I've met this year. I wasn't any too gentle with her. It don't pay.'

'Your methods, of course, had amazing success?'

'Oh — she stuck to her story. But you take it from me, she knows more than she's telling. Too many tears for an innocent bystander. I'll bet you a hundred dollars right now that she's Eve Durand.'

Chan shrugged. 'My race,' he said, 'possesses great fondness for gambling. Not to go astray into ruin, I am compelled to overlook even easy methods of gain in that line.'

Captain Flannery was driven back to his favourite phrase. 'Is that so?' he replied, and they entered Kirk's office.

When they were all in the middle room, Barry Kirk shut the door on the interested Mr. Kinsey. Captain Flannery faced Gloria Garland.

'I want to see you. You know who I am. I was upstairs last night. So your name's Gloria Garland, is it?'

She looked up at him a bit apprehensively. 'Yes, of course.'

'Are you telling your real name, lady?'

'Well, it's the name I have used for many years. I — '

'Oh? So it isn't the real one?'

'Not exactly. It's a name I took — '

'I see. You took a name that didn't belong to you.' The Captain's tone implied a state's prison offence. 'You had reasons, I suppose?'

'I certainly had.' The woman looked at him with growing anger. 'My name was Ida Pingle, and I didn't think that would go well in the theatre. So I called myself Gloria Garland.'

'All right. You admit you travel under an assumed name?'

'I don't care for the way you put it. A great many people on the stage have taken more attractive names than their own. I have done nothing to justify your rudeness — '

'I can quite understand your feeling,' said Miss Morrow, with a disapproving glance at the Captain. 'From this point I will take up the inquiry.'

'I wish you would,' remarked Miss Garland warmly.

'Had you ever met Sir Frederic Bruce before you came to Mr. Kirk's dinner party last night?' the girl inquired.

'No, I had not.'

'He was, then, a complete stranger to you?'

'He certainly was. Why should you ask me that?'

'You had no private interview with him last night?'

'No. None.'

Captain Flannery stepped forward, his mouth open, about to speak. Miss Morrow raised her hand. 'Just a moment, Captain. Miss Garland, I warn you this is a serious business. You should tell the truth.'

'Well — ' Her manner became uncertain. 'What makes you think I'm — '

'Lying? We know it,' exploded Flannery.

'You broke the string of your necklace last night on your way to the bungalow,' Miss Morrow continued. 'Where did that accident happen?'

'On the stairs — the stairs leading up from the twentieth floor to the roof.'

'Did you recover all the pearls?'

'Yes — I think so. I wasn't quite sure of the number. Of course, I needn't tell you they're only imitation. I couldn't afford the real thing.'

Miss Morrow opened her hand-bag, and laid a solitary pearl on the desk. 'Do you recognize that, Miss Garland?'

'Why — why, yes. It belongs to me, of course. Thank you so much. Where — er — where did you find it?'

'We found it,' said Miss Morrow slowly, 'under the desk in this room.' The woman flushed, and made no reply. There was a moment's strained silence. 'Miss Garland,' the girl went on, 'I think you had better change your tactics. The truth, if you please.'

The actress shrugged. 'I fancy you're right. I was only trying to keep out of this. It's not the sort of publicity I want. And as a matter of fact, I'm not in it very deep.'

'But you really broke the string in this office, where you had come for a talk with Sir Frederic?'

'Yes, that's true. I caught the necklace on a corner of the desk, when I got up to go.'

'Please don't start with the moment when you got up to go. Take it from the beginning, if you will.'

'Very good. When I said I had never seen Sir Frederic before last night, I was telling the truth. I had left the elevator and was crossing the hall to the stairs, when the door of these offices opened and a man stood on the threshold. He said: 'You are Miss Garland, I believe?' I told him that was my name, and he said he was Sir Frederic Bruce, Mr. Kirk's guest, and that he wanted to have a talk with me, alone, before we met upstairs.'

'Yes — go on.'

'Well, it seemed odd, but he was such a

distinguished-looking man I felt it must be all right, so I followed him in here. We sat down, and he started in to tell me who he was — Scotland Yard, and all that. I'm English, of course, and I have the greatest respect for anyone from the Yard. He talked around for a minute, and then he went to the point.'

'Ah, yes,' smiled Miss Morrow. 'That's what we are waiting for. What was the point?'

'He — he wanted to ask me something.'

'Yes? What?'

'He wanted to ask me if I could identify a woman who disappeared a great many years ago. A woman who just stepped off into the night, and was never heard of again.'

A tense silence followed these words. Quietly Chan moved a little closer. Barry Kirk's eyes were fixed with interest on Gloria Garland's face. Even Captain Flannery stood eagerly at attention.

'Yes,' said Miss Morrow calmly. 'And why did Sir Frederic think you could identify this woman?'

'Because I was her best friend. I was the last person who saw her on the night she disappeared.'

Miss Morrow nodded. 'Then you were present at a picnic party in the hills near Peshawar on a certain night fifteen years ago?'

The woman's eyes opened wide. 'Peshawar? That's in India', isn't it? I have never been in India in my life.'

Another moment of startled silence. Then Flannery roared at her. 'Look here — you promised to tell the truth — '

'I am telling the truth,' she protested.

'You are not. That woman he asked you about was Eve Durand, who disappeared from a party one night outside Peshawar — '

Chan cut in on him. 'Humbly asking pardon, Captain,' he said, 'you shouldn't be so agile in jumping upon the lady's story.' He picked up a couple of clippings from the desk. 'Will you be so kind,' he added to Miss Garland, 'as to mention name of place from which your friend disappeared?'

'Certainly. She disappeared from Nice.'

'Nice? Where the hell's that?' Flannery asked.

'Nice is a resort city on the French Riviera,' replied Miss Garland, sweetly. 'I am afraid your duties keep you too much at home, Captain.'

'Nice,' repeated Chan slowly. 'Then the name of your friend was perhaps Marie Lantelme?'

'That was her name,' the actress replied.

Chan selected a clipping, and handed it to Miss Morrow. 'Will you condescend to read words out loud?' he inquired. 'Most interesting, to be sure.'

Again, as in the dining-room of the St. Francis the day before, Miss Morrow read one of Sir Frederic's treasured clippings.

'What became of Marie Lantelme? It is now eleven years since that moonlit June night when a company under English management played *The Dollar Princess* on the stage of the Theatre de la Jetée-Promenade, in the city of Nice. It was a memorable evening for all concerned. The house was sold out, packed with soldiers on leave, and the manager was frantic. At the last moment word had come that his leading lady was seriously ill and with many misgivings he sent for the under-study, a pretty, inconspicuous little chorus girl named Marie Lantelme. It was her big chance at last. She stepped out on the blazing stage and became a woman trans-formed. The performance she gave will never be forgotten by anyone who was in that audience — an audience that went wild, that was on its feet cheering for her when the curtain fell.

'After the performance the manager rushed in high glee to Marie Lantelme's dressing-room. She was a discovery, and she was his. He would star her in London, in New York. She listened to

137

him in silence. Then she put on her simple little frock and stepped from the stage door out into the open. Fame and riches were waiting for her, if she chose to take them. Whether she chose or not will never be known. All that is known is that when she left the theatre she walked off into nothingness. Eleven years have passed, and from that day to this no one has ever heard from Marie Lantelme.'

Miss Morrow stopped reading, her countenance again in great need of ironing out. Captain Flannery stood with open mouth. Only Chan seemed to have retained his cheerful composure.

'Marie Lantelme was your friend?' he said to Miss Garland.

'She was,' replied the actress, 'and somehow Sir Frederic knew it. I was appearing in that same company. I must say the clipping exaggerates a bit — I suppose they have to do it to make things interesting. It was an adequate performance — that's what I would have called it. I don't remember any cheering. But there isn't any doubt about her making good. She could have had other parts — better ones than she had ever had before. Yet it's true enough — she left the theatre, and that was the last of her.'

'You had final view of her?' Chan suggested.

'Yes. On my way home, I saw her standing talking to some man on the Promenade des Anglais, at the entrance to the jetty. I went on, thinking nothing of it at the time. Afterwards, of course — '

'And it was this girl Sir Frederic asked you about?' Miss Morrow inquired.

'It was. He showed me that clipping, and asked me if I wasn't in the same company. I said I was. He wanted to know if I thought I could identify Marie Lantelme if I met her again, and I said I was quite sure I could. 'Very good,' he said. 'I may call upon you for that service before the evening is over. Please do not leave to-night until we have had another talk.' I told him I wouldn't, but of course, at the end — well, he wasn't talking to anyone any more.'

They sat for a moment in silence. Then Miss Morrow spoke.

'I think that is all,' she said. 'Unless Captain Flannery — '

She glanced at the Captain. An expression of complete bewilderment decorated that great red face. 'Me? No — no, I guess not. Nothing more from me, now,' he stammered.

'Thank you very much, Miss Garland,' the girl continued. 'You are going to be in the city for some time?'

139

'Yes. I've been promised a part at the Alcazar.'

'Well, don't leave town without letting me know. You may go now. So good of you to come.'

Miss Garland nodded towards the desk. 'May I have the pearl?'

'Oh — certainly.'

'Thanks. When an actress has been out of a shop for some time, even the imitation jewels are precious. You understand?'

Miss Morrow let her out, and returned to the silent little group in the inner room. 'Well?' she remarked.

'It's incredible,' cried Barry Kirk. 'Another lost lady. Good lord, Eve Durand and Marie Lantelme can't both be hanging out around here. Unless this is the Port of Missing Women. What do you say, Sergeant?'

Chan shrugged. 'All time we get in deeper,' he admitted 'Free to announce I find myself sunk in bafflement.'

'I'll get to the bottom of it,' Flannery cried. 'You leave it to me. I'll stir things up.'

Chan's eyes narrowed. 'My race has old saying, Captain,' he remarked gently. ' "Muddy water, unwisely stirred, grows darker still. Left alone, it clears itself." '

Flannery glared at him and without a word strode from the room, slamming the outer door behind him.

140

8

Willie Li's Good Turn

Thoughtfully Charlie Chan picked up Sir Frederic's clippings from the desk and taking out a huge wallet, stowed them away inside. Barry Kirk's eyes were on the door through which Flannery had taken his unceremonious departure.

'I'm very much afraid,' he said, 'that the policeman's lot is not a happy one. The dear old Captain seemed a bit — what's a good word for it? Nettled? Ah, yes, nettled is a very good word.'

Miss Morrow smiled. 'He's frightfully puzzled, and that always makes a policeman cross.'

'I hope it doesn't have that effect on you.'

'If it did, I'd be so cross right at this moment you'd order me out of your life for ever.'

'A trifle baffled, eh?'

'Can you wonder? Was there ever a case like this?' She picked up her coat, which she had brought with her from the bungalow. 'All that about Marie Lantelme — '

'Humbly making suggestion,' remarked Chan, 'do not think too much about Marie Lantelme. She is — what you say — an issue from the side. Remember always one big fact — Sir Frederic Bruce dead on this very floor, the velvet shoes absent from his feet. Wandering too far from that, we are lost. Think of Eve Durand, think of Hilary Galt, but think most of all regarding Sir Frederic and last night. Bestow Marie Lantelme in distant pigeonhole of mind. That way alone, we progress, we advance.'

The girl sighed. 'Shall we ever advance? I doubt it.'

'Take cheer,' advised Chan. 'A wise man said, 'The dark clouds pass, the blue heavens abide.'' He bowed low and disappeared towards the stairs leading up to the bungalow.

Barry Kirk held the girl's coat. As he placed it about her shoulders the words of a familiar advertisement flashed into his mind. 'Obey that impulse.' But one couldn't go through life obeying every chance impulse.

''All time we get in deeper,'' he quoted. 'It begins to look like a long and very involved case.'

'I'm afraid it does,' Miss Morrow replied.

'What do you mean, afraid? You and I are very brainy people — thanks for including me — and we should welcome a good stiff test of

142

our powers. Let's get together for a conference very soon.'

'Do you think that's necessary?'

'I'm sure of it.'

'Then it's all settled,' she smiled. 'Thanks for the lunch — and good-bye.'

When Kirk reached the bungalow, Charlie called to him from the room formerly occupied by the man from Scotland Yard. Going in, he found the detective standing thoughtfully before Sir Frederic's luggage, now piled neatly in a corner.

'You have investigated these properties of Sir Frederic?' Chan asked.

Kirk shook his head. 'No, I haven't. That's hardly in my line. Flannery went through them last night, and evidently found nothing. He told me to turn them over to the British Consul.'

'Flannery travels with too much haste,' protested Chan. 'You have the keys, perhaps? If so, I experience a yearning of my own to look inside.'

Kirk handed him the keys, and left him alone. For a long time Chan proceeded with his search. Finally he appeared in the living-room with a great collection of books under his arm.

'Find anything?' Kirk asked.

'Nothing at all,' Chan returned, 'with these

somewhat heavy exceptions. Deign to come closer, if you will be kind enough.'

Kirk rose and casually examined the books. His off hand manner vanished, and he cried excitedly: 'Great Scott!'

'The same from me,' Chan smiled. 'You have noted the name of the author of these volumes.' He read off the titles. '*Across China and Back. Wanderings in Persia. A Year in the Gobi Desert. Tibet, the Top of the World. My Life as an Explorer.*' His eyes narrowed as he looked at Kirk. 'All the work of our good friend, Colonel Beetham. No other books amid Sir Frederic's luggage. Does it not strike you as strange, his keen interest in one solitary author?'

'It certainly does,' agreed Kirk. 'I wonder — '

'I have never ceased to wonder. When I look into deep eyes of the lonely explorer last night, I ask myself, what make of man is this? No sooner is Sir Frederic low on the floor than my thoughts fly back to that mysterious face. So cold, so calm, but who knows with what hot fires beneath.' He selected one enormous volume, the *Life*. 'I feel called upon to do some browsing amid Sir Frederic's modest library. I will advance first on this, which will grant me bird's-eye look over an adventurous career.'

144

'A good idea,' Kirk nodded.

Before Chan could settle to his reading, the bell rang and Paradise admitted Mrs. Dawson Kirk. She came in as blithely as a girl.

'Hello, Barry. Mr. Chan, I rather thought I'd find you here. Didn't sail after all, did you?'

Chan sighed. 'I have encountered some difficulty in bringing vacation to proper stop. History is a grand repeater.'

'Well, I'm glad of it,' said Mrs. Kirk. 'They'll need you here. Frightful thing, this is. And to think, Barry, it happened in your building. The Kirks are not accustomed to scandal. I never slept a wink all night.'

'I'm sorry to hear it,' her grandson said.

'Oh, you needn't be. Not sleeping much anyhow, of late. Seems I got all my sleeping done, years ago. Well, what's happened? Have they made any progress?'

'Not much,' Kirk admitted.

'How could they? That stupid police captain — he annoyed me. No subtlety. Sally Jordan's boy here will show him up.'

'Humbly accept the flattery,' Chan bowed.

'Flattery — rot. The truth, nothing else. Don't you disappoint me. All my hopes are pinned on you.'

'By the way,' said Kirk, 'I'm glad you came alone. How long has that woman — Mrs. Tupper-Brock — been with you?'

145

'About a year. What's she got to do with it?'

'Well — what do you know about her?'

'Don't be a fool, Barry. I know everything. She's all right.'

'You mean all her past is an open book to you?'

'Nothing of the sort. I never asked about it. I didn't have to. I'm a judge of people. One look — that's enough for me.'

Kirk laughed. 'What a smart lady. As a matter of fact, you don't know a thing about her, do you?'

'Oh, yes, I do. She's English — born in Devonshire.'

'Devonshire, eh?'

'Yes. Her husband was a clergyman — you'd know that by her starved look. He's dead now.'

'And that's the extent of your knowledge?'

'You're barking up the wrong tree — but you would. A nice boy, but never very clever. However, I didn't come here to discuss Helen Tupper-Brock. It has just occurred to me that I didn't tell all I knew last night.'

'Concealing evidence, eh?' smiled Kirk.

'I don't know — it may be evidence — probably not. Tell me — have they dug up any connexion between Sir Frederic and that little Mrs. Enderby?'

'No, they haven't. Have you?'

'Well — it was just after the pictures started. I went out into the kitchen — '

'You would.'

'My throat was dry. I didn't see any water in the living-room. But what could I expect in a man-run house? In the passageway I came upon Sir Frederic and Mrs. Enderby engaged in what appeared to be a quite serious talk.'

'What were they saying?'

'I'm no eavesdropper. Besides, they stopped suddenly when I appeared, and remained silent until I had gone by. When I returned a few moments later, both were gone.'

'Well, that may be important,' Kirk admitted. 'Perhaps not. Odd, though — Sir Frederic told me he had never met Mrs. Enderby when he suggested I invite the pair to dinner. I'll turn your information over to Miss Morrow.'

'What's Miss Morrow got to do with it?' snapped the old lady.

'She's handling the case for the district attorney's office.'

'What! You mean to say they've put an important case like this in the hands of — '

'Calm yourself. Miss Morrow is a very intelligent young woman.'

'She couldn't be. She's too good-looking.'

'Miracles happen,' laughed Kirk.

His grandmother regarded him keenly.

'You look out for yourself, my boy.'

'What are you talking about?'

'The Kirk men always did have a weakness for clever women — the attraction of opposites, I presume. That's how I came to marry into the family.'

'You don't happen to have an inferiority complex about you, do you?'

'No, sir. That's one thing the new generation will never be able to pin on me. Well, go ahead and tell Miss Morrow about Eileen Enderby. But I fancy the important member of the investigating committee has heard it already. I'm speaking of Mr. Chan.' She rose. 'I wrote Sally Jordan this morning that I'd met you,' she went on, to the detective. 'I said I thought the mainland couldn't spare you just yet.'

Chan shrugged. 'Mainland enjoys spectacle of weary postman plodding on his holiday walk,' he replied. 'No offence is carried, but I am longing for Hawaii.'

'Well, that's up to you,' remarked Mrs. Kirk bluntly. 'Solve this case quickly and run before the next one breaks. I must go along. I've a club meeting. That's what my life's come to — club meetings. Barry, keep me posted on this thing. First excitement in my neighbourhood in twenty years. I don't want to miss any of it.'

Kirk let her out, and returned to the living-room. The quick winter dusk was falling, and he switched on the lights.

'All of which,' he said, 'brings little Eileen into it again. She did seem a bit on edge last night — even before she saw that man on the fire-escape. If she really did see him. I'll put Miss Morrow on her trail, eh?'

Chan looked up from his big book, and nodded without interest. 'All you can do.'

'She doesn't intrigue you much, does she?' Kirk smiled.

'This Colonel Beetham,' responded Chan. 'What a man!'

Kirk looked at his watch. 'I'm sorry, but I'm dining to-night at the Cosmopolitan Club, with a friend. I made the engagement several days ago.'

'Greatly pained,' said Chan, 'if I interfered with your plans in any way. Tell me — our Colonel Beetham — you have seen him at Cosmopolitan Club?'

'Yes. Somebody's given him a card. I meet him around there occasionally. I must take you over to the club one of these days.'

'The honour will be immense,' Chan said gravely.

'Paradise will give you dinner,' Kirk told him.

'Not to be considered,' Chan protested.

'Your staff in kitchen deserves holiday after last night's outburst. I am doing too much eating at your gracious board. I too will dine elsewhere — there are little matters into which I would peer inquiringly.'

'As you wish,' nodded Kirk. He went into his bedroom, leaving Chan to the book.

At six-thirty, after Kirk had left, Chan also descended to the street. He had dinner at an inexpensive little place and when it was finished, strolled with what looked like an aimless step in the direction of Chinatown.

The Chinese are a nocturnal race; Grant Avenue's shops were alight and thronged with customers; its pavement crowded with idlers who seemed at a loose end for the evening. The younger men were garbed like their white contemporaries; the older, in the black satin blouse and trousers of China, shuffled along on felt shod feet. Here and there walked with ponderous dignity a Chinese matron who had all too obviously never sought slimming. A sprinkling of bright-eyed flappers lightened the picture.

Chan turned up Washington Street, then off into the gloomy stretch of Waverly Place. He climbed dimly lighted stairs and knocked at a familiar door.

Surprise is not in the lexicon of the race, and Chan Kee Lim admitted him with stolid

150

face. Though they had said farewell only that morning, the detective's call was accepted calmly by his cousin.

'I am here again,' Chan said in Cantonese. 'It was my thought that I was leaving the mainland, but the fates have decreed otherwise.'

'Enter,' his cousin said. 'Here in my poor house the welcome never cools. Deign to sit on this atrociously ugly stool.'

'You are too kind,' Charlie returned. 'I am, as you must surmise, the victim of my despicable calling. If you will so far condescend, I require information.'

Kee Lim's eyes narrowed, and he stroked his thin grey beard. He did not approve of that calling, as Charlie well knew.

'You are involved,' he said coldly, 'with the white devil police?'

Chan shrugged. 'Unfortunately, yes. But I ask no betrayal of confidence from you. A harmless question, only. Perhaps you could tell me of a stranger, a tourist, who has been guest of relatives in Jackson Street? The name Li Gung.'

Kee Lim nodded. 'I have not met him, but I have heard talk at the Tong House. He is one who has travelled much in foreign lands. For some time he has been domiciled with his cousin Henry Li, the basket importer, who lives American style in the big apartment-house on Jackson Street. The Oriental Apartments, I believe. I have not been inside, but I understand there are bathrooms and other strange developments of what the white devil is pleased to call his civilization.'

'You are an acquaintance of Henry Li?' Charlie asked.

Kee Lim's eyes hardened. 'I have not the honour,' he replied.

Charlie understood. His cousin would have no part in whatever he proposed. He rose from his ebony stool.

'You are extremely kind,' he said. 'That was the extent of my desire. Duty says I must walk my way.'

Kee Lim also rose. 'The briefness of your stop makes it essential you come again. There is always a welcome here.'

'Only too well do I know it,' nodded Charlie. 'I am busy man, but we will meet again. I am saying good-bye.'

His cousin followed to the door. 'I hope you have a safe walk,' he remarked, and there was, it seemed, something more in his mind than the conventional farewell wish.

Chan set out at once for Jackson Street. Half-way up the hill he encountered the gaudy front of the Oriental Apartments. Here the more prosperous members of the Chinese colony lived in the manner of their adopted country.

He entered the lobby and studied the letter boxes. Henry Li, he discovered, lived on the second floor. Ignoring the push buttons, he tried the door. It was unlocked, and he went inside. He climbed to the third floor, walking softly as he passed the apartment occupied by Henry Li. For a moment he stood at the head of the stairs, then started down. He had proceeded about half-way to the floor below, when suddenly he appeared to lose his footing, and descended with a terrific clatter to the second-floor landing. The door of Henry Li's apartment opened, and a fat little Chinese in a business suit peered out.

'You are concerned in an accident?' he inquired solicitously.

'Haie!' cried Chan, picking himself up, 'the evil spirits pursue me. I have lost my footing on these slippery stairs.' He tried to walk, but limped painfully. 'I fear I have given my ankle a bad turn. If I could sit quietly for a moment — '

The little man threw wide his door. 'Condescend to enter my contemptible house. My chairs are plain and uncomfortable, but you must try one.'

Profuse in thanks, Chan followed him into an astonishing living-room. Hang-chau silk hangings and a few pieces of teak-wood mingled with blatant plush furniture from some department store. A small boy, about thirteen, was seated at a radio, which ground out dance music. He wore the khaki uniform of a boy scout, with a bright yellow handkerchief about his throat.

'Please sit here,' invited Henry Li, indicating a huge chair of green plush. 'I trust the pain is not very acute.'

'It begins to subside,' Chan told him. 'You are most kind.'

The boy had shut off the radio, and was standing before Charlie Chan with keen interest in his bright eyes.

'A most regrettable thing,' explained his father. 'The gentleman has turned his ankle on our detestable stairs.'

'So sorry,' the boy announced. His eyes grew even brighter. 'All boy scouts know how to make bandages. I will get my first-aid kit — '

'No, no,' protested Chan hastily. 'Do not trouble yourself. The injury is not serious.'

'It would be no trouble at all,' the boy assured him. With some difficulty Charlie dissuaded him, and to the detective's great relief, the boy disappeared.

'I will sit and rest for a moment,' Chan said to Henry Li. 'I trust I am no great obstacle here. The accident overwhelmed me when I was on the search for an old friend of mine — Li Gung by name.'

Henry Li's little eyes rested for a moment on the picture of a middle-aged Chinese in a silver frame on the mantel. 'You are a friend of Li Gung?' he inquired.

The moment had been enough for Chan. 'I am — and I see his photograph above there, tastefully framed. Is it true, then, that he is stopping here? Has my search ended so fortunately after all?'

'He was here,' Li replied, 'but only this morning he walked his way.'

'Gone!' Chan's face fell. 'Alas, then I am too late. Would you be so kind as to tell me where he went?'

Henry Li became discreet. 'He disappeared on business of his own, with which I have no concern.'

'Of course. But it is a great pity. A friend of mine, an American gentleman who goes on a long hazardous journey, required his services. The recompense would have been of generous amount.'

Li shook his head. 'The matter would have held no interest for Gung. He is otherwise occupied.'

'Ah, yes. He still remains in the employ of Colonel John Beetham?'

'No doubt he does.'

'Still the reward in this other matter would have been great. But it may be that he is very loyal to Colonel Beetham. A loyalty cemented through many years. I am trying to figure, but I cannot. How long is it your honourable cousin is in Colonel Beetham's service?'

'Long enough to cement loyalty, as you say,' returned Li, noncommittally.

'Fifteen years, perhaps?' hazarded Chan.

'It might be.'

'Or even longer?'

'As to that, I do not know.'

Chan nodded. 'When you know, to know that you know, and when you do not know, to know that you do not know — that is true knowledge, as the master said.' He moved his foot, and a spasm of pain spread over his fat face. 'A great man, Colonel Beetham. A most remarkable man. Li Gung has been fortunate. With Colonel Beetham he has seen Tibet, Persia — even India. He has told you, perhaps, of his visits to India with Colonel Beetham?'

In the slanting eyes of the host a stubborn expression was evident. 'He says little, my cousin,' Henry Li remarked.

'Which point of character no doubt increases his value to a man like the Colonel,' suggested Chan. 'I am very sorry he has gone. While I would no doubt have failed, owing to his feeling of loyalty for his present employer, I would nevertheless have liked to try. I promised my friend — '

The outer door opened, and the active little boy scout burst into the room. After him came a serious, prematurely bearded young American with a small black case.

'I have brought a physician,' cried Willie Li triumphantly.

Chan gave the ambitious boy a savage look.

'An accident, eh?' said the doctor briskly. 'Well — which one of you — '

Henry Li nodded towards Chan. 'This gentleman's ankle,' he said.

The white man went at once to Chan's side. 'Let's have a look at it.'

'It is nothing,' Chan protested. 'Nothing at all.'

He held out his foot, and the doctor ripped off shoes and stocking. He made a quick examination with his fingers, turned the foot this way and that, and studied it thoughtfully for a moment. Then he stood up.

'What are you trying to do — kid me?' he said with disgust. 'Nothing wrong there.'

'I remarked the injury was of the slightest,' Chan said.

He looked at Henry Li. An expression of complete understanding lighted the basket merchant's face.

'Five dollars, please,' said the doctor sternly.

Chan produced his purse, and counted out the money. With an effort he refrained from looking in the boy's direction.

The white man left abruptly. Chan drew on his stocking, slipped into his shoe, and stood up. His dignity requiring that he still maintain the fiction, he limped elaborately.

'These white devil doctors,' he remarked glumly. 'All they know is five dollars, please.'

Henry Li was looking at him keenly. 'I recall,' he said, 'there was one other who came to ask questions about Li Gung. An Englishman — a large man. They are clever and cool, the English, like a thief amid the fire. Was it not his death I read about in the morning paper?'

'I know nothing of the matter,' responded Chan stiffly.

'Of course.' Henry Li followed to the door. 'If you will accept advice offered in humble spirit,' he added, 'you will walk softly. What a pity if you encountered a really serious accident.'

Mumbling a good-bye, Chan went out. By the door he passed young Willie Li, who was grinning broadly. The event had come to an unexpected ending, but none the less the lad was happy. He was a boy scout, and he had done his good turn for the day.

Chan returned to the street, thoroughly upset. Rarely had any of his little deceptions ended so disastrously. His usefulness on the trail of Li Gung was no doubt over for all time. He consigned all boy scouts to limbo with one muttered imprecation.

Entering a drug store, he purchased a quantity of lampblack and a camel's hair brush. Then he went on to the Kirk Building. The night watchman took him up to the bungalow, and he let himself in with a key Kirk had given him. The place was dark and silent. He switched on the lights, and made a round of the rooms. No one seemed to be about.

He unlocked the compartment in Kirk's desk, and carefully removed the sheet of paper that had arrived in the envelope from Scotland Yard. With satisfaction he noted the paper was of a cheap variety, highly glazed. Along the lines where it had been folded, someone's fingers must have pressed hard.

Seated at the desk, with a floor lamp glowing brightly at his side, he cautiously sprinkled the black powder in the most likely place. Then he carefully dusted it with his brush. He was rewarded by the outline of a massive thumb — the thumb of a big man. He considered. Carrick Enderby was a big

159

man. He was employed at Cook's. In some way he must procure impressions of Enderby's thumb.

He returned the paper to the compartment, and with it the tools of his investigation. Turning over ways and means in his mind, he sat down in a comfortable chair, took up Colonel John Beetham's story of his life, and began to read.

About an hour later Paradise came in from outside. He was absent for a moment in the pantry. Then, entering the living-room with his inevitable silver platter, he removed a few letters and laid them on Kirk's desk.

'The last mail is in, sir,' he announced. 'There is, I believe, a picture postcard for you.'

He carried card and tray negligently at his side, as though to express his contempt for picture postcards. Chan looked up in surprise; he had telephoned the hotel to forward any mail to him here, and this was quick work. Paradise offered the tray, and Chan daintily took up the card.

It was from his youngest girl, designed to catch him just before he left.

'Hurry home, honourable father, we miss you all the time. There is Kona weather here now, and we have ninety degrees of climate every day. Wishing to see you soon. Your loving daughter, ANNA.'

160

Chan turned over the card. He saw a picture of Waikiki, the surf boards riding the waves, Diamond Head beyond. He sighed with homesickness, and sat for a long moment immobile in his chair.

But as Paradise left the room, the little detective leaped nimbly to his feet and returned to the desk. For Paradise had glued the postcard to his tray with one large, moist thumb, a thumb which had fortunately rested on the light blue of Hawaii's lovely sky.

Quickly Chan applied lamp-black and brush. Then he removed the blank paper from the compartment, and with the aid of a reading glass, studied the impressions.

He leaned back in his chair with a puzzled frown. He knew now that he need not investigate the finger-prints of Carrick Enderby. The thumb-print of Paradise was on the postcard, and the same print was on the blank sheet of paper that had arrived in the envelope from Scotland Yard. It was Paradise, then, who had tampered with Sir Frederic's mail.

9

The Port of Missing Women

Thursday morning dawned bright and fair. Stepping briskly from his bed to the window, Chan saw the sunlight sparkling cheerily on the waters of the harbour. It was a clear, cool world he looked upon, and the sight was invigorating. Nor for ever would he wander amid his present dark doubts and perplexities; one of these days he would see the murderer of Sir Frederic as plainly as he now saw the distant towers of Oakland. After that — the Pacific, the lighthouse on Makapuu Point, Diamond Head and a palm-fringed shore, and finally his beloved town of Honolulu nestling in the emerald cup of the hills.

Calm and unhurried, he prepared himself for another day, and left his bedroom. Barry Kirk, himself immaculate and unperturbed, was seated at the breakfast table reading the morning paper. Chan smiled at thought of the bomb he was about to toss at his gracious host. For he had not seen Kirk the previous night after his discovery. Though he had waited until midnight, the young man had not returned, and Chan had gone sleepily to bed.

'Good morning,' Kirk said. 'How's the famous sleuth to-day?'

'Doing as well as could be predicted,' Chan replied. 'You are tip-top yourself. I see it without the formal inquiring.'

'True enough,' Kirk answered. 'I am full of vim, vigour and ambition, and ready for a new day's discoveries. By the way, I called Miss Morrow last night and gave her my grandmother's story about Eileen Enderby. She's going to arrange an interview with the lady, and you're invited. I hope I won't be left out of the party, either. If I am, it won't be my fault.'

Chan nodded. 'Interview is certainly indicated,' he agreed.

Paradise entered, haughty and dignified as always, and after he had bestowed on each a suave good morning, placed orange juice before them. Kirk lifted his glass.

'Your very good health,' he said, 'in the wine of the country. California orange juice — of course you read our advertisements. Cures anything from insomnia to a broken heart. How did you spend last evening?'

'Me?' Chan shrugged. 'I made slight sally into Chinatown.'

'On Li Gung's trail, eh? What luck?'

'The poorest,' returned Chan, grimacing at the memory. 'I encounter Chinese boy scout panting to do good turn, and he does me one of the worst I ever suffered.' He recounted his adventure, to Kirk's amusement.

'Tough luck,' laughed the young man. 'However, you probably got all you could, at that.'

'Later,' continued Chan, 'the luck betters itself.' Paradise came in with the cereal, and Chan watched him in silence. When the butler had gone, he added: 'Last night in living-room out there I make astonishing discovery.'

'You did? What was that?'

'How much you know about this perfect servant of yours?'

Kirk started. 'Paradise? Good lord! You don't mean — '

'He came with references?'

'King George couldn't have brought better. Dukes and earls spoke of him in glowing terms. And why not? He's the best servant in the world.'

'Too bad,' commented Chan.

'What do you mean, too bad?'

'Too bad best servant in world has weakness for steaming open letters — ' He stopped suddenly, for Paradise was entering with bacon and eggs. When he had gone out, Kirk leaned over and spoke in a low tense voice.

'Paradise opened that letter from Scotland Yard? How do you know?'

Briefly Charlie told him, and Kirk's face grew gloomy at the tale.

'I suppose I should have been prepared,' he sighed. 'The butler is always mixed up in a thing like this. But Paradise! My paragon of all the virtues. Oh, well — 'twas ever thus. 'I never loved a young gazelle — '? What's the rest of it? What shall I do? Fire him?'

'Oh, no,' protested Chan. 'For the present, silence only. He must not know we are aware of his weakness. Just watchfully waiting.'

'Suits me,' agreed Kirk. 'I'll hang on to him until you produce the handcuffs. What a pity it will seem to lock up such competent hands as his.'

'May not happen,' Chan suggested.

'I hope not,' Kirk answered fervently.

After breakfast Chan called the *Globe* office, and got Bill Rankin's home address. He routed the reporter from a well-earned sleep, and asked him to come at once to the bungalow.

An hour later Rankin, brisk and full of enthusiasm, arrived on the scene. He grinned broadly as he shook hands.

'Couldn't quite pull it off, eh?' he chided. 'The cool, calm Oriental turned back at the dock.'

Chan nodded. 'Cool, calm Oriental gets too much like mainland Americans from circling in such lowering society. I have remained to assist Captain Flannery, much to his well-concealed delight.'

Rankin laughed. 'Yes — I talked with him last night. He's tickled pink but he won't admit it, even to himself. Well, what's the dope? Who killed Sir Frederic?'

'A difficult matter to determine,' Chan replied. 'We must go into the past, upearthing here and there. Just at present I am faced by small problem with which you can assist. So I have ventured to annoy you.'

'No annoyance whatever. I'm happy to have you call on me. What are your orders?'

'For the present, keep everything shaded by darkness. No publicity. You understand it?'

'All right — for the present. But when the big moment comes, I'm the fair-haired boy. You understand it?'

Chan smiled. 'Yes — you are the chosen one. That will happen. Just now, a little covered investigation. You recall the story of Eve Durand?'

'Will I ever forget it? I don't know when anything has made such an impression on me. Peshawar — the dark hills — the game of hide-and-seek — the little blonde who never came back from the ride. If that isn't what the flappers used to call intriguing, I don't know what is.'

'You speak true. Fifteen years ago, Sir Frederic said. But from neither Sir Frederic nor the clipping did I obtain the exact date, and for it I am yearning. On what day of what month, presumably in the year 1913, did Eve Durand wander off into unlimitable darkness of India? Could you supply the fact?'

Rankin nodded. 'A story like that must have been in the newspapers all over the world. I'll have a look at our files for 1913 and see what I can find.'

'Good enough,' said Chan. 'Note one other matter, if you please. Suppose you find accounts. Is the name of Colonel John Beetham anywhere mentioned?'

'What! Beetham! That bird? Is he in it?'

'You know him?'

'Sure — I interviewed him. A mysterious sort of guy. If he's in it, the story's even better than I thought.'

'He may not be,' warned Chan. 'I am curious, that is all. You will then explore in files?'

'I certainly will. You'll hear from me *pronto*. I'm on my way now.'

The reporter hurried off, leaving Chan to his ponderous book. For a long time he wandered with Colonel Beetham through lonely places, over blazing sands at one moment, at another over wastelands of snow. Men and camels and mules lay dead on the trail, but Beetham pushed on. Nothing stopped him.

During lunch the telephone rang, and Kirk answered. 'Hello — oh, Miss Morrow. Of course. Good — he'll be there. So will I — I beg your pardon? . . . No trouble at all. Mr. Chan's a stranger here, and I don't want him to get lost . . . Yes . . . Yes, I'm coming, so get resigned, lady, get resigned.'

He hung up. 'Well, we're invited to Miss Morrow's office at two o'clock to meet the Enderbys. That is, you're invited, and I'm going anyhow.'

At two precisely Chan and his host entered the girl's office, a dusty, ill-lighted room piled high with law books. The deputy district attorney rose from behind an orderly desk and greeted them smilingly.

Kirk stood looking about the room. 'Great Scott — is this where you spend your days?' He walked to the window. 'Charming view of the alley, isn't it? I must take you out in the country some time and show you the grass and the trees. You'd be surprised.'

'Oh, this room isn't so bad,' the girl answered. 'I'm not like some people. I keep my mind on my work.'

Flannery came in. 'Well, here we are again,' he said. 'All set for another tall story. Mrs. Enderby this time, eh? More women in this case than in the League of Women Voters.'

'You still appear in baffled stage,' Chan suggested.

'Sure I do,' admitted the Captain. 'I am. And how about you? I don't hear any very illuminating deductions from you.'

'At any moment now,' grinned Chan, 'I may dazzle you with great light.'

'Well, don't hurry on my account,' advised Flannery. 'We've got all the year on this, of course. It's only Sir Frederic Bruce of Scotland Yard who was murdered. Nobody cares — except the whole British Empire.'

'You have made progress?' Chan inquired.

'How could I? Every time I get all set to go at the thing in a reasonable way, I have to stop and hunt for a missing woman. I tell you, I'm getting fed up on that end of it. If there's any more nonsense about — '

The door opened and a clerk admitted Carrick Enderby and his wife. Eileen Enderby, even before she spoke, seemed flustered and nervous. Miss Morrow rose.

'How do you do,' she said. 'Sit down,

169

please. It was good of you to come,'

'Of course we came,' Eileen Enderby replied. 'Though what it is you want, I for one can't imagine — '

'We must let Miss Morrow tell us what is wanted, Eileen,' drawled her husband.

'Oh, naturally.' Mrs. Enderby's blue eyes turned from one to the other and rested at last on the solid bulk of Captain Flannery.

'We're going to ask a few questions, Mrs. Enderby,' began Miss Morrow. 'Questions that I know you'll be glad to answer. Tell me — had you ever met Sir Frederic Bruce before Mr. Kirk's dinner party the other night?'

'I'd never even heard of him,' replied the woman firmly.

'Ah, yes. Yet just after Colonel Beetham began to show his pictures, Sir Frederic called you out into a passageway. He wanted to speak to you alone.'

Eileen Enderby looked at her husband, who nodded. 'Yes,' she admitted. 'He did. I was never so surprised in my life.'

'What did Sir Frederic want to speak to you about?'

'It was a most amazing thing. He mentioned a girl — a girl I once knew very well.'

'What about the girl?'

'Well — it was quite a mystery. This girl Sir Frederic spoke of — she disappeared one

170

night. Just walked off into the dark and was never heard of again.'

There was a moment's silence. 'Did she disappear at Peshawar in India?' Miss Morrow inquired.

'India? Why, no — not at all,' replied Eileen Enderby.

'Oh, I see. Then he was speaking of Marie Lantelme, who disappeared from Nice?'

'Nice? Marie Lantelme? I don't know what you're talking about.' Mrs. Enderby's pretty forehead wrinkled in amazement.

For the first time, Chan spoke. 'It is now how many years,' he asked, 'since your friend was last seen?'

'Why — it must be — let me think. Seven — yes — seven years.'

'She disappeared from New York, perhaps?'

'From New York — yes.'

'Her name was Jennie Jerome?'

'Yes. Jennie Jerome.'

Chan took out his wallet and removed a clipping. He handed it to Miss Morrow. 'Once more, and I am hoping for the last time,' he remarked, 'I would humbly request that you read aloud a scrap of paper from Sir Frederic's effects.'

Miss Morrow took the paper, her eyes wide. Captain Flannery's face was a study in scarlet. The girl began to read:

'What happened to Jennie Jerome? A famous New York modiste and an even more famous New York illustrator are among those who have been asking themselves that question for the past seven years.

'Jennie Jerome was what the French call a mannequin, a model employed by the fashionable house of DuFour et Cie, on Fifth Avenue, in New York. She was something more than a model, a rack for pretty clothes; she was a girl of charming and marked personality and a beauty that will not be forgotten in seven times seven years. Though employed but a brief time by DuFour she was the most popular of all their models among the distinguished patrons of the house. A celebrated New York illustrator saw her picture in a newspaper and at once sought her out, offering her a large sum of money to pose for him.

'Jennie Jerome seemed delighted at the opportunity. She invited a number of her friends to a little dinner party at her apartment, to celebrate the event. When these friends arrived, the door of her apartment stood open. They entered. The table was set, the candles lighted, preparations for the dinner apparent. But the hostess was nowhere about.

'The boy at the telephone switchboard in the hall below reported that, a few minutes before, he had seen her run down the stairs and vanish into the night. He was the last person who saw Jennie Jerome. Her employer, Madame DuFour, and the illustrator who had been struck by her beauty, made every possible effort to trace her. These efforts came to nothing. Jennie Jerome had vanished into thin air. Eloped? But no man's name was ever linked with hers. Murdered? Perhaps. No one knows. At any rate, Jennie Jerome had gone without leaving a trace, and there the matter has rested for seven years.'

'Another one of 'em,' cried Flannery, as Miss Morrow stopped reading. 'Great Scott — what are we up against?'

'A puzzle,' suggested Chan calmly. He restored the clipping to his pocket-book.

'I'll say so,' Flannery growled.

'You knew Jennie Jerome?' Miss Morrow said to Eileen Enderby.

Mrs. Enderby nodded. 'Yes. I was employed by the same firm — DuFour. One of the models, too. I was working there when I met Mr. Enderby, who was in Cook's New York

173

office at the time. I knew Jennie well. If I may say so, that story you just read has been touched up a bit. Jennie Jerome was just an ordinarily pretty girl — nothing to rave about. I believe some illustrator did want her to pose for him. We all got offers like that.'

'Leaving her beauty out of it,' smiled Miss Morrow, 'she did disappear?'

'Oh, yes. I was one of the guests invited to her dinner. That part of it is true enough. She just walked off into the night.'

'And it was this girl whom Sir Frederic questioned you about?'

'Yes. Somehow, he knew I was one of her friends — how he knew it, I can't imagine. At any rate, he asked me if I would know Jennie Jerome if I saw her again. I said I thought I would. He said: 'Have you seen her in the Kirk Building this evening?''

'And you told him — '

'I told him I hadn't. He counselled me to stop and think a minute. I couldn't see the need of that. I hadn't seen her — I was sure of it.'

'And you still haven't seen her?'

'No — I haven't.'

Miss Morrow rose. 'We are greatly obliged to you, Mrs. Enderby. That is all, I believe. Captain Flannery — '

'That's all from me,' said Flannery.

'Well, if there's any more I can tell you — '
Mrs. Enderby rose, with evident relief.

Her husband spoke. 'Come along, Eileen,'
he said sternly. They went out. The four left
behind in the office stared at one another in
wonder.

'There you are,' exploded Flannery, rising.
'Another missing woman. Eve Durand, Marie
Lantelme and Jennie Jerome. Three — count
'em — three — and if you believe your ears,
every damn one of 'em was in the Kirk
Building night before last. I don't know how
it sounds to you, but to me it's all wrong.'

'It does sound fishy,' Barry Kirk admitted.
'The Port of Missing Women — and I
thought I was running just an ordinary office
building.'

'All wrong, I tell you,' Flannery went on
loudly. 'It never happened, that's all. Somebody's kidding us to a fare-ye-well. This last
story is one too many — ' He stopped, and
stared at Charlie Chan. 'Well, Sergeant
— what's on your mind?' he inquired.

'Plenty,' grinned Chan. 'On one side of our
puzzle, at least, light is beginning to break.
This last story illuminates darkness. You
follow after me, of course.'

'I do not. What are you talking about?'

'You do not? A great pity. In good time, I
show you.'

'All right — all right,' cried Flannery. 'I leave these missing women to you and Miss Morrow here. I don't want to hear any more about 'em — I'll go dippy if I do. I'll stick to the main facts. Night before last Sir Frederic Bruce was murdered in an office on the twentieth floor of the Kirk Building. Somebody slipped away from that party, or somebody got in from outside, and did for him. There was a book beside him, and there were marks on the fire-escape — I didn't tell you that, but there were — and the murderer nabbed a pair of velvet shoes off his feet. That's my case, my job, and by heaven I'm going after it, and if anybody comes to me with any more missing women stories — '

He stopped. The outer door had opened, and Eileen Enderby was coming in. At her heels came her husband, stern and grim. The woman appeared very much upset.

'We — we've come back,' she said. She sank into a chair. 'My husband thinks — he has made me see — '

'I have insisted,' said Carrick Enderby, 'that my wife tell you the entire story. She has omitted a very important point.'

'I'm in a terrible position,' the woman protested. 'I do hope I'm doing the right thing. Carry — are you sure — '

'I am sure,' cut in her husband, 'that in a

176

serious matter of this sort, truth is the only sane course.'

'But she begged me not to tell,' Eileen Enderby reminded him. 'She pleaded so hard. I don't want to make trouble for her — '

'You gave no promise,' her husband said. 'And if the woman's done nothing wrong, I don't see — '

'Look here,' broke in Flannery. 'You came back to tell us something. What is it?'

'You came back to tell us that you have seen Jennie Jerome?' suggested Miss Morrow.

Mrs. Enderby nodded, and began to speak with obvious reluctance.

'Yes — I did see her — but not before I talked with Sir Frederic. I told him the truth. I hadn't seen her then — that is, I had seen her, but I didn't notice — one doesn't, you know — '

'But you noticed later.'

'Yes — on our way home. Going down in the elevator. I got a good look at her then, and that was when I realized it. The elevator girl in the Kirk Building night before last was Jennie Jerome.'

10

The Letter From London

Captain Flannery got up and took a turn about the room. He was a simple man and the look on his face suggested that the complexities of his calling were growing irksome. He stopped in front of Eileen Enderby.

'So — the elevator girl in the Kirk Building was Jennie Jerome? Then you lied a few minutes ago when you told Miss Morrow you hadn't seen her?'

'You can't hold that against her,' Enderby protested. 'She's come back of her own free will to tell you the truth.'

'But why didn't she tell it in the first place?'

'One doesn't care to become involved in a matter of this sort. That's only natural.'

'All right, all right.' Flannery turned back to Mrs. Enderby. 'You say you recognised this girl when you were going down in the elevator, on your way home after the dinner? And you let her see that you recognized her?'

'Oh, yes. I cried out in surprise: 'Jennie! Jennie Jerome! What are you doing here?''

'You saw what she was doing, didn't you?'

'It was just one of those questions — it didn't mean anything.'

'Yeah. And what did she say?'

'She just smiled quietly and said: 'Hello, Eileen. I was wondering if you'd know me.''

'Then what?'

'There were a thousand questions I wanted to ask, of course. Why she ran away that time — where she had been — But she wouldn't answer, she just shook her head, still smiling, and said maybe some other time she'd tell me everything. And then she asked me if I'd do this — this favour for her.'

'You mean, keep still about the fact that you'd seen her?'

'Yes. She said she'd done nothing wrong, but that if the story about how she left New York came out it might create a lot of suspicion — '

'According to your husband, you made no promise?' Flannery said.

'No, I didn't. Under ordinary conditions, of course, I'd have promised at once. But I thought of Sir Frederic's murder, and it seemed to me a very serious thing she was asking. So I just said I'd think it over and let her know when I saw her again.'

'And have you seen her again?'

'No, I haven't. It was all so strange. I hardly knew what to do.'

'Well, you'd better keep away from her,' Flannery suggested.

'I'll keep away from her all right. I feel as though I'd betrayed her.' Eileen Enderby glanced accusingly at her husband.

'You were not in her debt,' said Enderby. 'Lying's a dangerous business in a matter of this kind.'

'You're lucky, Mrs. Enderby,' said the Captain. 'You've got a sensible husband. Just listen to him, and you'll be O.K. I guess that's all now. You can go. Only keep this to yourself.'

'I'll certainly do that,' the woman assured him. She rose.

'If I want you again, I'll let you know,' Flannery added.

Chan opened the door for her. 'May I be permitted respectful inquiry,' he ventured. 'The beautiful garment marked by iron rust stains — it was not ruined beyond reclaim?'

'Oh, not at all,' she answered. She paused, as though she felt the matter called for an explanation. 'When I saw that man on the fire-escape I became so excited I leaned against the garden railing. It was dripping with fog. Careless of me, wasn't it?'

'In moment of stress, how easy to slip into careless act,' returned Chan. Bowing low, he closed the door after the Enderbys.

'Well,' said Flannery, 'I guess we're getting somewhere at last. Though if you ask me where, I can't tell you. Anyhow, we know that Sir Frederic was looking for Jennie Jerome the night he was killed, and that Jennie Jerome was running an elevator just outside his door. By heaven, I've a notion to lock her up right now.'

'But you haven't anything against her,' Miss Morrow objected. 'You know that.'

'No, I haven't. However, the newspapers are howling for an arrest. They always are. I could give 'em Jennie Jerome — a pretty girl — they'd eat it up. Then, if nothing else breaks against her, I could let her off, sort of quiet.'

'Such tactics are beneath you, Captain,' Miss Morrow said. 'I trust that when we make an arrest, it will be based on something more tangible than any evidence we've got so far. Are you with me, Mr. Chan?'

'Undubitably,' Chan replied. He glanced up at the frowning face of the Captain. 'If I may make humble suggestion — '

'Of course,' agreed Miss Morrow.

But Chan, it seemed, changed his mind. He kept his humble suggestion to himself. 'Patience,' he finished lamely, 'always brightest plan in these matters. Acting as champion of that lovely virtue, I have fought many fierce battles. American has always the urge to leap too quick. How well it was said, retire a step and you have the advantage.'

'But these newspaper men — ' protested the Captain.

'I do not wish to infest the picture,' Chan smiled, 'but I would like to refer to my own habit in similar situation. When newspapers rage, I put nice roll of cotton in the ears. Simmered down to truth, I am responsible party, not newspaper reporter. I tell him with exquisite politeness to fade off and hush down.'

'A good plan,' laughed Miss Morrow. She turned to Barry Kirk. 'By the way, do you know anything about this elevator girl? Grace Lane was, I believe, the name she gave the other night.'

Kirk shook his head. 'Not a thing. Except that she's the prettiest girl we've ever employed in the building. I'd noticed that, of course.'

'I rather thought you had,' Miss Morrow said.

'Lady, I'm not blind,' he assured her. 'I notice beauty anywhere — in elevators, in cable cars — even in a lawyer's office. I tried to talk to this girl once or twice, but I didn't get very far. If you like, I'll try it again.'

'No thanks. You'd probably be away off the subject.'

'Well, it all sounds mighty mysterious to me,' he admitted. 'We thought Sir Frederic was on the trail of Eve Durand, and now it seems it must have been a couple of other women. The poor chap is gone, but he's left a most appalling puzzle on my doorstep. You're all such nice detectives — I don't want to hurt your feelings — but will you kindly tell me whither we are drifting? Where are we getting? Nowhere, if you ask me.'

'I'm afraid you're right,' Miss Morrow sighed.

'Maybe if I locked this woman up — ' began Flannery, attached to the idea.

'No, no,' Miss Morrow told him. 'We can't do that. But we can shadow her. And since she is one who has some talent for walking off into the night, I suggest that you arrange the matter without delay.'

Flannery nodded. 'I'll put the boys on her trail. I guess you're right — we might get on to something that way. But Mr. Kirk has said it — we're not progressing very fast. If there was only some clue I could get my teeth into — '

Chan cut in. 'Thanks for recalling my wandering ideas,' he said. 'So much has happened the matter was obscure in my mind. I have something here that might furnish excellent teeth-hold.' He removed an envelope from his pocket and carefully extracted a folded sheet of paper and a picture postcard. 'No doubt, Captain, you have more cleverness with finger-prints than stupid man like me. Could you say — are these thumb prints identically the same?'

Flannery studied the two items. 'They look the same to me. I could put our expert on them — but say, what's this all about?'

'Blank sheet of paper,' Chan explained, 'arrive in envelope marked Scotland Yard. Without question Miss Morrow has told you?'

'Oh, yes — she mentioned that. Somebody tampering with the mail, eh? And this thumb print on the postcard?'

'Bestowed there last night by digit of Paradise, Mr. Kirk's butler,' Chan informed him.

Flannery jumped up. 'Well, why didn't you say so? Now we're getting on. You've got the makings of a detective after all, Sergeant. Paradise, eh — fooling with Uncle Sam's mail. 'That's good enough for me — I'll have him behind the bars in an hour.'

Chan lifted a protesting hand. 'Oh, no — my humblest apologies. Again you leap too sudden. We must watch and wait — '

'The hell you say,' Flannery cried. 'That's not my system. I'll nab him. I'll make him talk — '

184

'And I,' sighed Barry Kirk, 'will lose my perfect butler. Shall I write him a reference — or won't they care, at the gaol?'

'Captain, pause and listen,' pleaded Chan. 'We have nothing here to prove Paradise fired fatal bullet into Sir Frederic. Yet somehow he is involved. We watch his every move. Much may be revealed by the unsuspecting. We hunt through his effects. To-day, I believe, he enjoys weekly holiday. Is that not so?' He looked at Kirk.

'Yes, it's Black Thursday — the servants' day off,' Kirk said. 'Paradise is probably at the movies — he adores them. Melodrama — that's his meat.'

'Fortunate event,' continued Chan. 'Cook too is out. We return to flat and do some despicable prying into private life of Paradise. Is that not better, Captain, than searching through crowded atmosphere of movie theatres to make foolish arrest?'

Flannery considered. 'Well, I guess it is, at that.'

'Back to the dear old home,' said Kirk rising. 'If Miss Morrow will lend a hand, I'll give you tea.'

'Count me out,' said Flannery.

'And other liquids,' amended Kirk.

'Count me in again,' added Flannery. 'You got your car?' Kirk nodded. 'You take Miss

Morrow then, and the Sergeant and I will follow in mine.'

In the roadster on their way to the Kirk Building, Barry Kirk glanced at Miss Morrow and smiled.

'Yes?' she inquired.

'I was just thinking. I do, at times.'

'Is it necessary?'

'Perhaps not. But I find it exhilarating. I was thinking at that moment about you.'

'Oh, please don't trouble.'

'No trouble at all. I was wondering. There are so many mysterious women hovering about this case. And no one is asking you any questions.'

'Why should they?'

'Why shouldn't they? Who are you? Where did you come from? Since you're not very like to investigate yourself, perhaps I should take over the job.'

'You're very kind.'

'I hope you won't object. Of course, you look young and innocent, but I have your word for it that men are easily fooled.' He steered round a lumbering truck, then turned to her sternly. 'Just what were you doing on the night Eve Durand slipped from sight at Peshawar?'

'I was probably worrying over my home work,' the girl replied. 'I was always very

186

conscientious, even in the lowest grades.'

'I'll bet you were. And where was this great mental effort taking place? Not in San Francisco?'

'No, in Baltimore. That was my home before I came West to law school.'

'Yes? Peering further into your dark past — why, in heaven's name, the law school? Disappointed in love, or something?'

She smiled. 'Not at all. Father was a judge, and it broke his heart that I wasn't a boy.'

'I've noticed how unreasonable judges are. Times when they've talked to me about my automobile driving. So the judge wanted a boy? He didn't know his luck.'

'Oh, he gradually discovered I wasn't a total loss. He asked me to study law, and I did.'

'What an obedient child,' Kirk said.

'I didn't mind — in fact, I rather liked it. You see, frivolous things never have appealed to me.'

'I'm afraid that's true. And it worries me.'

'Why should it?'

'Because, as it happens, I'm one of those frivolous things.'

'But surely you have your serious side?'

'No — I'm afraid that side was just sketched in — never finished. However, I'm working on it. Before I get through you'll be calling me deacon.'

'Really? I'm afraid I've never cared much for deacons, either.'

'Well, not exactly deacon, then. I'll try to strike a happy medium.'

'I'll help you,' smiled the girl.

Kirk parked his car in a side street, and they went round the corner to the Kirk Building. It was Grace Lane who took them aloft. Kirk studied her with a new interest. Strands of dark red hair crept out from beneath her cap; her face was pale, but unlined and young. Age uncertain, Kirk thought, but beauty unmistakable. What was the secret of her past? Why had Sir Frederic brought to the Kirk Building that clipping about Jennie Jerome?

'I'll be along in a minute,' Miss Morrow said, when the elevator stopped at the twentieth floor. Kirk nodded and preceded her to the roof. She followed almost immediately. 'I wanted to ask a question or two,' she explained. 'You see, I gave Grace Lane very little attention on the night Sir Frederic was killed.'

'What do you think of her — now that you've looked again?'

'She's a lady — if you don't mind an overworked word. This job she has now is beneath her.'

'Think so?' Kirk took Miss Morrow's coat. 'I should have said that most of the time, it's over her head.'

The girl shrugged. 'That from you, deacon,' she said, reproachfully.

Chan and Captain Flannery were at the door, and Kirk let them in. The Captain was all business.

'Hello,' he said. 'Now if you'll show us that butler's room, Mr. Kirk, we'll get busy right away. I've brought a few skeleton keys. We'll go over the place like a vacuum cleaner.' Kirk led them into the corridor.

'How about the cook's room?' Flannery added. 'We might take a look at that.'

'My cook's a Frenchman,' Kirk explained. 'He sleeps out.'

'Humph. He was here the other night at the time of the murder?'

'Yes, of course.'

'Well, I'd better have a talk with him sometime.'

'He speaks very little English,' Kirk smiled. 'You'll enjoy him.' He left the two in the butler's bedroom, and returned to Miss Morrow.

'I suppose you hate the sight of a kitchen,' he suggested.

'Why should I?'

'Well — a big lawyer like you — '

'But I've studied cook-books, too. You'd be surprised. I can cook the most delicious — '

'Rarebit,' he finished. 'I know. And your chocolate fudge was famous at the sorority house. I've heard it before.'

'Please let me finish. I was going to say, pot roast. And my lemon pie is not so bad, either.'

He stood solemnly regarding her. 'Lady,' he announced, 'you improve on acquaintance. And if that isn't gilding the lily, I don't know what is. Come with me and we'll dig up the tea things.'

She followed him to the kitchen. 'I've got a little apartment,' she said. 'And when I'm not too tired, I get my own dinner.'

'How are you on Thursday nights?' he asked. 'Pretty tired?'

'That depends. Why?'

'Servants' night out. Need I say more?'

Miss Morrow laughed. 'I'll remember,' she promised. With deft hands she set the water on to boil, and began to arrange the tea tray. 'How neat everything is,' she remarked. 'Paradise is a wonder.'

'Tell that to my grandmother,' Kirk suggested. 'She believes that a man who lives alone wallows in grime and waste. Every home needs a woman's touch, according to her story.'

'Absurd,' cried the girl.

'Oh, well — grandmother dates back a few years. In her day women were housekeepers. Now they're movie fans, club members, lawyers — what have you? Must have been a rather comfortable age at that.'

'For the men, yes.'

'And men don't count any more.'

'I wouldn't say that. I guess we're ready now.'

Kirk carried the tray to the living-room, and placed it on a low table before the fire. Miss Morrow sat down behind it. He threw a couple of logs on to the glowing embers, then, visiting the dining-room, returned with a bottle, a siphon and glasses.

'Mustn't forget that Captain Flannery doesn't approve of tea,' she said.

Miss Morrow looked towards the passage. 'They'd better hurry, or they'll be late for the party,' she remarked.

But Chan and Flannery did not appear. Outside the March dusk was falling; a sharp wind swept through the little garden and rattled insistently at the casements. Kirk drew the curtains. On the hearth the fresh logs flamed, filling the room with a warm, satisfying glow. He took from Miss Morrow's hand his cup of tea, selected a small cake, and dropped into a chair.

'Cosy — that would be my word for this,'

he smiled. 'To look at you now, no one would ever suspect that old affair between you and Blackstone.'

'I'm versatile, anyhow,' she said.

'I wonder,' he replied.

'Wonder what?'

'I wonder just how versatile you are. It's a matter I intend to investigate further. I may add that I am regarded throughout the world as the greatest living judge of a lemon pie.'

'You frighten me,' Miss Morrow said.

'If your testimony has been the truth, so help you,' he answered, 'what is there to be frightened about?'

At that moment Chan and Flannery appeared in the doorway. The Captain seemed very pleased with himself.

'What luck?' Kirk inquired.

'The best,' beamed Flannery. He carried a piece of paper in his hand. 'Ah — shall I help myself?'

'By all means,' Kirk told him. 'A congratulatory potion. Mr. Chan — what's yours?'

'Tea, if Miss Morrow will be so kind. Three lumps of sugar and the breath of the lemon in passing.'

The girl prepared his cup. Flannery dropped into a chair.

'I see you've found something,' Kirk suggested.

'I certainly have,' the Captain replied. 'I've found the letter from Scotland Yard that Paradise nabbed from the mail.'

'Good enough,' cried Kirk.

'A slick bird, this Paradise,' Flannery went on. 'Where do you think he had it? All folded up in a little wad and tucked into the toe of a shoe.'

'How clever of you to look there,' Miss Morrow approved.

Flannery hesitated. 'Well — er — come to think of it, I didn't. It was Sergeant Chan here dug it up. Yes, sir — the Sergeant's getting to be a real sleuth.'

'Under your brilliant instruction,' smiled Chan.

'Well, we can all learn from each other,' conceded the Captain. 'Anyhow, he found it, and turned it right over to me. The letter that came in the Scotland Yard envelope — no question about it. See the print at the top!'

'If it's not asking too much,' said Kirk, 'what's in the letter?'

Flannery's face fell. 'Not a whole lot. We'll have to admit that. But little by little — '

'With brief steps we advance,' put in Chan. 'Humbly suggest you read the epistle.'

'Well, it's addressed to Sir Frederic, care of Cook's, San Francisco,' said Flannery. He read:

'Dear Sir Frederic:

'I was very glad to get your letter from Shanghai and to know that you are near the end of a long trail. It is indeed surprising news to me that the murder of Hilary Galt and the disappearance of Eve Durand from Peshawar are, in your final analysis, linked together. I know you always contended they were, but much as I admire your talents, I felt sure you were mistaken. I can only apologize most humbly. It is a matter of regret to me that you did not tell me more; what you wrote roused my interest to a high pitch. Believe me, I shall be eager to hear the end of this strange case.

'By the way, Inspector Rupert Duff will be in the States on another matter at about the time you reach San Francisco. You know Duff, of course. A good man. If you should require his help, you have only to wire him at the Hotel Waldorf, New York.

'With all good wishes for a happy outcome to your investigation,

'I am, sir, always, your obedient servant,

'MARTIN BENFIELD, Deputy-Commissioner.'

Flannery stopped reading and looked at the others. 'Well, there you are,' he said. 'The Galt affair and Eve Durand are mixed up together. Of course that ain't exactly news

— I've known it right along. What I want to find out now is, why did Paradise try to keep this information from us? What's his stake in the affair? I could arrest him at once, but I'm afraid that if I do, he'll shut up like a clam and that will end it. He doesn't know we're wise to him, so I'm going to put this letter back where we found it and give him a little more rope. The Sergeant here has agreed to keep an eye on him, and I rely on you, too, Mr. Kirk, to see that he doesn't get away.'

'Don't worry,' said Kirk. 'I don't want to lose him.'

Flannery rose. 'Sir Frederic's mail isn't coming here any more?' he inquired of Miss Morrow.

'No, of course not. I arranged to have it sent to my office. There's been nothing of interest — purely personal matters.'

'I must put this letter back, and then I'll have to run along,' the Captain said. He went into the passage.

'Well,' remarked Kirk, 'Paradise hangs on a little longer. I see your handiwork there, Sergeant, and you have my warmest thanks.'

'For a brief time, at least,' Chan said. 'You will perceive I am no person's fool. I do not arrange arrest of butler in house where I am guest. I protect him, and I would do same for the cook.'

Flannery returned. 'I got to get back to the station,' he announced. 'Mr. Kirk, thanks for your — er — hospitality.'

Miss Morrow looked up at him. 'You are going to wire to New York for Inspector Duff?' she asked.

'I am not,' the Captain said.

'But he might be of great help — '

'Nix,' cut in Flannery stubbornly. 'I got about all the help I can stand on this case now. Get him here and have him under foot? No, sir — I'm going to find out first who killed Sir Frederic. After that, they can all come. Don't you say so, Sergeant?'

Chan nodded. 'You are wise man. The ship with too many steersmen never reaches port.'

11

The Muddy Water Clears

Flannery departed, and Miss Morrow picked up her coat. Reluctantly, Kirk held it for her. 'Must you go?' he protested.

'Back to the office — yes,' she said. 'I've oceans of work. The district attorney keeps asking me for results in this investigation, and so far all I have been able to report is further mysteries. I wonder if I'll ever have anything else.'

'It was my hope,' remarked Chan, 'that to-day we take a seven-league step forward. But it is fated otherwise. Not before Monday now.'

'Monday,' repeated the girl. 'What do you mean, Mr. Chan?'

'I mean I experience great yearning to bring Miss Gloria Garland to this building again. I have what my cousin Willie Chan, a vulgar speaker, calls a hunch. But this morning when I call Miss Garland on the telephone I learn that she is absent in Del Monte, and will not return until Sunday night.'

'Miss Garland? What has she to do with it?'

'Remains to be observed. She may have

much, or nothing. Depends on the authentic value of my hunch. Monday will tell.'

'But Monday,' sighed Miss Morrow. 'This is only Thursday.'

Chan also sighed. 'I too resent that with bitter feelings. Do not forget that I have sworn to be on boat departing Wednesday. My little son demands me.'

'Patience,' laughed Barry Kirk. 'The doctor must take his own medicine.'

'I know,' shrugged Chan. 'I am taking same in plenty large doses. Mostly when I talk of patience, I am forcing it on others. Speaking for myself in this event, I do not much enjoy the flavour.'

'You said nothing about your hunch to Captain Flannery,' Miss Morrow remarked.

Chan smiled. 'Can you speak of the ocean to a well frog, or of ice to a summer insect? The good Captain would sneer — until I prove to him I am exceedingly correct. I am praying to do that on Monday.'

'In the meantime, we watch and wait,' said Miss Morrow.

'You wait, and I will watch,' suggested Chan.

Kirk accompanied Miss Morrow to the door. '*Au revoir*,' he said. 'And whatever you do, don't lose that lemon pie recipe.'

'You needn't keep hinting,' she replied. 'I won't forget.'

Upon Kirk's return, Charlie regarded him keenly. 'A most attracting young woman,' he remarked.

'Charming,' agreed Kirk.

'What a deep pity,' Chan continued, 'that she squanders glowing youth in a man's pursuit. She should be at mothering work.'

Kirk laughed. 'You tell her,' he suggested.

On Friday, Bill Rankin called Chan on the telephone. He had been through the *Globe's* files for the year 1913, he said — a long, arduous job. His search had been without result; he could find no story about Eve Durand. Evidently cable news had not greatly interested the *Globe's* staff in those days.

'I'm going to the public library for another try,' he announced. 'No doubt some of the New York papers carried the story. They seem our best bet now. I'm terribly busy, but I'll speed all I can.'

'Thanks for your feverish activity,' Chan replied. 'You are valuable man.'

'Just a real good wagon,' laughed Rankin. 'Here's hoping I don't break down. I'll let you know the minute I find something.'

Saturday came; the life at the bungalow was moving forward with unbroken calm. Through it Paradise walked with his accustomed dignity and poise, little dreaming of the dark cloud of suspicion that hovered over his head. Chan was busy with the books of Colonel John Beetham; he had finished the *Life* and was now going methodically through the others as though in search of a clue.

On Saturday night Kirk was dining out, and after his own dinner Chan again went down into Chinatown. There was little he could do there, he knew, but the place drew him none the less. This time he did not visit his cousin, but loitered on the crowded pavement of Grant Avenue.

Catching sight of the lights outside the Mandarin Theatre, he idly turned his footsteps towards the doorway. The Chinese have been a civilized race for many centuries; they do not care greatly for moving-pictures, preferring the spoken drama. A huge throng was milling about the door of the theatre, and Chan paused. There was usually enough drama in real life to satisfy him, but to-night he felt the need of the painted players.

Suddenly in the mob he caught sight of Willie Li, the boy scout whose good deed had thwarted his best laid plans on the previous Wednesday evening. Willie was gazing wistfully at the little frame of actors' pictures in the lobby. Chan went up to him with a friendly smile.

'Ah, we meet again,' he said in Cantonese. 'How fortunate, since the other night I walked my way churlishly, without offering my thanks for the great kindness you did me in bringing a physician.'

The boy's face brightened in recognition. 'May I be permitted to hope that the injury is improved?' he said.

'You have a kind heart,' Chan replied. 'I now walk on the foot with the best of health. Be good enough to tell me, have you performed your kind act for to-day?'

The boy frowned. 'Not yet. Opportunities are so seldom.'

'Ah, yes — how true. But if you will deign to come into the theatre as my guest, opportunities may increase. Each of the actors, as you know, receives in addition to his salary a bonus of twenty-five cents for every round of applause that is showered upon him. Come, and by frequent applauding you may pile up enough kind acts to spread over several days.'

The boy was only too willing, and buying a couple of tickets, Chan led him inside. The horrible din that greeted them they did not find disconcerting. It was, in fact, music to their ears. Even at this early hour the house was crowded. On the stage, with the casual, off-hand manner they affected, the Chinese company was enacting a famous historical play. Chan and the boy were fortunate enough to find seats.

Looking about, the detective from Hawaii saw that he was in a gathering of his own race exclusively. The women members of the audience were arrayed in their finest silks; in a stage box sat a slave girl famous in the colony. Little, slant-eyed children played in the aisles; occasionally a mother sent out to the refreshment booth in the lobby a bottle of milk, to be heated for the baby in her arms.

The clatter of the six-piece orchestra never ceased; it played more softly at dramatic moments, but comedy lines were spoken to the accompaniment of a terrific fusillade. Chan became engrossed in the play, for the actors were finished artists, the women players particularly graceful and accomplished. At eleven o'clock he suggested that they had better go, lest the boy's family be troubled about him.

'My father will not worry,' said Willie Li. 'He knows a boy scout is trustworthy.'

Nevertheless, Chan led him to the lobby, and there stood treat to a hot dog and a cup of coffee — for the refreshment booth alone was Americanized. As they climbed the empty street to the Oriental Apartments, Charlie looked inquiringly at the boy.

'Tell me,' he said, still speaking in Cantonese, 'of your plans for the future. You are ambitious. What profession calls you?'

'I would be an explorer, like my cousin Li Gung,' the boy answered in the same rather stilted tongue.

'Ah, yes — he who is attached to Colonel John Beetham,' nodded Chan. 'You have heard from your cousin stories of Colonel Beetham?'

'Many exciting ones,' the boy replied.

'You admire the Colonel? You think him very great character?'

'Why not? He is man of iron, stern but just. Discipline is with him important thing, and all boy scouts know that is right thinking. Many examples of this our cousin told us. Sometimes, Li Gung said, the caravan would revolt. Then the Colonel would snatch out gun, facing them with his bravery, alone. The caravan would tremble and proceed.'

'They knew, perhaps, that the Colonel would not hesitate to fire?'

'They had seen him do it. One event Li Gung spoke about I can never forget.' The boy's voice rose in excitement. 'It was on the desert, and the Colonel had told them what they must do, and what they must not do. A dirty keeper of camels, a man of low character, he did a thing which the Colonel had forbidden. In an instant he lay on the sand, with a bullet in his heart.'

'Ah, yes,' said Chan, 'I would expect that. However, it is an incident I have not encountered in any of the Colonel's books.'

They were at the door of the apartment-house. 'Accept my thanks, please,' Willie Li said. 'You have done a very kind deed to me.'

Chan smiled. 'Your company was a real pleasure. I hope we meet again.'

'I hope it, too,' answered Willie Li warmly. 'Good night.'

Chan walked slowly back to the Kirk Building. He was thinking of Colonel Beetham. A hard man, a man who did not hesitate to kill those who opposed their will to his. Here was food for thought.

On Sunday Barry Kirk called up Miss Morrow and suggested a ride into the country and dinner at a distant inn. 'Just to clear the cobwebs from your brain,' he put it.

'Thanks for the ad,' she answered. 'So that's how my brain strikes you? Cobwebby.'

'You know what I mean,' he protested. 'I want you to keep keen and alert. Nothing must happen to that pie.'

They spent a happy, care-free day on roads far from the rush of city traffic. When Kirk helped the girl out of the car before her door that night, he said: 'Well, to-morrow morning Charlie springs his hunch.'

'What do you imagine he has up his sleeve?'

'I haven't an idea. The more I see of him, the less I know him. But let's hope it's something good.'

'And illuminating,' added Miss Morrow. 'I feel the need of a little light.' She held out her hand. 'You've been lovely to me to-day.'

'Give me another chance,' he said. 'Give me lots of 'em. I'll get lovelier and lovelier as time goes on.'

'Is that a threat?' she laughed.

'A promise. I hope you don't mind.'

'Why should I? Good night.' She entered the lobby of her apartment-house.

On Monday morning Chan was brisk and business-like. He called Gloria Garland and was much relieved to hear her answering voice. She agreed to come to Kirk's place at ten o'clock, and Charlie at once got in touch with Miss Morrow and asked her to come at the same hour, bringing Captain Flannery. Then he turned to Kirk.

'Making humble suggestion,' he said, 'would you be so kind as to dispatch Paradise on lengthy errand just as ten o'clock hour approaches. I do not fancy him in place this morning.'

'Surely,' agreed Kirk. 'I'll send him out for some fishing tackle. I never get time to fish, but a man can't have too much tackle.'

At fifteen minutes to ten Chan rose and got

his hat. He would, he said, himself escort Miss Garland to the bungalow. Going below, he took up his stand in the doorway of the Kirk Building.

He saw Miss Morrow and Flannery enter, but gave them only a cool nod as they passed. Mystified, they went on upstairs. Kirk met them at the door.

'Here we are,' growled Flannery. 'I wonder what the Sergeant's up to. If he's got me here on a wild goose chase, I'll deport him to Hawaii. I'm too busy to-day to feel playful.'

'Oh, Chan will make good,' Kirk assured him. 'By the way, I suppose you've got that elevator girl — Jennie Jerome, or Grace Lane, or whatever her name is — under your eagle eye?'

'Yes. The boys have been shadowing her.'

'Find out anything?'

'Not a thing. She's got a room on Powell Street. Stays in nights and minds her own business, as far as I can learn.'

Down at the door, Chan was greeting Gloria Garland.

'You are promptly on the minute,' he approved. 'A delectable virtue.'

'I'm here, but I don't know what you want,' she replied. 'I told you everything the other day — '

'Yes, of course. Will you be kind enough to

walk after me? We rise aloft.'

He took her up in a car run by a black-haired Irish girl, and they entered the living-room of the bungalow.

'Ah, Captain — Miss Morrow — we are all here. That is correct,' Charlie said. 'Miss Garland, will you kindly recline on chair.'

The woman sat down, obviously puzzled. Her eyes sought Flannery's. 'What do you want with me now?' she asked.

The Captain shrugged his broad shoulders. 'Me — I don't want you. It's Sergeant Chan here. He's had a mysterious hunch.'

Chan smiled. 'Yes, I am guilty party, Miss Garland. I hope I have not rudely unconvenienced you?'

'Not a bit,' she answered.

'One day you told us of the girl Marie Lantelme, who disappeared so oddly out of Nice,' Chan continued. 'Will you kindly state — you have still not encountered her?'

'No, of course not,' the woman replied.

'You are quite sure you would recognize her if you met her?'

'Of course. I knew her well.'

Chan's eyes narrowed. 'There would be no reason why you would conceal act of recognition from us? I might humbly remind you, this is serious affair.'

'No — why should I do that? I'll tell you if

I see her — but I'm sure I haven't — '

'Very good. Will you remain in present posture until my return?' Chan went rapidly out to the stairs leading to the floor below.

They looked at one another in wonder, but no one spoke. In a moment, Chan returned. With him came Grace Lane, the elevator girl whom Mrs. Enderby had identified as Jennie Jerome.

She came serenely into the room, and stood there. The sunlight fell full upon her, outlining clearly her delicately modelled face. Gloria Garland started, and half rose from her chair.

'Marie!' she cried. 'Marie Lantelme! What are you doing here?'

They gasped. A look of triumph shone in Chan's narrow eyes.

The girl's poise did not desert her. 'Hello, Gloria,' she said softly. 'We meet again.'

'But where have you been, my dear?' Miss Garland wanted to know. 'Where did you go — and why — '

The girl stopped her. 'Some other time — ' she said.

In a daze, Flannery rose to his feet. 'Look here,' he began. 'Let me get this straight.' He moved forward accusingly, 'You are Marie Lantelme?'

'I was — once,' she nodded.

'You were singing in the same troupe as Miss Garland here — eleven years ago, at Nice? You disappeared?'

'I did.'

'Why?'

'I was tired of it. I found I didn't like the stage. If I had stayed, they would have forced me to go on. So I ran away.'

'Yeah. And seven years ago you were in New York — a model for a dressmaker. Your name then was Jennie Jerome. You disappeared again?'

'For the same reason. I didn't care for the work. I — I'm restless, I guess — '

'I'll say you're restless. You kept changing names?'

'I wanted to start all over. A new person.'

Flannery glared at her. 'There's something queer about you, my girl. You know who I am, don't you?'

'You appear to be a policeman.'

'Well, that's right. I am.'

'I have never done anything wrong. I am not afraid.'

'Maybe not. But tell me this — what do you know about Sir Frederic Bruce?'

'I know that he was a famous man from Scotland Yard, who was killed in Mr. Kirk's office last Tuesday night.'

'Ever see him before he came here?'

'No, sir — I never had.'

'Ever hear of him?'

'I don't believe so.'

Her even, gentle answers put Flannery at a loss. He stood, considering. His course was far from clear.

'You were running the elevator here last Tuesday night?' he continued.

'Yes, sir, I was.'

'Have you any idea why Sir Frederic was hunting for you? For Marie Lantelme, or Jennie Jerome, or whoever you really are?'

She frowned. 'Was he hunting for me? How strange. No, sir — I have no idea at all.'

'Well,' said Flannery, 'let me tell you this. You're a pretty important witness in the matter of Sir Frederic's murder, and I don't intend you shall get away.'

The girl smiled. 'So I judge. I seem to have been followed rather closely the past few days.'

'Well, you'll be followed even more closely from now on. One false move, and I lock you up. You understand that?'

'Perfectly, sir.'

'All right. Just tend to your work, and when I want you, I'll tell you so. You can go now.'

'Thank you, sir,' the girl replied, and went out.

Flannery turned to Miss Garland. 'You

210

recognized her the other night, didn't you?' he demanded.

'Oh, but I assure you, I didn't. I recognized her to-day for the first time.'

'Which is plenty time enough,' said Chan. 'Miss Garland, we are sunk deep in your debt. I permit you now to depart — '

'Yeah — you can go,' added Flannery. 'Take some other car and keep away from your old friend until this thing's cleared up.'

'I'll do that,' Miss Garland assured him. 'I'm afraid she didn't want me to identify her. I do hope I haven't got her into trouble.'

'That depends,' answered Flannery, and Kirk showed the actress out.

Chan was beaming. 'Hunch plenty good, after all,' he chuckled.

'Well, where are we?' Flannery said. 'The elevator girl is Jennie Jerome. Then she's Marie Lantelme. What does that mean?'

'It means only one thing,' said Miss Morrow softly.

'The Captain is pretending to be dense,' suggested Chan. 'He could not really be so thick.'

'What are you talking about?' Flannery demanded.

'My hunch, which has come so nicely true,' Chan told him. 'The elevator girl is Jennie Jerome. Next, she is Marie Lantelme. What does it mean, you ask? It means one thing only. She is also Eve Durand.'

'By heaven!' Flannery cried.

'Consider how the muddy water clears,' Chan went on. 'Eve Durand flees from India one dark night fifteen years ago. Four years later she is found in Nice, playing in theatre. Something happens — maybe she is seen and recognized — again she runs away. Another four years elapse and we encounter her in New York, walking in model gowns. Again something happens, again she disappears. Where does she go? Eventually to San Francisco. Here opportunities are not so good, she must take more lowly position. And here Sir Frederic comes, always seeking for Eve Durand.'

'It's beautifully clear,' approved Miss Morrow.

'Like lake at evening,' nodded Chan. 'Sir Frederic, though he has looked long for this woman, has never seen her. He can upearth here no one who can identify Eve Durand, but he remembers once she was Marie Lantelme, once Jennie Jerome. In this great city, he learns, are two people who have known her when she was wearing these other names. He asks that they be invited to dinner, hoping that one or both will point out to him the woman he has trailed so long.'

Flannery was walking the floor. 'Well — I don't know. It's almost too good to be true. But if it is — if she's Eve Durand — then I can't let her wander around loose. I'll have to lock her up this morning. If I could only be sure — '

'I am telling you,' persisted Chan.

'I know, but you are guessing. You've identified her as those other two, but as for Eve Durand — '

The telephone rang. Kirk answered, and handed it to Flannery. 'For you, Captain,' he said.

Flannery took the telephone. 'Oh — hello, Chief,' he said. 'Yeah — yeah. What's that? Oh — oh, he is? Good enough. Thank you, Chief. I sure will.'

He hung up the receiver and turned to the others. A broad smile was on his face.

'We're going to find out, Sergeant, just how good a guesser you are,' he said. 'I'll put a couple of extra men to following this dame, but I won't do anything more until to-morrow. Yes, sir — by to-morrow evening I'll know whether she's Eve Durand or not.'

'Your words have obscure sound,' Chan told him.

'The Chief of Police has just had a wire,' Flannery explained. 'Inspector Duff of Scotland Yard is getting in tomorrow afternoon at two-thirty. And he's bringing with him the one man in all the world who's sure to know Eve Durand when he sees her. He's bringing the woman's husband, Major Eric Durand.'

12

A Misty Evening

When Chan and Kirk were left alone, the little detective sat staring thoughtfully into space. 'Now Tuesday becomes the big day for keen anticipation,' he remarked. 'What will it reveal? Much, I hope, for my time on the mainland becomes a brief space indeed.'

Kirk looked at him in wonder. 'Surely you won't go on Wednesday if this thing isn't solved?'

Chan nodded stubbornly. 'I have made unspoken promise to Barry Chan. Now I put it into words. To-morrow Eve Durand's husband arrives. In all the world we could have selected no more opportune person. He will identify this elevator woman as his wife, or he will not. If he does, perhaps case is finished. If he does not' — Charlie shrugged — 'then I have done all possible. Let Captain Flannery flounder alone after that.'

'Well, we won't cross our oceans until we get to them,' Kirk suggested. 'A lot may happen before Wednesday. By the way, I've been meaning to take you over to the

Cosmopolitan Club. How about lunching there this noon?'

Chan brightened. 'I have long nursed desire to see that famous interior. You are most kind.'

'All set, then,' replied his host. 'I have some business in the office. Come downstairs for me at twelve-thirty. And when Paradise returns, please tell him we're lunching out.'

He took his hat and coat and went below. Chan strolled aimlessly to the window and stood looking down on the glittering city. His eyes strayed to the Matson dock, the pier-shed and, beyond, the red funnels of a familiar ship. A ship that was sailing, day after to-morrow, for Honolulu harbour. Would he be on it? He had sworn, yes — and yet — He sighed deeply. The door-bell rang, and he admitted Bill Rankin, the reporter.

'Hello,' said Rankin. 'Glad to find you in. I spent all day yesterday at the public library, and say, I'll bet I stirred up more dust than the chariot in *Ben Hur*.'

'With any luck?' Chan inquired.

'Yes. I finally found the story in the files of the *New York Sun*. A great newspaper in those days — but I won't talk shop. It was just a brief item with the Peshawar date line — I copied it down. Here it is.'

Charlie took the sheet of yellow paper, and

read a short cable story that told him nothing he did not already know. Eve Durand, the young wife of a certain Captain Eric Durand, had disappeared under mysterious circumstances two nights previously, while on a picnic party in the hills outside Peshawar. The authorities were greatly alarmed, and parties of British soldiers were scouring the wild country-side.

'Item has date, May fifth,' remarked Chan. 'Then Eve Durand was lost on night of May third, the year 1913. You found nothing else?'

'There were no follow-up stories,' Rankin replied. 'And no mention of Beetham, as you hoped. Say — what in Sam Hill could he have to do with this?'

'Nothing,' said Chan promptly. 'It was one of my small mistakes. Even great detective sometimes steps off on wrong foot. My wrong foot often weary from too much use.'

'Well, what's going on, anyhow?' Rankin wanted to know. 'I've hounded Flannery, and I've tried Miss Morrow, and not a thing do I learn. My city editor is waxing very sarcastic. Can't you give me a tip to help me out?'

Chan shook his head. 'It would be plenty poor ethics for me to talk about the case. I am in no authority here, and already Captain Flannery regards me with the same warm feeling he would show pickpocket from Los

217

Angeles. Pursuing the truth further, there is nothing to tell you anyhow. We are not as yet close to anything that might indicate happy success.'

'I'm sorry to hear it,' Rankin said.

'Situation will not continue,' Chan assured him. 'Light will break. For the present we swim with one foot on the ground, but in good time we will plunge into centre of the stream. Should I be on scene when success is looming, I will be happy to give you little secret hint.'

'If you're on the scene? What are you talking about?'

'Personal affairs call me home with a loud megaphone. On Wednesday I go whether case is solved or not.'

'Yes — like you did last Wednesday,' Rankin laughed. 'You can't kid me. The patient Oriental isn't going to get impatient at the wrong minute. Well, I must run. Remember your promise about the hint.'

'I have lengthy memory,' Chan replied. 'And already I owe you much. Good-bye.'

When the reporter had gone, Charlie stood staring at the copy of that cable story. 'May third, nineteen hundred thirteen,' he said aloud. With a surprisingly quick step he went to a table and took from it the *Life* of Colonel John Beetham. He ran hastily through the pages until he found the thing he sought. Then for a long moment he sat in a chair with the book open on his knee, staring into space.

At precisely twelve-thirty he entered Kirk's office. The young man rose and, accepting some papers from his secretary, put them into a leather brief-case. 'Got to see a lawyer after lunch,' he explained. 'Not a nice lawyer, either — a man this time.' They went to the Cosmopolitan Club.

When they had checked their hats and coats and returned to the lobby in that imposing building, Chan looked about him with deep interest. The Cosmopolitan's fame was widespread; it was the resort of men active in the arts, in finance and in journalism. Kirk's popularity there was proved by many jovial greetings. He introduced Chan to a number of his friends, and the detective was presently the centre of a pleasant group. With difficulty they got away to lunch in one corner of the big dining-room.

It was towards the close of the lunch that Chan, looking up, saw approaching the man who interested him most at the moment. Colonel John Beetham's hard-bitten face was more grim than ever, seen in broad daylight. He paused at their table.

'How are you, Kirk?' he said. 'And Mr.

Chan. I'll sit down a moment, if I may.'

'By all means,' Kirk agreed cordially. 'How about lunch? What can I order for you?'

'Thanks, I've just finished,' Beetham replied.

'A cigarette, then.' Kirk held out his case.

'Good of you.' The Colonel took one and lighted it. 'I haven't seen you since that beastly dinner. Oh — I beg your pardon — you get my meaning? . . . What a horrible thing that was — a man like Sir Frederic — by the way, have they any idea who did it?'

Kirk shrugged. 'If they have, they're not telling me.'

'Sergeant Chan — perhaps you are working on the case?' Beetham suggested.

Chan's eyes narrowed. 'The affair concerns mainland police. I am stranger here, like yourself.'

'Ah, yes, of course,' responded Beetham. 'I just happened to recall that you were on the point of leaving, and I thought, seeing you had stayed over — '

'If I can help, I will do so,' Chan told him. He was thinking deeply. A man like Colonel Beetham did not note the comings and goings of a Charlie Chan without good reason.

'How's the new expedition shaping up?' Kirk inquired.

'Slowly — rather slowly,' Beetham frowned. 'Speaking of that, I have wanted a chat with

220

you on the subject. Your grandmother has offered to help with the financing, but I have hesitated — it's a stiff sum.'

'How much?'

'I have part of the money. I still need about fifty thousand dollars.'

Kirk's eyebrows went up. 'Ah, yes — quite a nest-egg. But if grandmother wants to do it — well, it's her own money.'

'Glad you feel that way about it,' said Beetham. 'I was fearful the other members of the family might think I was using undue influence. The whole idea was hers — I give you my word.'

'Naturally,' Kirk answered. 'I'm sure she would enjoy it, at that.'

'The results will be most important from a scientific point of view,' Beetham continued. 'Your grandmother's name would be highly honoured. I would see that she had full credit.'

'Just what sort of expedition is it?' Kirk asked.

The tired eyes lighted for the first time. 'Well, I had a bit of luck when I was last on the Gobi Desert. I stumbled on to the ruins of a city that must have been flourishing early in the first century. Only had time to take a brief look — but I turned up coins that bore the date of 7 A.D. I unearthed the oldest papers in existence — papers that bore the scrawl of little children — arithmetic — seven times seven and the like. Letters written by the military governor of the city, scraps of old garments, jewellery — amazing mementos of the past. I am keen to go back and make a thorough investigation. Of course, the trouble in China will interfere, rather — but there is always trouble in China. I have waited long enough. I shall get through somehow. I always have.'

'Well, I don't envy you,' Kirk smiled. 'The way I've always felt, when you've seen one desert, you've seen 'em all. But you have my best wishes.'

'Thanks. You're frightfully kind,' Beetham rose. 'I hope to settle the matter in a few days. I am hoping, also, that before I leave, the murderer of Sir Frederic will be found. Struck me as a good chap, Sir Frederic.'

Chan looked up quickly. 'A great admirer of yours, Colonel Beetham,' he said.

'Admirer of mine? Sir Frederic? Was he really?' The Colonel's tone was cool and even.

'Undubitable fact. Among his effects we find many books written by you.'

Beetham threw down his cigarette. 'That was good of him. I am quite flattered. If by any chance you are concerned in the hunt for the person who killed him, Sergeant Chan, I wish you the best of luck.'

He strolled away from the table, while

Chan looked after him thoughtfully.

'Reminds me of the snows of Tibet,' Kirk said. 'Just as warm and human. Except when he spoke of his dead city. That seemed to rouse him. An odd fish, isn't he, Charlie?'

'An odd fish from icy waters,' Chan agreed. 'I am wondering — '

'Yes?'

'He regrets Sir Frederic's passing. But might it not happen that beneath his weeping eyes are laughing teeth?'

They went to the cloak-room, where they retrieved their hats and coats and Kirk's brief-case. As they walked down the street, Kirk looked at Chan.

'Just remembered the Cosmopolitan Club year book,' he said. 'You don't imagine it meant anything, do you?'

Chan shrugged. 'Imagination does not seem to thrive on mainland climate,' he replied.

Kirk went off to his lawyer's and Charlie returned home to await a more promising to-morrow.

On Tuesday afternoon, Miss Morrow was the first to arrive at Kirk's place. She came in about three-thirty. The day was dark, with gusts of wind and rain, but the girl was glowing.

Kirk helped her off with her raincoat. 'You seem to be filled with vim and vigour,' he said.

'Walked all the way,' she told him. 'I was too excited to sit calmly in a taxi. Just think — in a few minutes we may see the meeting between Major Durand and his long-lost wife.'

'The Major has arrived?' Chan inquired.

'Yes — he and Inspector Duff came half an hour ago. Their train was a trifle late. Captain Flannery went to the station to meet them. He telephoned me they'd be along shortly. It seems that, like a true Englishman, the Major didn't care to talk with anybody until he'd gone to a hotel and had his tub.'

'Don't blame him, after that trip from Chicago,' Kirk said. 'I believe little Jennie Jerome Marie Lantelme is on the elevator.'

Miss Morrow nodded. 'She is. I saw her when I came up. I wonder if she is really Eve Durand? Won't it be thrilling if she is!'

'She's got to be. She's Charlie's hunch.'

'Do not be too certain,' Chan objected. 'In the past it has often happened I was hoarsely barking up uncorrect tree.'

Kirk stirred the fire, and drew up a wide chair for the girl. 'Here you are — a trifle large for you, but you may grow. I'll give you tea later. These Englishmen probably can't do a thing until they've had their Oolong.'

The girl sat down, and, dropping into a chair at her side, Kirk began to talk airily of nothing in particular. He was conscious that at his back Chan was nervously walking the floor.

'Better sit down, Charlie,' he suggested. 'You act like a man in a dentist's waiting-room.'

'Feel that way,' Chan told him. 'Much is at stake now for me. If I have taken wrong turning, I shall have to endure some Flannery sneers.'

It was four o'clock, and the dusk was falling outside the lofty windows, when the bell rang. Kirk himself went to the door. He admitted Flannery and a thick-set young Englishman. Two men only — Kirk peered past them down the stairs, but the third man was not in evidence.

'Hello,' Flannery said, striding in. 'Major Durand not here yet, eh?'

'He is not,' Kirk replied. 'Don't tell me you've mislaid him.'

'Oh, no,' Flannery answered. 'I'll explain in a minute. Miss Morrow, meet Inspector Duff, of Scotland Yard.'

The girl came forward, smiling. 'I'm so glad,' she said.

'Charmed,' remarked Duff in a hearty, roast-beef-of-old-England voice. He was surprisingly young, with rosy cheeks, and the look of a farmer about him. And indeed it had been from a farm in Yorkshire that he had come to London and the Metropolitan police.

'The Inspector and I went from the train to my office,' Flannery explained. 'I wanted to go over the records of our case with him. The Major stopped at the hotel to brush up — he'll be along in a minute. Oh, yes — Mr. Kirk, Inspector Duff. And this, Inspector, is Sergeant Charlie Chan, of the Honolulu police.'

Chan bowed low. 'A moment that will live for ever in my memory,' he said.

'Oh — er — really?' Duff replied. 'The Captain's told me of you, Sergeant. We're in the same line — some miles apart.'

'Many miles apart,' conceded Charlie gravely.

'Look here,' said Flannery, 'it will be just as well if the Major doesn't meet that girl in the elevator until we're all set for it. Somebody should go below and steer him into a different elevator.'

'I will be happy to perform that service,' Chan offered.

'No — I know him by sight — I'll do it,' Flannery replied. 'I want to have a word with the men I've got watching her. I saw one of them in front of the building when I came in. Inspector — I'll leave you here. You're in good hands.' He went out.

Kirk drew up a chair for the English detective. 'Give you tea when the Major comes,' he said.

'You're very kind, I'm sure,' Duff answered.

'You have been all over the case with Captain Flannery?' Miss Morrow inquired.

'I have — from the beginning,' Duff replied. 'It's a shocking affair — shocking. Sir Frederic was deeply respected — I might even say loved — by all of us. It appears that he was killed in the line of duty, though he had retired and was, supposedly, out of all that. I can assure you that the murder of one of its men is not taken lightly by Scotland Yard. We shall not rest until we have found the guilty person — and in that task, Sergeant, we shall welcome help from every possible source.'

Chan bowed. 'My abilities are of the slightest, but they are lined up beside your very great ones.'

'I had hoped, Inspector,' Miss Morrow said, 'that you would be able to throw considerable light on this affair.'

Duff shook his head. 'I'm frightfully sorry. There are so many other men — older men — on our force who would have been of much greater service. Unfortunately, I am the only Scotland Yard man in the States at the moment. You see — I'm a bit young — '

'I'd noticed that,' smiled the girl.

'All these events that appear to be linked up with Sir Frederic's murder happened before my day. I shall do my best — but — '

'Will you have a cigarette?' Kirk suggested.

'No, thanks. My pipe, if the young lady doesn't object.'

'Not at all,' said Miss Morrow. 'It's quite in the Sherlock Holmes tradition.'

Duff smiled. 'But the only point of similarity, I fear. As I say, I have been with the police a comparatively brief time — a mere matter of seven years. Of course, I have heard of the Hilary Galt murder, though it happened many years ago. As a young policeman I was shown, in the Black Museum, the famous velvet slippers they found Galt wearing that disastrous night. Coming to Eve Durand, I am familiar in a casual way with the story of her disappearance. In fact, I had once a very slight connexion with the case. Five years ago there was a rumour that she had been seen in Paris, and Sir Frederic sent me across the Channel to look into it. It was merely another false alarm, but while making the investigation I chanced to encounter Major Durand, who was also on the ground. Poor chap — that was one of a long series of disappointments for him. I hope he is not to suffer another here to-night.'

'How did the Major happen to come to America at this time?' Miss Morrow inquired.

'He came in answer to a cable from Sir Frederic,' Duff explained. 'Sir Frederic asked his help, and of course he hastened to comply, landing in New York a week ago. When I got off the Twentieth Century in Chicago I discovered Durand had been on the same train. We joined forces and hurried on to San Francisco together.'

'Well, he at least can help us,' Miss Morrow suggested.

'I fancy he can. I repeat, I have been over the case carefully, but I have had no inspiration as yet. One angle of it interests me tremendously — those velvet slippers. Why were they taken? Where are they now? They appear to be again the essential clue. What do you say, Sergeant?'

Chan shrugged. 'Slippers were exactly that, long time ago,' he said. 'On which occasion they led positively no place.'

'I know,' smiled Duff. 'But I'm not superstitious. I shall follow them again. By the way, there is one point on which I may be able to offer some help.' He turned suddenly to Kirk. 'You have a butler named Paradise?' he inquired.

Kirk's heart sank. 'Yes — and a very good one,' he answered.

'I have been interested in Paradise,' said Duff. 'And Paradise, I understand, has been interested in Sir Frederic's mail. Where is he now?'

'He's in the kitchen, or his room,' Kirk replied. 'Do you want to see him?'

'Before I go — yes,' Duff said.

Flannery came through the hall, followed by a big blond man in a dripping Burberry coat. Major Eric Durand, retired, looked to be the sportsman type of Englishman; his cheeks were tanned and weather-beaten, as though from much riding in the open, his blue eyes alert. Indoors, one would picture him sitting in a club with a cigar, a whisky and soda, and a copy of the *Field*.

'Come in, Major,' Flannery said. He introduced the Englishman to the company, and Kirk hurried forward to take the Burberry coat. There followed a moment of awkward silence.

'Major,' Flannery began, 'we haven't told you why we got you here. You have come to San Francisco in response to a cablegram from Sir Frederic Bruce?'

'I have,' said Durand quietly.

'Did he give you any idea of why he wanted you to come?'

'He intimated that he was on the point of finding — my wife.'

'I see. Your wife disappeared under unusual circumstances some fifteen years ago, in India?'

'Precisely.'

'Did you ever hear of her after that?'

'Never. There were many false reports, of course. We followed them all up, but none of them came to anything in the end.'

'You never heard of her at Nice? Or in New York?'

'No — I don't think those were among the places. I'm sure they weren't.'

'You would, of course, know her if you saw her now?'

Durand looked up with sudden interest. 'I fancy I would. She was only eighteen when she was — lost.' Miss Morrow felt a quick twinge of pity for the man. 'But one doesn't forget, you know.'

'Major,' said Flannery slowly, 'we have every reason to believe that your wife is in this building to-night.'

Durand took a startled step backward. Then he sadly shook his head. 'I wish it were true. You've no idea — fifteen years anxiety — it rather takes it out of a chap. One stops hoping, after a time. Ah, yes — I wish it were true — but there have been so many disappointments. I cannot hope any more.'

'Please wait just a minute,' Flannery said, and went out.

A strained silence followed his exit. The ticking of a tall clock in a corner became suddenly like the strokes of a hammer. Durand began to pace the floor.

'It can't be,' he cried to Duff. 'No — it can't be Eve. After all these years — in San Francisco — no, no — I can't believe it.'

'We shall know in a moment, old chap,' Duff said gently.

The moments lengthened horribly. Chan began to wonder. Durand continued to pace back and forth, silently, over the rug. Still the hammer strokes of the clock. Five minutes — ten —

The outer door was flung open and Flannery burst into the room. His face was crimson, his grey hair dishevelled.

'She's gone!' he cried. 'Her elevator's standing at the seventh floor with the door open. She's gone, and no one saw her go!'

Durand gave a little cry and sinking into a chair, buried his face in his hands.

13

Old Friends Meet Again

Major Durand was not the only one to whom Flannery's news came as a shock and a disappointment. On the faces of the four other people in that room dismay was clearly written.

'Gone, and no one saw her go,' Chan repeated. He looked reprovingly at the Captain. 'Yet she was under watchful eye of clever mainland police.'

Flannery snorted. 'She was, but we're not supermen. That woman's as slippery as an eel. There were two of my boys on the job — both keen lads — well, no use crying over spilt milk. I'll get her. She can't — '

The door opened and a plain clothes man entered, bringing with him a little old cleaning woman with straggling grey hair.

'Hello, Petersen — what is it?' Flannery asked.

'Listen to this, Chief,' said Petersen. 'This woman was working in an office on the seventh floor.' He turned to her. 'Tell the Captain what you told me.'

The woman twisted her apron nervously. 'In 709 I was, sir. They go home early, and I was alone there at my work. The door opens and this red-headed elevator girl runs in. She's got on a raincoat, and a hat. 'What's the matter?' I says, but she just runs on into the back room, and sort of wondering, I follow her. I'm just in time to see her climb on to the fire-escape. Never a word she said, sir — she just disappeared in the night.'

'The fire-escape,' repeated Flannery. 'I thought so. Have you looked at it, Petersen?'

'Yes, sir. It's one of those — you know — a person's weight lets down the last flight of steps to the ground. A simple matter to go like that.'

'All right,' Flannery answered. 'Someone must have seen her when she came out of the alley. We'll go down and have a look round.' He turned to the cleaning woman. 'That's all. You can go.'

The woman passed a second plain clothes man in the hall. He came quickly into the living-room.

'I've got a lead, Captain,' he said. 'Boy in the cigar store on the corner. He says a girl with a Kirk Building uniform under her coat rushed in a few minutes ago and used his telephone.'

'Did he hear the call?'

'No, sir. It's a booth phone. She was there only a few minutes, and then she hurried out again.'

'Well, that's something,' Flannery said. 'You boys wait for me — I've got a car. First of all, I'll send out the alarm. I'll have men at the ferries and the railroad stations — she's a marked woman with that uniform. I'll pick her up before midnight — '

'On what charge?' asked Miss Morrow gently.

'Oh — oh, well — as a witness. I'll take her as a witness. Still that will mean a lot of publicity I don't want at this time. I have it. I'll take her on a charge of stealing. The uniform is your property, Mr. Kirk?'

'Yes — but I don't like that,' protested Kirk.

'Oh, it's just a fake. We won't press it. I've got to get her on some pretext. Now — if I can use your phone — '

Flannery talked to some purpose to the station house, and the hue and cry after that elusive woman was once more under way. He rose full of energy.

'I'll get her,' he promised. 'It's a bad set-back to our plans, but it's only for a minute. She can't get away — '

'She is one who has had some success at getting away in the past,' Chan reminded him.

'Yeah — but not this time,' answered the

Captain. 'She's never had me on her trail before.' He blustered out, followed by his two men.

Major Durand slumped dejectedly in his chair. Inspector Duff was puffing calmly on his well-seasoned pipe.

'It's a bit of hard luck,' he remarked. 'But patience — that's what counts in this work, eh, Sergeant Chan?'

Charlie beamed. 'At last I meet fellow detective who talks same language with me.'

Barry Kirk rose and rang the bell. 'How about a cup of tea?' he said. He stepped to the window and looked out. Swords of light marking the streets floated dimly in the mist, far below. The wind howled, rain spattered on the panes, the city was shrouded and lost. 'It's one of those nights — a little something to warm us up — ' He was silent. What a night it was — made to order for the man or woman who sought to slip away and never be seen again.

Paradise entered with calm dignity and stood in the brightly lighted room, his shock of snow-white hair lending him an air of stern respectability.

'You rang, sir?' he said.

'Yes,' Kirk replied. 'We'll have tea, Paradise. Five of us here — ' He stopped. The butler's eyes were on Inspector Duff, and his face was suddenly as white as his hair.

There was a moment of silence. 'Hello, Paradise,' Duff said quietly.

The butler muttered something, and turned as though to go out.

'Just a moment!' The Inspector's voice was steely cold. 'This is a surprise, my man. A surprise for both of us, I fancy. When I last saw you, you were standing in the dock at Old Bailey.' Paradise bowed his head. 'Perhaps I shouldn't have been inclined to give you away, Paradise, if you had behaved yourself. But you've been opening mail — haven't you? You've been tampering with a letter addressed to Sir Frederic Bruce?'

'Yes, sir, I have.' The servant's voice was very low.

'So I understand,' Duff continued. He turned to Barry Kirk. 'I'm sorry to distress you, Mr. Kirk. I believe Paradise has been a good servant?'

'The best I ever had,' Kirk told him.

'He was always a good servant,' went on Duff. 'As I recall, that fact was brought out clearly at the trial. A competent, faithful man — he had many references to prove it. But unfortunately a few years ago, in England, there was some suspicion that he had put hydrocyanic acid in a lady's tea.'

'What an odd place for hydrocyanic acid,'

237

said Kirk. 'But then, of course, I speak without knowing the lady.'

'The lady was his wife,' Duff explained. 'It seemed to some of us that he had rather overstepped a husband's privileges. He was brought to trial — '

Paradise raised his head. 'Nothing was ever proved,' he said firmly. 'I was acquitted.'

'Yes, our case collapsed,' admitted Inspector Duff. 'That doesn't often happen, Mr. Kirk, but it did in this instance. Technically, at least, Paradise cannot be adjudged guilty. In the eyes of the law, I mean. And for that reason I might have been inclined to keep all this to myself, if I had not heard of his queer work with that letter. Tell me, Paradise — do you know anything about Eve Durand?'

'I have never heard the name before, sir.'

'Have you any information in the matter of an old murder in Ely Place — the murder of Hilary Galt?'

'None whatever, sir.'

'But you opened an envelope addressed to Sir Frederic Bruce and substituted a blank sheet for the letter you found inside. I think you had better explain, my man.'

'Yes, sir. I will do so.' The servant turned to Barry Kirk. 'This is very painful for me, Mr. Kirk. In the two years I have been with you I have done nothing dishonourable before

— before this act. The gentleman has said that I poisoned my wife. I may call attention to the fact that he has some animus in the matter, as he conducted the investigation and was bitterly disappointed when a jury acquitted me. A natural feeling — '

'Never mind that,' said Duff sharply.

'At any rate, sir,' the butler continued to Kirk, 'I was acquitted, for the very good reason that I was an innocent man. But I knew that, innocent or not, the fact of my having been tried would not be — er — pleasant news for you.'

'Anything but,' agreed Kirk.

'I thought it would be best if the matter remained in its former oblivion. I have been happy here — it is an excellent post — the very fact of its height above the ground has inspired me. I was always fond of high places. So I was in a bit of a funk, sir, when you told me Sir Frederic Bruce was coming. I had never had the pleasure of his acquaintance, but I'd had my brief moment in the public eye and I feared he might do me the honour to remember me. Well, he arrived and — unfortunately — he recognized me at once. We had a long talk here in this room. I assured him that I had been unjustly accused, that I had never done anything wrong, and that I was living a model life. I begged

239

him to keep my secret. He was a just man. He said he would look into the matter — I presumed he wanted to hear Scotland Yard's opinion of the evidence — and would let me know his decision later. And there the matter stood, sir, on the night Sir Frederic met his unhappy end.'

'Ah, yes,' said Kirk. 'I begin to see.'

'What I did later was done from a misguided wish to retain your respect and confidence, sir. A messenger from Cook's put into my hand that packet of letters, and I saw on the top what I thought was the dreaded missive from Scotland Yard. If I may be allowed to say so, I went a bit balmy then. I believed that Sir Frederic had cabled about me to the Yard, and that this was the answer. It would no doubt fall into the hands of the police — '

'It was too early for any answer yet,' Kirk told him.

'How could I be sure, sir? In this day of the air-mail and other time-saving devices. I determined to have a look at that letter, and if it did not concern me, to put it back in place — '

'But it didn't concern you, Paradise,' said Kirk.

'Not directly, sir. However, it mentioned that Inspector Duff was in New York. I had enjoyed the honour of Inspector Duff's personal attention in my — er — my ordeal, and I was panic-stricken. The local police, reading the letter, might send for him with results that are all too apparent now. So in my madness I slipped a blank sheet of paper into the envelope and resealed it. It was a clumsy subterfuge, sir, and one I deeply regret. Not the clumsiness, but the deceit, sir — that pains me. Everything has always been above the table with us, sir.'

'I should hope it had,' said Kirk.

'I am perhaps going too far when I ask you to overlook my defection, Mr. Kirk. I assure you, however, that it was my fondness for you, my keen desire to remain in your service, that prompted my rash act. If we could only go back to the old basis, sir — of mutual confidence and esteem — '

Kirk laughed. 'I don't know. I shall have to think this over. Are you sure you're fond of me, Paradise?'

'Very, sir.'

'Have you analyzed your emotions carefully? No little hidden trace of resentment, or disapproval?'

'None whatever, sir. I give you my word.'

Kirk shrugged. 'Very well. Then you might go and prepare the — er — the tea. In the usual manner, please.'

'Thank you, sir,' answered Paradise, and departed.

'The poor old dear,' said Miss Morrow. 'I'm sure he never did it. He was the victim of circumstances.'

'Perhaps,' admitted Duff. 'Personally, however, I thought the evidence very strong. But I was new to the work at that time, and I may have been mistaken. At any rate, I am happy to have been able to eliminate Paradise from our case. It clears the air a bit.'

'He may be eliminated from the case,' Barry Kirk remarked. 'But I'm free to admit that to me he is more important than ever.'

'You don't believe he had anything to do with killing Sir Frederic?' Miss Morrow inquired.

'No — but I'm afraid he may have something to do with killing me. I'm faced by a private and personal problem — and a very pretty one, too. I'd hate to lose Paradise, but I'd hate to lose myself even more. Imagine taking the glass of good old orange juice every morning from a hand that has been up to tricks with hydrocyanic acid. Not so good. Charlie, as a guest here, you're interested. What do you say?'

Chan shrugged. 'It may be he disliked his wife,' he suggested.

'I should hate to think he was fond of her,'

Kirk replied. 'But at that, he's a good old soul. And some wives, no doubt, drive a man too far. I think I'll let him stay a while. However' — he looked at Miss Morrow — 'something tells me I'll do an awful lot of eating out.'

'Sergeant Chan,' Duff said, 'you have not been idle. What discoveries have you made in our case so far?'

'None but the slightest,' Chan told him. 'I am very bright in tracking down Paradise here, and we have just seen the value of that. Alas, there are sprouting crops that never ripen into grain.'

'True enough,' agreed the Inspector. 'But you must have had ideas along other lines, too. I should be interested to hear them.'

'Sometime we have little talk,' Charlie promised. 'For the present — I hesitate to speak of it. I am not without tender feeling to my heart, and I know only too well the topic must be one of deep pain to Major Durand. He must pardon my rudeness if I have keen desire to hear something of that far-away night when Eve Durand was lost.'

Durand came out of a deep reverie. 'Ah, yes — what's that? The night when Eve — of course, it was all so long ago.'

'Yet a moment you are not likely to forget,' suggested Chan.

Durand smiled ruefully. 'I'm afraid not. I have tried to forget — it seemed the best way. But I have never succeeded.'

'The date was the third of May, in the year 1913,' Chan prompted.

'Precisely. We had been living in Peshawar just six months — I was assigned to a regiment there only a month after our marriage in England. A God-forsaken place, Peshawar — an outpost of empire, with a vengeance. No place to bring a woman like Eve, who had known nothing save the civilized life of the English countryside.'

He paused deep in thought. 'Yet we were very happy. We were young — Eve was eighteen, I was twenty-four — young and tremendously in love. The discomforts of that far garrison meant nothing — we had each other.'

'And on this night under question,' Chan persisted.

'There was a gay social life at the garrison, and Eve took an important part in it, as was natural. On the evening you ask about, we had arranged a picnic party in the hills. We were to ride our ponies out of the town and up a narrow dirt road to a small plateau from which we could watch the moon rise over the roofs of Peshawar. The plan was rather foolhardy — the hills were full of bandits — I was a bit fearful at the time. But the ladies — they insisted — you know how women are. And there were five men in the party, all fully armed. There seemed no real danger.'

Again he paused. 'Eve wore her jewels — a pearl necklace her uncle had given her — I remember protesting against it before we set out. She only laughed at me. Sometimes I have thought — But no, I do not like to think that. Was she killed for her necklace, her rings? I have had to face it.

'At any rate, we packed our supper and rode out of the town. Everything went well until the hour arrived to go home. Then some-one suggested a game of hide-and-seek — '

'You recall who suggested that?' asked Chan.

'Yes — it was Eve. I objected, but — well, one doesn't like to be a spoil-sport, and the party was in a gay humour. The women scattered among the tamarisks — disappeared into the shadows, laughing and chatting. Within the half-hour we had found them all — save one. We have not found her yet.'

'How terrible,' Miss Morrow cried.

'You can scarcely realize the true horror of it,' Durand returned. 'Those black hills filled with innumerable dangers — oh, it was a foolish thing, that game. It should never have happened. Of the night that followed — and the long, hot dreadful days after that — I need not go on, I'm sure.' He bowed his head.

'There were five men,' said Chan. 'Yourself already counted.'

'Five men, yes,' Durand replied. 'And five charming girls.'

'Five men — the other four officers, like yourself?' Charlie continued.

'Three of them were officers. One was not.'

Chan's face lighted. 'One was not?'

'No. The party was given in his honour, in a way. You see, he was a famous man — everyone was eager to pay tribute to him. He had just been a guest at the Viceregal Lodge, he'd spoken in the throne-room, and they'd pinned medals and things on him. All India was ringing with his praises. He'd recently come back from a beastly perilous journey through Tibet — '

Chan's eyes narrowed. 'He was an explorer?'

'One of the best. A brave man.'

'You are referring to Colonel John Beetham?'

'Yes, of course. Then you knew?'

Kirk and Miss Morrow sat up with sudden interest. Chan nodded. 'I had guessed,' he said. He was silent for a moment. 'Colonel Beetham is at this moment in San Francisco,' he added.

'Really?' answered the Major. 'An odd coincidence. I should like to meet him again.

He was most sympathetic.'

'The party was in his honour, you have said?' Charlie went on.

'Yes — a sort of farewell. You see, he was leaving the next day. Leaving for home, but not by the conventional route — not Beetham. He was going by caravan through the wilds of Afghanistan and across the great salt desert of Persia to Teheran.'

'Through Khyber Pass?' Chan asked.

'Oh, yes — through the Khyber. A dangerous business, but he had a big retinue of servants who had been with him on other expeditions — and the Emir of Afghanistan had invited him. He left early the next morning and I have never seen him since.'

'Early the next morning,' Chan repeated slowly. 'Going home.' He stared for a moment at the misty window. 'I had hoped to go home in the morning myself. But always something rises up making me break my word to my little son. What a despicable father he will think me. However' — he shrugged — 'what is to be, will be.'

Paradise came into the room, pompously wheeling a tea-wagon. There was a moment of uncomfortable silence.

'Tea, sir,' said the butler.

'I hope so, I'm sure,' replied Kirk.

Paradise served Miss Morrow, and then

turned to Inspector Duff. 'What will you have in yours, sir?' he inquired.

The Inspector looked him firmly in the eye. 'One lump of sugar,' he said. 'And — nothing else.'

14

Dinner for Two

With a grave face Paradise served the tea, passed sandwiches and cakes, and then silently withdrew. Barry Kirk paused with his cup at his lips, an inquiring look in his eyes. Inspector Duff saw it and smiled.

'I may tell you,' he said, 'that hydrocyanic acid has a quite distinctive odour. A pungent odour of peach blossoms.'

'That's very good of you,' answered Kirk. 'I shall remember what you say. And you, Charlie — you'd better do the same. At the first intimation that we are in a peach orchard, we call up the employment agency and engage a new butler.'

'I have made a note,' Chan told him.

'At any rate,' Kirk continued, 'life's going to be rather a sporting proposition from now on. 'To be, or not to be': that is the question.'

'We must treat Paradise with kindly consideration,' Chan suggested. 'We must bear in mind that a good word has heat enough for three winters, while a hard one wounds like six months of cold. It is going to improve our characters.'

'I'll say it is,' agreed Kirk. He looked at Major Durand and reflected that perhaps the conversation was a bit flippant in view of that gentleman's mission in San Francisco. Poor devil — what a life he must have led. Seeking about to include him in the talk, Kirk was able to hit upon nothing save the aged and obvious bromide. 'Tell us, Major,' he said. 'What do you think of the States?'

'Ah, yes,' replied Durand. 'My impressions. Well, really, I'm afraid I can't be very original. My sole impression so far is one of — er — bigness. Size, you know. My word — your country is tremendous.'

Duff nodded. 'We could talk of little else on the train coming out. You can scarcely imagine the effect of America on the minds of men who hail from a country like England. There, a ride of a few miles in any direction and you are on the coast. But here — day after day we looked from the car windows incredulous, amazed. We thought we should never come to the end of our journey.'

'No doubt about it,' Kirk returned, 'there's plenty of the United States. Too much, some people think.'

'We haven't said that,' Durand reminded him, smiling faintly. 'However, the possibilities of such a country seem endless. I may add' — he looked at Miss Morrow — 'that I find your young women charming.'

'How very polite of you,' she smiled.

'Oh, not at all. I really mean it. If you will pardon me — I did not quite catch your connexion with this affair?'

'I am in the district attorney's office,' she told him.

'Like our crown prosecutor, the district attorney,' Duff explained. 'This young woman is, I believe, a student of the law.'

'My word,' said Durand. 'Just fancy. Then it surprises me there is not more respect for law in the States.'

'Thank you,' Miss Morrow answered. 'That's flattering to me, if not to the States.'

Durand rose. 'You must forgive me if I run along,' he said. 'I have found the long journey somewhat fatiguing — and added to that is the disappointment I suffered a few moments ago. I pretended, of course, that I had no hope, but it wasn't quite true. As a matter of fact, despite all the false rumours in the past, I still go on hoping. And this time, with the word of a man like Sir Frederic Bruce involved — well, my mind will never be at rest until I have seen the woman who left so suddenly to-night.'

'She may yet be found,' Duff suggested.

'I hope so, I'm sure. Are you coming, old chap?'

'Of course,' Duff replied, rising.

'You and I must have that talk soon, Inspector,' Chan said.

Duff stopped. 'Well, I've always thought there's no time like the present. You go ahead, Major, and I'll follow.'

'Very good,' Durand answered. 'I have engaged a room for you at the St. Francis Hotel. I trust you'll approve of my choice.'

'That was thoughtful of you,' Duff told him. 'I'll see you shortly.'

Durand turned to Barry Kirk. 'You've been very hospitable to a stranger.'

'Not at all,' Kirk said. 'You must drop in often. I hope you won't be lonely here. I'll send you a card for a club or two, and if you like, we'll have a little party occasionally.'

'Frightfully kind, I'm sure,' Durand replied warmly. 'A thousand thanks.' He added his farewells and went out.

'Poor man,' Miss Morrow said.

'A nice chap,' Duff remarked. He turned briskly to Charlie. 'But this isn't getting us forward, Sergeant. Where shall we begin? I learned from Captain Flannery that no records of any case were found among Sir Frederic's effects?'

'None whatsoever,' Chan corroborated.

'Then it looks like theft as well as murder, for unquestionably such records were kept.

Somewhere — unless they have been destroyed by the same hand that killed Sir Frederic — there must be in existence detailed accounts of the Hilary Galt case, as well as the disappearance of Eve Durand — '

'You have heard that, in Sir Frederic's thinking, these two matters boast some obscure connexion?' Chan asked.

Duff nodded. 'Yes, I saw the copy of the letter from my Chief at the Yard. I should say from the sound of it that he's as much in the dark as we are. But I have already cabled him for any information he may have.'

'You act with beautiful speed,' Chan approved. 'One thing this Major Durand has told us puts new face on whole matter. Up to now, it was entirely unknown round here that Colonel John Beetham attended picnic that unforgotten night at Peshawar.'

'What about Beetham? He's in San Francisco, you say?'

'Very much so. He was present at dinner. A strange, silent, mind-beguiling man.'

Miss Morrow spoke suddenly. 'Why, of course,' she cried. 'Colonel Beetham at the picnic — that means he knew Eve Durand. On the night he came here to dinner, he must have been brought up in the elevator by little Jennie Jerome Marie Lantelme. If she was Eve Durand, he probably recognized her.'

253

'Undubitably,' Chan agreed.

'Why, that makes it all very simple,' Miss Morrow continued. 'I'll get hold of him at once, and ask him — '

Chan raised his hand. 'Humbly begging pardon to cut in — would you ask a blind man the road?'

'Why — I — what do you mean?'

'I have known for some days that the Colonel was in neighbourhood of Peshawar that early May, 1913. Until to-night I did not dream he was member of picnic party. Even so, the last act I would consider would be to make inquiries.'

'Surely you don't think — '

'I have not decided what to think. A member of that party — the fact may mean much, or it may mean nothing at all. On chance that it means much, let us say nothing to the Colonel just yet. To do so might defeat our own ends. There was once a man who pinched the baby while rocking the cradle. His work was not regarded a very large success.'

Miss Morrow smiled. 'I shall take your advice, of course.'

'Thank you. Before we act, permit that I dig about some more amid events of past.' Chan turned to the Inspector. 'Dropping the Colonel for the moment, I mention those velvet slippers.'

'Yes,' said Duff. 'The velvet slippers. A bit of a mystery, they are. Carried off by the murderer, it seems. But why? And what did he — or she — do with them? It's not unreasonable to suppose they were hurriedly chucked away somewhere. In England, we have a system in such a case — we advertise and offer a reward.'

'Splendid idea,' agreed Chan.

'Surely Captain Flannery has thought of it?'

Chan shrugged. 'Captain acts much like little child caught in cross-woven net. He can only struggle, always getting deeper. But I must restrain my criticism. Free to admit the plan had not occurred even to me.'

Duff laughed. 'Well, I'll look the Captain up after dinner and suggest that he try it. By the way, I'm quite at a loss — the city is new to me. Could I prevail on you, Sergeant, to dine with me? We can talk things over, and afterwards you can show me about and direct me to Flannery's office.'

'Deeply pleased at the invitation,' Chan beamed. 'I have much to learn. Where better could I study than in your distinguished company?'

'Well — er — that's a bit strong,' returned Duff. 'However, we'll have a jolly little dinner. Any time you're ready — '

'I procure hat and coat with instant action,' Chan replied.

Duff turned to Kirk and the girl. 'Great pleasure to meet you both,' he said. 'Miss Morrow, to work with a charming young woman on a case will be a new experience for me — and a delightful one.'

'You must think it an utterly ridiculous situation,' she remarked.

'I haven't said so,' he smiled.

Chan returned, and he and Duff went out together. Miss Morrow took up her coat.

'Just a minute,' Kirk protested. 'Where are you going?'

'Home,' she told him.

'To a lonely dinner,' he suggested.

'You needn't hint. I can't invite you to-night. I shall need loads of time to prepare that pie — '

'Of course. I wasn't hinting. But oddly enough, I've gone sort of cold on the idea of dining here in my cosy little nest. I propose to go where there are lights, laughter, and a waiter I can trust. And unless you prove more cruel than you look, I'm not dining alone.'

'But I really should go home — and freshen up.'

'Nonsense — you're blooming now. Like a peach tree covered with blossoms — I wonder how I came to think of that? No matter — will you join me?'

'If you want me to.'

Kirk rang the bell, and Paradise appeared at once. 'Ah — er — I'm dining out to-night,' the young man explained.

Paradise looked distressed. 'Very good, sir. But if I may make so bold — '

'Yes — what is it?'

'I trust this is not a sign of waning confidence in me, sir? I have been hoping for the old relations between us — '

'Nonsense. I often dine out. You know that.'

'Certainly, sir.' The butler made a gloomy exit.

'Good lord,' sighed Kirk, 'I'm afraid he's going sensitive on my hands. I suppose that just to show I trust him, I'll have to give a large dinner and invite all the people of whom I'm especially fond.'

'A large dinner?'

'Well — fairly large. My grandmother, and Charlie Chan, and a few old friends from the club. And — er — would you come?'

'If I didn't, it wouldn't be because I was afraid of Paradise.'

They descended to the street. It was a night of mist, with occasional fierce rain. Kirk found his car and helping the girl in, drove from the deserted business district to Union Square, where bright lights were gleaming on the wet pavements. The cable-car bells rang cheerily, a flotilla of umbrellas bobbed jauntily along the streets; the spirits of the people of San Francisco, habitually high, are not to be damped by a little rain. 'How about Marchetti's?' Kirk inquired.

'Sounds good to me,' Miss Morrow answered.

They entered the little restaurant. On the dance floor the first of the cabaret acts was under way; a young, good-looking chorus pranced about to the strains of a popular air. Barry Kirk was known there, and the result was a good table and an obsequious head waiter. They gave their order.

'I like this place,' said Kirk. 'They never confuse noise with merriment.' A pretty little blonde awarded him a sweet smile in passing. 'Awfully cute girls, don't you think?'

'Yes, aren't they?' Miss Morrow answered. 'Do you like cute girls?'

'Like to see 'em going by — on the other side. Never cared much for their conversation. It has no weight. Now, you take a lawyer, for instance — '

'Please,' she said. 'Don't make fun of me. I'm not in the mood for it to-night. I'm tired — and discouraged.'

'Tired — that's all right,' he replied. 'But discouraged — what about? As I understand it, you've been a big success in your work.'

'Oh, no, I haven't. I've got on — a little way — but am I going any farther? Have you forgotten — this is an anniversary. A week ago to-night — '

'You dined with me for the first time. I hope — '

'A week ago to-night Sir Frederic was killed, and I embarked on my first big case. Up to this minute I haven't contributed a thing to its solution — '

'Oh, yes, you have. Of course, you haven't solved the puzzle, but there's plenty of time — '

'Oh, no, there isn't. At any moment the district attorney may tell me I'm out. I've got to make good quickly — and how can I? Look back — what have we accomplished to date?'

'Well, you've found Eve Durand.'

'And lost her. That is — if the little elevator girl was Eve Durand.'

'She must be. Charlie says so.'

Miss Morrow shook her head. 'Charlie's clever, but he's been wrong. He admits it freely. You know, something happened to-night while we were waiting for Captain Flannery to lead that girl into the room. Something inside me. Just a hunch — a woman's intuition — I suddenly felt quite sure that she wasn't Eve Durand after all.'

'You don't say. And what basis did you have for that hunch?'

'None whatever. But I felt we were on the wrong trail altogether. She might very well be Jennie Jerome, and Marie Lantelme too, and still not be Durand's lost wife. Don't forget there are many other possibilities for that rôle.'

'For example?'

'How about Lila Barr — the girl in the office of the Calcutta Importers? You remember what you told us — how interested Sir Frederic was in her? Just what did that mean?'

'I'd be happy to tell you — if I knew.'

'But you don't. Then there's Eileen Enderby and Gloria Garland. In spite of their stories about why Sir Frederic wanted to see them — are they out of it? And Mrs. Tupper-Brock. No — we can't be sure that the elevator girl was Eve Durand. We've just been guessing — Chan's been guessing. And we'll never know now.'

'Why not? Flannery will find her.'

'You don't really believe that? If you do, you've more faith in the poor old Captain than I have. Suppose he does find her, and she is Eve Durand — what of it? She'll simply refuse to talk, and we'll be no nearer knowing who killed Sir Frederic than we ever were.'

'I brought you here for an evening of gaiety,' Kirk said sternly, 'and you sit there thinking black thoughts.'

'Just a minute — let me go on. It's such a comfort to talk things over. Who killed Sir Frederic — that's my problem. The identity of Eve Durand may not have as much to do with the matter as we think. It may even prove to have nothing to do with it at all. Who pulled that trigger in your office last Tuesday night? Carrick Enderby? It's quite possible. Eileen Enderby? There were those stains on her frock — did she climb down the fire-escape on some sinister errand? Dismissing the Enderby family, there are others. How about Gloria Garland? Mrs. Tupper-Brock?'

'Each of whom, of course, arrived at my dinner with a pistol hidden under her gown?' smiled Kirk.

'Each of whom knew she was to meet Sir Frederic that night. The pistol could have been arranged. To go on with the list — there's Paradise. I like him, but I can't see that his story of this afternoon puts him completely beyond suspicion. On the contrary. Outside your flat, there was that pale young man from the accountants' office.'

'Oh, yes — name of Smith,' said Kirk. 'I'd forgotten all about him.'

'I haven't,' Miss Morrow replied. 'Then,

261

there's Li Gung. The Chinese who fled to Honolulu next day. What was his hurry? Isn't it possible that he climbed up the fire-escape — Oh, what's the use? The list seems endless.' Miss Morrow sighed.

'And incomplete, as you give it,' added Kirk.

'You mean — '

'I mean the man who accompanied Li Gung to the dock. Colonel John Beetham.'

'Absurd! A man like Colonel Beetham — famous throughout the world — a man who has won all the medals and distinctions there are for gallant conduct — as though he could do anything base, anything despicable.'

'Just there,' said Kirk, 'your sex betrays you. Not one of you women can resist a handsome, distinguished-looking Englishman. Speaking as a less romantic male, I must say that the Colonel doesn't strike me quite so favourably. He has courage, yes — and he has a will that gets him where he wants to go, and damn the consequences. I shouldn't care to be one of his party on the top floor of Tibet and too weak to go on. He'd give me one disgusted look, and leave me. But wait a minute — I believe he'd do me one last kindness before he left.'

'What's that?'

'I think he'd pull out a gun and shoot me.

Yes, I'm certain he would, and he'd go on his way happy to know there was one weakling who would never trouble him again.'

'Yes, he's a hard, determined man,' Miss Morrow admitted. 'Nevertheless, he wouldn't kill Sir Frederic. Poor Sir Frederic wasn't interfering with his plans in any way.'

'Oh, wasn't he? How do you know he wasn't?'

'Well — I can't see — '

'Let's leave Beetham to Chan,' Kirk suggested. 'The little man has an air about him — I believe he knows what he's doing. And now will you drop all this and dance with me — or must I dance alone?'

'I don't know. In my position, I have to give an impression of being serious — the public — '

'Oh, forget your public. He wouldn't venture out on a night like this. Come along.'

Miss Morrow laughed, and they danced together on the tiny floor. For the rest of the evening she permitted Kirk to lead the conversation into more frivolous channels — a task at which he excelled. The change seemed to do her good.

'Well,' said Kirk, as he signed the check, 'you can be gay, after all. And I must say it becomes you.'

'I've forgot all my worries,' replied the girl,

her eyes sparkling. 'I feel as though I should never think of them again.'

'That's the talk,' Kirk approved.

But before they got out of the room, Miss Morrow's worries were suddenly brought back to her. Along one wall was a series of booths, beside which they walked on their way to the door. Opposite the final booth the girl half stopped, and glanced back over her shoulder at Barry Kirk. In passing he too looked into the compartment, and then hastily moved on. He need not have effaced himself so hurriedly, for the two people who were dining together in the booth were so deep in serious conversation they were oblivious to everything.

In the street Miss Morrow turned to Kirk. 'What did I tell you?' she cried. 'There are other women involved in this affair besides that poor little elevator girl.'

'And what did I tell you,' Kirk answered, 'about your handsome British hero?'

Miss Morrow nodded. 'To-morrow,' she said, 'I shall look into this. Just what, I wonder, is the connexion between Colonel Beetham and Mrs. Helen Tupper-Brock?'

15

The Discreet Mr. Cuttle

When Charlie Chan rose on Wednesday morning, the rain was over and the fog was lifting. Bravely struggling through remnants of mist, the sun fell on a sparkling town, washed clean for a new day. Chan stood for a long time looking out at the magnificent panorama over bay and harbour, at the green of Goat Island and the prison fortress of Alcatraz. Along the water-front stretched a line of great ships as though awaiting a signal that should send them scurrying off to distant treaty ports and coral islands.

Chan's heart was heavy despite the bright morning. At twelve noon would sail the ship on which he had sworn to depart, the ship that would come finally to rest under the tower that bore the word *Aloha*. There would be keen disappointment in the little house beneath the algaroba trees on Punchbowl Hill, as there was disappointment in the detective's heart now. He sighed. Would this holiday never end? This holiday so filled with work and baffling problems? This holiday that was no holiday at all?

When he entered the dining-room Barry Kirk was already at the table, but his glass of orange juice stood before him, untouched.

'Hello,' said the host. 'I waited for you.'

'You grow increasingly kind with every dawn,' Chan grinned.

'Oh, I don't know. It isn't exactly kindness. Somehow, I don't seem in any hurry to quaff California's favourite beverage this morning. Take a look at it. Does it strike you as being — er — the real thing?'

As Chan sat down, Paradise appeared in the doorway. Without a moment's hesitation, Chan lifted his glass. 'Your very good health,' he remarked.

Kirk glanced at the butler, and raised his own glass. 'I sincerely trust you're right,' he murmured, and drank heartily.

Paradise gravely said his good mornings and, setting down two bowls of oatmeal, departed. 'Well,' Barry Kirk smiled, 'we seem to be O.K. so far.'

'Suspicion,' Chan told him, 'is a wicked thing. That is written in many places.'

'Yes — and where would you be in your work without it?' Kirk inquired. 'By the way, did you get anything out of Duff last night?'

'Nothing that demands heavy thought. One point he elucidated carried slight interest.'

'What was that?'

'Begging respectful pardon, for the present I will ponder same with my customary silence. You dined here?'

'No. Miss Morrow and I went to a restaurant.'

'Ah — a moment's pleasant recreation,' said Chan approvingly.

'That was the idea.'

'You enjoy society of this young woman?'

'I do not precisely pine in her presence. You know, she's not so serious as she pretends to be.'

'That is good. Women were not invented for heavy thinking. They should decorate scene, like blossom of the plum.'

'Yes, but they can't all be movie actresses. I don't mind a girl's having a brain if she doesn't act up-stage about it — and Miss Morrow never does. We had a very light-hearted evening, but we weren't blind. As we left the restaurant, we made a little discovery.'

'Good, what was it?'

Kirk shrugged. 'Shall I ponder same with my customary silence? No, I won't be as mean as you are, Charlie. We saw your old friend Colonel John Beetham relaxing from the stern realities of life. We saw him dining with a lady.'

'Ah, yes. Which lady?'

'A lady we have rather overlooked so far. Mrs. Helen Tupper-Brock.'

'That has interest. Miss Morrow will investigate?'

'Yes. I'm going to pick up Mrs. Tupper-Brock this morning and take her down to the district attorney's office. I don't look for any brilliant results, however. She's cold and distant, like the winter stars. Good lord — I'm getting poetic. You don't suppose it could be something I've had for breakfast?'

'More likely memories of last night,' Chan answered.

When the meal was finished, Kirk announced that he was going down to the office to attend to a few letters. Chan rose quickly.

'I will accompany, if I may,' he said. 'I must produce letter of explanation for my wife, hoping it will yet catch outgoing boat. It will be substitute for me — a smaller substitute.' He sighed.

'That's right,' Kirk remembered. 'You were going out on the tide to-day, weren't you? It's a shame you can't.'

'What will little Barry think of me?'

'Oh, he's probably sensible, like his namesake. He'll want you to stay where duty lies. And how proud he'll be — in the future — over your success in running down the murderer of Sir Frederic Bruce.'

'Still have some running to do,' Chan admitted. 'One more week — I give myself that. Then, whatever has happened, I shift mainland dust off my shoes and go. I swear it, and this time I am firm like well-known Gibraltar rock.'

'A week,' repeated Kirk. 'Oh, that will be ample. You'll be sitting pretty then.'

'On deck of boat bound for Honolulu,' Chan said firmly. 'Quoting local conversation, you bet I will.'

They went below, and Kirk seated himself at the big desk. Kinsey was out; 'collecting rents,' Kirk explained. Chan accepted paper and an envelope and took his place at the stenographer's desk by the wall.

But his mind did not seem to be on the letter he was writing. Out of the corner of his eye he watched Kirk's movements carefully. In a moment he rose and came over to Kirk's desk. 'Pen enjoys stubborn spasm,' he explained. 'The ink will not gush. Who calls it fountain pen?'

'There are pens in here,' Kirk said, leaning over to open a lower drawer. Chan's keen eyes were on the papers atop the desk. Noted for his courtesy, his actions were odd. He appeared to be spying on his host.

Charlie accepted a pen and returned to his writing. Still he watched Kirk from the corner of his eye.

The young man finished his letter and started another. When he had completed the second, he stamped them both. Simultaneously Chan sealed his own letter, stamped it, and rose quickly to his feet. He held out his long thin hand.

'Permit me,' he said, 'that I deposit our mail in the hall chute.'

'Why — thank you,' Kirk replied, giving him the letters.

When Charlie returned, Kirk was on his feet, consulting his watch. 'Want to hear Mrs. Tupper-Brock's life story?' he inquired.

The detective shook his head. 'Thanking you all the same, I will not interpolate myself. Miss Morrow is competent for work. Already, I have several times squirmed about in the position of fifth, unnecessary wheel. This once I will loiter elsewhere.'

'Suit yourself,' Kirk answered carelessly. He took up his hat and coat and disappeared.

When Chan went upstairs by the inner route, he found Bill Rankin waiting for him in the living-room of the bungalow. The reporter looked at him with amusement.

'Good morning,' he said. 'I presume you're sailing this noon?'

Chan frowned. 'Missing boats is now a regular habit for me,' he replied. 'I cannot go. Too many dark clouds shade the scene.'

'I knew it,' smiled Rankin. 'Before you go you've got to give me a story that will thrill the town. I was sure I could depend on you. A great little people, the Chinese.'

'Thanks for advertising my unassuming race,' Chan said.

'Now to get down to business,' Rankin continued. 'I've brought you a little present this bright morning.'

'You are pretty good.'

'I'm a clever boy,' Rankin admitted. 'You know, your rather foggy remarks about Colonel John Beetham have set me thinking. And when I think — get out from under. I have read the Colonel's *Life*, from cover to cover. I imagine I need not tell you that on May fourth, nineteen hundred and thirteen, Beetham set out on an eight months' journey from Peshawar to Teheran, by way of Afghanistan and the Kevir desert of Persia?'

'I too have upearthed that,' nodded Chan.

'I thought you had. But did you know that he had written a book — a separate book — about that little jaunt? A bit of a holiday, he called it. Not real exploring, but just his way of going home.'

Chan was interested. 'I have been unaware of that volume,' he replied.

'It isn't as well known as his other books,' went on Rankin. 'Out of print now. *The Land*

Beyond the Khyber, he called it. I tried every book store in town, and finally picked up a copy over in Berkeley.'

He produced a volume bound in deep purple. 'It's the little present I mentioned,' he added.

Chan took it eagerly. 'Who shall say? This may be of some value. I am in your debt and sinking all the time.'

'Well, I don't know about its value. Maybe you can find something I have overlooked. I've been through it carefully, but I haven't found a thing.'

Chan opened the book. 'Interesting item flashes up immediately,' he said. 'Unlike Colonel Beetham's other books, this has dedication.' Slowly he read the inscription on the dedicatory page: 'To one who will remember, and understand.'

'I noticed that,' Rankin told him. 'It begins to look as though the Colonel has his tender moments, doesn't it? To one who will remember and understand. A boyhood sweetheart, probably. One who will remember the time he kissed her under the lilacs at the gate, and understand that he goes on his daring trips with her image in his heart.'

Chan was deep in thought. 'Possible,' he muttered.

'You know, these Englishman aren't as

272

hard-boiled as they seem,' Rankin continued. 'I knew a British aviator in the war — a tough baby, he ate nails for breakfast. Yet he always carried a sprig of heather on his 'plane — the memento of an old love-affair. A sentimentalist at heart. Perhaps Colonel Beetham is the same type.'

'May very well be,' Charlie agreed.

Rankin got up. 'Well, I suppose my dear old Chief is crying his eyes out because I haven't shown up. He loves me, even though he does threaten to cast me off because I haven't solved the mystery of Sir Frederic's murder.'

'You are not alone in that fault,' Chan told him.

'I — I don't suppose you could give me any little morsel for our million panting readers?'

'Nothing of note may yet be revealed.'

'Well, it does seem high time we were getting a glimpse behind that curtain,' Rankin remarked.

Charlie shook his head. 'The matter is difficult. If I were in Peshawar — but I am not. I am in San Francisco fifteen years after the event, and I can only guess. I may add, guessing is poor business that often leads to lengthy saunters down the positively wrong path.'

'You hang on,' advised Rankin. 'You'll win yet and when you do, just let me be there, with a direct line to the office at my elbow.'

'We will hope that happy picture eventuates,' Chan replied.

Rankin went out, leaving Charlie to the book. He sat down before the fire and began to read eagerly. This was better than interviewing Mrs. Tupper-Brock.

At about the same time, Barry Kirk was going blithely up the steps of his grandmother's handsome house on Pacific Heights. The old lady greeted him in the drawing-room.

'Hello,' she said. 'How do you happen to be up and about so early? And wide awake, if I can believe my failing eyesight.'

'Detective work,' he laughed.

'Good. What can I do for you? I seem to have been left entirely out of things and it annoys me.'

'Well, you're still out, so don't get up any false hopes,' he returned. 'I'm not here to consult with you, wise as I know you to be. I'm looking for Mrs. Tupper-Brock. Where is she?'

'She's upstairs. What do you want with her?'

'I want to take her for a little ride — down to see Miss Morrow.'

'Oh, so that young woman is still asking questions? She seems a bit lacking in results, so far.'

'Is that so? Well, give her time.'

'I rather fancy she'll need a lot of it. Mixing up in affairs that should be left to the men — '

'You're a traitor to your sex. I think it's mighty fine of her to be where she is. Give this little girl a great big hand.'

'Oh, I imagine she doesn't lack for applause when you are about. You seem very much taken with her.'

'I am, and don't forget it. Now, how about calling Mrs. Tupper-Brock? Please tell her to come, and bring her hyphen.'

Mrs. Kirk gave him a scornful look, and departed. In a few minutes the secretary appeared in the room. Poised and cool, as always, she greeted Barry Kirk without enthusiasm.

'Good morning,' he said. 'I'm sorry to disturb you, but Miss Morrow — you met her at my dinner — would like to see you. If you can come now, I'll drive you down in my car.'

'Why, of course,' returned the woman calmly. 'I'll be just a moment.'

She went out, and Mrs. Kirk reappeared. 'What's the matter with that boy of Sally Jordan's?' she demanded. 'I thought he'd have this thing solved long ago. I've been watching the papers like a bargain hunter.'

'Oh, Charlie's all right,' Kirk said. 'He's slow, but sure.'

'He's slow enough,' admitted the old lady. 'You might tell him that I'm growing impatient.'

'That'll speed him up,' Kirk smiled.

'I wish something would,' his grandmother snapped. 'What's all this about Helen? Surely she's not entangled in the case?'

'I'm not free to say, one way or another. Tell me, have you given Colonel Beetham that money yet?'

'No — but I believe I will.'

'Take my advice and hold off for a few days.'

'What? He isn't in it, is he? Why — he's a gentleman.'

'Just take my advice — ' began Kirk. Mrs. Tupper-Brock was in the hall, waiting for him.

'Now you've got me all excited,' complained Mrs. Kirk.

'That's bad, at your age,' Kirk said. 'Calm down.'

'What do you mean — my age? I read of a woman the other day who is a hundred and two.'

'Well, there's a mark to shoot at,' Kirk told her. 'So long. See you later.'

Mrs. Tupper-Brock sat at his side in the roadster, stiff and obviously not inclined to talk. A few remarks on the weather yielding no great flood of conversation, Kirk abandoned the effort. They rode on in silence, and finally he ushered her into Miss Morrow's office.

The deputy district attorney made a charming picture against that gloomy background. Such was not, however, her aim at the moment. Alert and businesslike, she greeted Mrs. Tupper-Brock and indicated a chair beside her desk.

'Sit down, please. So good of you to come. I hope I haven't inconvenienced you?'

'Not in the least,' the woman replied, seating herself. There was a moment's silence.

'You know, of course, that we are hunting the murderer of Sir Frederic Bruce,' Miss Morrow began.

'Naturally,' Mrs. Tupper-Brock's tone was cool. 'Why did you wish to see me?'

'I wondered whether you have any information that might help us.'

'That's hardly likely,' responded Mrs. Tupper-Brock. She took out a lace-edged handkerchief and began to turn it slowly in her hands.

'No, perhaps not,' Miss Morrow smiled. 'Still, we are not justified in ignoring anyone in this terrible affair. Sir Frederic was a complete stranger to you?'

'Yes, quite. I met him for the first time on that Tuesday night.'

'Did you also meet Colonel Beetham for the first time that night?'

The handkerchief was suddenly a tiny ball in her hand. 'No — I did not.'

'You had met him before?'

'Yes. At Mrs. Dawson Kirk's. He had been to the house frequently.'

'Of course. You and the Colonel are quite good friends, I hear. Perhaps you knew him before he came to San Francisco?'

'No, I did not.'

'While the Colonel was showing his pictures, you remained on the davenport with Miss Garland. You saw nothing of a suspicious nature?'

'Nothing whatever.' The handkerchief lay in a crumpled heap in her lap. She took it up and once more began to smooth it.

'Have you ever lived in India?'

'No — I have never been there.'

'Did you ever hear of a tragic event that happened in India — at Peshawar? The disappearance of a young woman named Eve Durand?'

Mrs. Tupper-Brock considered. 'I may have read about it in the newspapers,' she admitted. 'It has a dimly familiar sound.'

'Tell me — did you by any chance notice

the elevator girl who took you up to the bungalow the night of Mr. Kirk's dinner?'

Again the handkerchief was crushed in the woman's hand. 'I did not. Why should I?'

'She was, then, quite unknown to you?'

'I fancy she was. Of course, one doesn't study — er — that sort of person.'

'Ah, yes.' Miss Morrow sought an inconsequential ending for the interview. 'You are English, Mrs. Tupper-Brock?'

'English, yes.'

'A Londoner?'

'No — I was born in Devonshire. I stayed there until my — my marriage. Then my husband took me to York, where he had a living. He was a clergyman, you know.'

'Thank you so much.'

'I'm afraid I have been of very little help.'

'Oh, but I hardly looked for anything else,' Miss Morrow smiled. 'These questions are a mere formality. Everyone at the dinner — you understand. It was good of you to come.' She rose.

Mrs. Tupper-Brock restored the handkerchief to her bag, and also stood up. 'That is all, I take it?'

'Oh, quite. It's a lovely day after the rain.'

'Beautiful,' murmured the woman, and moved towards the door. Kirk came from the corner where he had been lolling.

'Any other little service I can do?' he asked.

'Not at present, thanks. You're immensely valuable.'

Mrs. Tupper-Brock had reached the outer room. Kirk spoke in a low voice. 'No word of the elevator girl?'

'Not a trace,' Miss Morrow sighed. 'The same old story. But just what I expected.'

Kirk looked towards the other room. 'And the lady who has just left,' he whispered. 'A complete dud, wasn't she? I'm awfully sorry. She told you nothing.'

The girl came very close, fragrant, young, smiling. Kirk felt a bit dizzy. 'You are wrong,' she said softly. 'The lady who has just left told me a great deal.'

'You mean?'

'I mean she's a liar, if I ever met one. A liar, and a poor one. I'm going to prove it, too.'

'Bright girl,' Kirk smiled, and, hurrying out, caught up with Mrs. Tupper-Brock in the hall.

The return ride to Mrs. Dawson Kirk's house was another strained, silent affair, and Kirk parted from the dark, mysterious lady with a distinct feeling of relief. He drove back to the Kirk Building and ascended to the twentieth floor. As he got out of the elevator, he saw Mr. Cuttle trying his office door. Cuttle was not only the night-watchman, but was also assistant superintendent of the building, a title in which he took great pride.

'Hello, Cuttle,' Kirk said. 'Want to see me?'

'I do, sir,' Cuttle answered. 'Something that may be important.' Kirk unlocked the office and they went in.

'It's about that girl, Grace Lane, sir,' Cuttle explained, when they reached the inner room. 'The one who disappeared last night.'

'Oh, yes.' Kirk looked at him with sudden interest. 'What about her?'

'The police asked me a lot of questions. Where did I get her, and all that. There was one point on which I was silent. I thought I had better speak to you first, Mr. Kirk.'

'Well, I don't know, Cuttle. It isn't wise to try to conceal things from the police.'

'But on this point, sir — '

'What point?'

'The matter of how I came to hire her. The letter she brought to me from a certain person — '

'From what person?'

'From your grandmother, sir. From Mrs. Dawson Kirk.'

'Good lord! Grace Lane came to you with a letter from my grandmother?'

'She did. I still have the letter. Perhaps you would like to see it?'

Cuttle produced a grey, expensive-looking

envelope. Kirk took out the enclosure and saw that the message was written in his grandmother's cramped, old-fashioned hand. He read:

'My dear Mr. Cuttle:
'The young woman who presents this letter is a good friend of mine, Miss Grace Lane. I should be very pleased if you could find some employment for her in the building — I have thought of the work on the elevators. Miss Lane is far above such work, but she has had a bad time of it, and is eager to take anything that offers. I am sure you will find her willing and competent. I will vouch for her in every way.
'Sincerely yours,
'MARY WINTHROP KIRK.'

Kirk finished, a puzzled frown on his face. 'I'll keep this, Cuttle,' he remarked, putting the letter in his pocket. 'And — I guess it was just as well you said nothing to the police.'
'I thought so, sir,' replied Cuttle with deep satisfaction, and retired.

16

Long Life and Happiness

Kirk hurried up to his study. He found Charlie Chan seated in a chair by the window, completely engrossed in Colonel John Beetham's description of *The Land Beyond the Khyber*.

'Well,' said Kirk, 'here's news for you. I've just got on the trail of another suspect in our little case.'

'The more the increased merriment,' Chan assured him. 'Kindly deign to name the newest person who has been performing queer antics.'

'Just my grandmother,' Kirk returned. 'That's all.'

Charlie allowed himself the luxury of a moment's surprise. 'You overwhelm me with amazement. That dear old lady. What misendeavour has she been up to?'

'It was she who got Grace Lane — or whatever her confounded name is — a job in the Kirk Building.' The young man repeated his talk with Cuttle and showed Chan the letter.

Charlie read Mrs. Dawson Kirk's warm endorsement with interest. He handed it back, smiling. 'Grandmother now becomes a lady to be investigated. Humbly suggest you place Miss Morrow on her track.'

Kirk laughed. 'I'll do it. The resulting display of fireworks ought to prove a very pretty sight.' He called Miss Morrow and, having heard his story, she suggested an interview with Mrs. Kirk at two o'clock.

The young man got his grandmother on the wire. 'Hello,' he said, 'this is Barry. Did I understand you to say this morning you'd like to be mixed up in the Bruce murder?'

'Well — in a nice way — I wouldn't mind. In fact, I'd rather enjoy it.'

'You've got your wish. Just at present the police are after you.'

'Mercy — what have I done?'

'I leave that to you. Think over your sins, and report here at two o'clock. Miss Morrow wants to question you.'

'She does, eh? Well, I'm not afraid of her.'

'All right. Only come.'

'I shall have to leave early. I promised to go to a lecture — '

'Never mind. You'll leave when the law has finished with you. I suggest that you come prepared to tell the truth. If you do, I may yet be able to keep you out of gaol.'

284

'You can't frighten me. I'll come — but only from curiosity. I should like to see that young woman in action. I haven't a doubt in the world but what I can hold my own.'

'I heard different,' replied Kirk. 'Remember — two o'clock. Sharp!'

He hung up the receiver and waited impatiently for the hour of the conflict. At a quarter before two Miss Morrow arrived on the scene.

'This is a strange turn,' she said, when Kirk had taken her coat. 'So your grandmother knows Jennie Jerome Marie Lantelme?'

'Knows her!' replied Kirk. 'They're great friends.' He handed over the letter. 'Read that. Vouches for her in every way. Good old grandmother!'

Miss Morrow smiled. 'I must handle her gently,' she remarked. 'Somehow, I don't believe she approves of me.'

'She's reached the age where she doesn't approve of anybody,' Kirk explained. 'Not even of me. A fine noble character, as you well know. Yet she discovers flaws. Can you imagine!'

'Absurd,' cried Miss Morrow.

'Don't be too nice to her,' Kirk suggested. 'She'll like you better if you walk all over her. Some people are made that way.'

Charlie entered from his room. 'Ah, Miss

Morrow. Again you add decoration to the scene. Am I wrong in presuming that Captain Flannery has apprehended Eve Durand?'

'If you mean the elevator girl, you are quite wrong. Not a trace of her. You still think she was Eve Durand?'

'If she wasn't, then I must bow my head in sack-cloth and ashes,' Chan replied.

'Well, that's no place for anybody's head,' Kirk remarked.

'None the less, mine has been there,' Chan grinned.

Mrs. Dawson Kirk bustled in. 'Here I am, on time to the minute. Please make a note of that.'

'Hello,' Kirk greeted her. 'You remember Miss Morrow, of course.'

'Oh, yes — the lawyer. How do you do. And Mr. Chan — look here, why haven't you solved this case?'

'A little more patience,' grinned Chan. 'We are getting warm now. You are under hovering cloud of suspicion at last.'

'So I hear,' snapped the old lady. She turned to Miss Morrow. 'Well, my dear, Barry said you wanted to cross-question me.'

'Nothing cross about it,' Miss Morrow said, with a smile. 'Just a few polite questions.'

'Oh, really. Don't be too polite. I'm always

suspicious of too polite people. You don't think I killed poor Sir Frederic, I hope?'

'Not precisely. But you've written a letter — '

'I suppose so. Have a habit of writing indiscreet letters. And old habits are hard to break. But I always put 'burn this' at the bottom. Somebody has failed to follow my instructions, eh?'

Miss Morrow shook her head. 'I believe you omitted that admonition in this case.' She handed the letter to Mrs. Kirk. 'You wrote that, didn't you?'

Mrs. Kirk glanced it through. 'Certainly I wrote it. What of it?'

'This Grace Lane was a good friend of yours?'

'In a way, yes. Of course, I scarcely knew the girl — '

'Oho,' cried Barry Kirk. 'You vouched for her in every way, yet you scarcely knew her.'

'Keep out of this, Barry,' advised the old lady. 'You're not a lawyer. You haven't the brains.'

'Then you knew Grace Lane only slightly, Mrs. Kirk?' the girl continued.

'That's what I said.'

'Yet you recommended her without reservation? Why did you do that?'

Mrs. Kirk hesitated. 'If you'll pardon me, I

287

regard it as my own affair.'

'I'm sorry,' Miss Morrow replied quickly, 'but you will have to answer. Please do not be deceived by the setting of this interview. It is not a social function. I am acting for the district attorney's office, and I mean business.'

Mrs. Kirk's eyes flashed. 'I understand. But now, if you don't mind, I'd like to ask a few questions.'

'You may do so. And when you have finished, I will resume.'

'What has this girl, Grace Lane, to do with the murder of Sir Frederic Bruce?'

'That is what we are trying to determine.'

'You mean she had something to do with it?'

'We believe she had. And that is why your recommendation of her is no longer your own affair, Mrs. Kirk.'

The old lady sat firmly on the edge of her chair. 'I shan't say a word until I know where all this is leading us.'

'It'll lead you to gaol if you don't stop being stubborn,' suggested Barry Kirk.

'Indeed? Well, I have friends among the lawyers, too. Miss Morrow, I want to know Grace Lane's connexion with Sir Frederic?'

'I have no objection to telling you — if you will keep the matter to yourself.'

'She's the most indiscreet woman on the west coast,' Kirk warned.

'Hush up, Barry. I can keep still if I have to, Miss Morrow — ?'

'When Sir Frederic came here,' Miss Morrow explained, 'he was seeking a woman named Eve Durand, who disappeared from India fifteen years ago. We suspect Grace Lane was that woman.'

'Well, why don't you ask her?'

'We'd be glad to, but we can't. You see, she's disappeared again.'

'What! She's gone?'

'Yes. Now I have answered your questions, and I expect you to do as much for me.' Miss Morrow became again very businesslike. 'Grace Lane was undoubtedly brought to you by a third person — a person you trusted. Who was it?'

Mrs. Kirk shook her head. 'I'm sorry. I can't tell you.'

'You realize, of course, the seriousness of your refusal?'

'I — well, I — good heavens, what have I got mixed up in, anyhow? A respectable woman like me — '

'Precisely,' said Miss Morrow sternly. 'A woman honoured throughout the city, a woman prominent in every forward-looking movement — I must say I am surprised, Mrs.

Kirk, to find you obstructing the course of justice. And all because this person who brought Grace Lane to you is now asking you to keep the matter secret — '

'I didn't say that.'

'But I did. It's true, isn't it?'

'Well — yes — it is. And I must say I think she's asking a good deal of me — '

'She? Then Grace Lane was brought to you by a woman?'

'What? Oh — oh, yes. Of course. I'll admit that.'

'You have admitted it,' chuckled Barry Kirk.

'Tell me this,' Miss Morrow went on, 'before you left to come down here, did you let Mrs. Tupper-Brock know where you were going?'

'I did.'

'Did you tell her you expected to be questioned by me when you got here?'

'Y-yes.'

'And was it then that she asked you not to reveal the fact that she was the person who brought Grace Lane to you, with a request that you help the girl?' Mrs. Kirk was silent. 'You needn't answer,' Miss Morrow smiled. 'As a matter of fact you have answered. Your face, you know.'

Mrs. Kirk shrugged. 'You're a clever young

290

woman,' she complained.

'Since that is settled, and I now know that it was Mrs. Tupper-Brock who introduced the Lane girl to you,' Miss Morrow continued, 'there is no real reason why you shouldn't give me the details. How long ago did it happen?'

Mrs. Kirk hesitated, and then surrendered. 'Several months ago,' she said. 'Helen brought the girl to the house. She told me she had met her on a ferry — that they were old friends — had known each other in Devonshire, a great many years back.'

'In Devonshire. Please go on.'

'Helen said this girl had been through a lot — '

'What?'

'I didn't ask. I have some delicacy. Also, that she was destitute and in desperate need of work. She was such a pretty, modest, feminine little thing, I took an immediate fancy to her. So I got her the job in this building.'

'Without consulting me,' Kirk suggested.

'Why should I? It was a matter requiring instant action. You were off somewhere as usual.'

'And that's all you know about Grace Lane?' inquired Miss Morrow.

'Yes. I made inquiries, and found she was

doing well and was, apparently, happy. When we came up here the other night, we spoke to her. She thanked me, very nicely. I'm sorry she's been hounded out of town.'

Miss Morrow smiled. 'One thing more. Have you noticed any signs of a close friendship between Mrs. Tupper-Brock and Colonel Beetham?'

'I believe they've gone out together occasionally. I don't spy on them.'

'Naturally not. I think that is all, Mrs. Kirk.'

Mrs. Kirk stood up. She appeared to be in a rather chastened mood. 'Thanks. Fortunately, I can still get to my lecture on time.'

'Just one point,' added the girl. 'I'd rather you didn't repeat this conversation to Mrs. Tupper-Brock.'

'Me — I won't repeat it to anybody.' The old lady smiled grimly. 'Somehow I don't seem to have come out of it as well as I expected.' She said good-bye and made a hasty exit.

'Bully for you,' cried Kirk, with an admiring look at Miss Morrow.

She stood frowning. 'What did I tell you this morning? Mrs. Tupper-Brock was lying, but I didn't expect confirmation so soon.'

'Going to have her on the carpet again?' Kirk asked.

'I am not. What's the good of more lies? Grace Lane was an old friend — which may mean that Grace Lane will write to Mrs. Tupper-Brock from wherever she is hiding. I am going to make immediate arrangements with the postal authorities. Mrs. Tupper-Brock's mail will reach her through my office from now on.'

'Excellent,' approved Chan. 'You have wise head on pretty shoulders. What an unexpected combination! May I inquire, what is our good friend Flannery doing?'

'The Captain has taken a sudden fancy to Miss Lila Barr. I believe he has ordered her to his office at five this afternoon, for what he calls a grilling. I can't be there, but if I were you I'd drop in on it.'

Chan shrugged. 'I fear I will look in vain for welcome inscribed in glowing characters on the mat. However, I will appear with off-hand air.'

Miss Morrow turned to Barry Kirk. 'I do hope your grandmother won't hold my inquisition against me.'

'Nonsense. You were splendid, and she's crazy about you. I saw it in her eyes when she went out.'

'I didn't,' smiled the girl.

'You didn't look carefully. That's where you make a mistake. Examine the eyes about you. You'll find a lot more approval than you suspect.'

'Really? I'm afraid I'm too busy — I must leave that sort of thing to the old-fashioned girls. Now, I must run along. There's just a chance I can find Grace Lane for Captain Flannery. Someone must.'

'And it might as well be you,' quoted Kirk. 'I'll hope to see you again soon.' He showed her out.

At four-thirty Charlie Chan strolled to the Hall of Justice and walked in on Captain Flannery. The Captain appeared to be in rare good humour.

'How are you, Sergeant,' he said. 'What's new with you?'

'With me, everything has aged look,' Chan replied.

'Not getting on as fast as you expected, are you?' Flannery inquired. 'Well, this should be a lesson to you. Every frog ought to stick to his own pond. You may be a world-beater in a village like Honolulu, but you're on the big time over here. You're in over your depth.'

'How true,' Charlie agreed. 'I am often dismayed, but I think of you and know you will not permit me to drown. Something has happened to elevate your spirit?'

'It sure has. I've just pulled off a neat little stunt. You see, I had a grand idea. I put an ad.

in the morning paper for those velvet slippers — '

'Ah, yes,' Chan grinned. 'Inspector Duff warned me you were about to be hit by that idea.'

'Oh, he did, did he? Well, I'm not taking orders from Duff. I was on the point of doing it some days ago, but it slipped my mind. Duff recalled it to me, that's all. I put a very cagy advertisement in the paper, and — '

'Results are already apparent?' Chan finished.

'Are they? I'll say so.' Flannery took up something wrapped in a soiled newspaper. The string had already been loosened, and casting it aside, he revealed the contents of the bundle. Before Chan's eyes lay the red velvet slippers from the Chinese Legation, the slippers found on the feet of Hilary Galt that tragic night in London, the slippers in which Sir Frederic Bruce had walked to his death little more than a week ago.

'What happy luck,' Charlie said.

'Ain't it?' agreed Flannery. 'A soldier from out at the Presidio brought them in less than an hour ago. It seems he was crossing to Oakland to visit his girl last Wednesday noon, and he picked this package up from one of the benches on the ferry-boat. There was nobody about to claim it, so he took it along.

Of course, he should have turned it over to the ferry people — but he didn't. I told him that was all right with me.'

'On ferry-boat to Oakland,' Chan repeated.

'Yes. This guy'd been wondering what to do with his find, and he was mighty pleased when I slipped him a five spot.'

Charlie turned the slippers slowly about in his hands. Again he was interested by the Chinese character which promised long life and happiness. A lying promise, that. The slippers had not brought long life and happiness to Hilary Galt. Nor to Sir Frederic Bruce.

'Just where,' Chan mused, 'do we arrive at now?'

'Well, I'll have to admit that we're still a long ways from home,' Flannery replied. 'But we're getting on. Last Wednesday, the day after the murder, somebody left these slippers on an Oakland ferry-boat. Left them intentionally, I'll bet — glad enough to be rid of 'em.'

'In same identical paper,' Charlie inquired, 'they were always wrapped?'

'Yes — that's the paper this fellow found them in. An evening paper dated last Wednesday night. A first edition, issued about ten in the morning.'

Chan spread out the newspaper and

studied it. 'You have been carefully over this journal, I suspect?'

'Why — er — I haven't had time,' Flannery told him.

'Nothing of note catches the eye,' Chan remarked. 'Except — ah, yes — here on margin of first page. A few figures, carelessly inscribed in pencil. Paper is torn in that locality, and they are almost obliterated.'

Flannery came closer, and Charlie pointed. A small sum in addition had evidently been worked out.

$$\begin{array}{r} \$79. \\ 23. \\ \hline 103. \end{array}$$

'A hundred three,' Flannery read. 'That's wrong. Seventy-nine and twenty-three don't add up to a hundred three.'

'Then we must seek one who is poor scholar of arithmetic,' Chan replied. 'If you have no inclination for objecting, I will jot figures down.'

'Go ahead. Put your big brain on it. But don't forget — I produced the slippers.'

'And the newspaper,' Charlie added. 'The brightest act you have performed to date.'

The door opened, and a man in uniform

entered. 'That dame's outside, Captain,' he announced. 'She's brought her fellow with her. Shall I fetch 'em in?'

'Sure,' Flannery nodded. 'It's Miss Lila Barr,' he explained to Chan. 'I got to thinking about her, and she don't sound so good to me. I'm going to have another talk with her. You can stay, if you want to.'

'Overwhelmed by your courtesy,' Chan responded.

Miss Lila Barr came timidly through the door. After her came Kinsey, Kirk's secretary. The girl seemed very much worried.

'You wanted me, Captain Flannery?'

'Yeah. Come in. Sit down.' He looked at Kinsey. 'Who's this?'

'Mr. Kinsey — a friend of mine,' the girl explained. 'I thought you wouldn't mind — '

'Your fellow, eh?'

'Well — I suppose — '

'The guy you was crying about that night you came out of the office where you saw Sir Frederic?'

'Yes.'

'Well, I'm glad to meet him. I'm glad you can prove you've got a fellow, anyhow. But even so — that story of yours sounds pretty fishy to me.'

'I can't help how it sounds,' returned the girl with spirit. 'It's the truth.'

'All right. Let it go. It's the next night I want to talk about now. The night Sir Frederic was killed. You were working in your office that night?'

'Yes, sir. Though I must have left before — the thing — happened.'

'How do you know you left before it happened?'

'I don't. I was just supposing — '

'Don't suppose with me,' bullied Flannery.

'She has good reason for thinking she left before the murder,' Kinsey put in. 'She heard no shot fired.'

Flannery swung on him. 'Say — when I want any answers from you, I'll ask for 'em.' He turned back to the girl. 'You didn't hear any shot?'

'No, sir.'

'And you didn't see anybody in the hall when you went home?'

'Well — I — I — '

'Yes? Out with it.'

'I'd like to change my testimony on that point.'

'Oh, you would, would you?'

'Yes. I have talked it over with Mr. Kinsey, and he thinks I was wrong to — to — say what I did — '

'To lie, you mean?'

'But I didn't want to be entangled in it,'

pleaded the girl. 'I saw myself testifying in court — and I didn't think — it just seemed I couldn't — '

'You couldn't help us, eh? Young woman, this is serious business. I could lock you up — '

'Oh, but if I change my testimony? If I tell you the truth now?'

'Well, we'll see. But make sure of one thing — that it's the truth at last. Then there was somebody in the hall?'

'Yes. I started to leave the office, but just as I opened the door, I remembered my umbrella. So I went back. But in that moment at the door, I saw two men standing near the elevators.'

'You saw two men. What did they look like?'

'One — one was a Chinese.'

Flannery was startled. 'A Chinese. Say — it wasn't Mr. Chan here?' Charlie smiled.

'Oh, no,' the girl continued. 'It was an older Chinese. He was talking with a tall, thin man. A man whose picture I have seen in the newspapers.'

'Oh, you've seen his picture in the papers? What's his name?'

'His name is Colonel John Beetham, and I believe he is — an explorer.'

'I see.' Flannery got up and paced the floor.

'You saw Beetham talking with a Chinese in the hall just before Sir Frederic was killed. Then you went back to get your umbrella?'

'Yes — and when I came out again they were gone.'

'Anything else?'

'No — I guess not.'

'Think hard. You've juggled the truth once.'

'She was not under oath,' protested Kinsey.

'Well, what if she wasn't. She obstructed our work, and that's no joking matter. However, I'll overlook it, now that she's finally come across. You can go. I may want you again.'

The girl and Kinsey went out. Flannery walked the floor in high glee.

'Now I'm getting somewhere,' he cried. 'Beetham! I haven't paid much attention to him, but I'll make up for lost time from here on. Beetham was in the hall talking with a Chinaman a few minutes before the murder. And he was supposed to be upstairs running his magic lantern. A Chinaman — do you get it? Those slippers came from the Chinese Legation. By heaven, it's beginning to tie up at last.'

'If I might presume,' said Chan, 'you now propose to — '

'I propose to get after Colonel Beetham. He told Miss Morrow he didn't leave the

301

room upstairs. Another liar — and a distinguished one this time.'

'Humbly asking pardon,' Chan ventured. 'Colonel Beetham very clever man. Have a care he does not outwit you.'

'I'm not afraid of him. He can't fool me. I'm too old at this game.'

'Magnificent confidence,' Charlie smiled. 'Let us hope it is justified by the finish.'

'It will be, all right. You just leave Colonel Beetham to me.'

'With utmost gladness,' agreed Chan. 'If you will allot something else to me.'

'What's that?' Flannery demanded.

'I refer to faint little figures on newspaper margin.'

'Poor arithmetic,' snorted Flannery. 'And a poor clue.'

'Time will reveal,' said Chan gently.

17

The Woman From Peshawar

Barry Kirk answered the ring of the telephone the next morning at ten, and was greeted by a voice that, even over the wire, seemed to afford him pleasure.

'Good morning,' he said. 'I'm glad to hear from you. This is what I call starting the day right.'

'Thanks ever so much,' Miss Morrow replied. 'Now that your day has begun auspiciously, would you mind fading away into the background and giving Mr. Chan your place at the telephone?'

'What — you don't want to talk to me?'

'I'm sorry — no. I'm rather busy to-day.'

'Well, I can take a hint as quickly as the next man. I know when I'm not wanted. That's what you meant to convey, isn't it — '

'Please, Mr. Kirk.'

'Here's Charlie now. I'm not angry, but I'm terribly, terribly hurt — ' He handed the telephone to Chan.

'Oh, Mr. Chan,' the girl said. 'Captain Flannery is going to interview Colonel

Beetham at eleven o'clock. He's all Beetham to-day. He's asked me to be on hand to remind the Colonel about his testimony the night of the murder, and I suggest you come too.'

'The Captain demands me?' Chan inquired.

'I demand you. Isn't that enough?'

'To me it is delicious plenty,' Charlie replied. 'I will be there — at Captain Flannery's office, I presume?'

'Yes. Don't fail me,' Miss Morrow said, and rang off.

'Something doing?' Kirk asked.

Chan shrugged. 'Captain Flannery has hot spasm about Colonel Beetham. He interrogates him at eleven, and I am invited.'

'How about me?'

'I am stricken by regret, but you are not mentioned.'

'Then I hardly think I'll go,' Kirk said.

At a little before eleven, Charlie went to the Hall of Justice. In Flannery's dark office he found Miss Morrow, brightening the dreary corner where she was.

'Good morning,' she said. 'The Captain is showing Inspector Duff about the building. I'm glad you're here. Somehow, I've got the impression Captain Flannery doesn't care much for me this morning.'

'Mainland police have stupid sinking

spells,' Chan informed her.

Flannery came in, followed by Inspector Duff. He stood for a minute glaring at Charlie and the girl.

'Well, a fine pair you are,' he roared. 'What's the idea, anyhow?'

'What *is* the idea, Captain?' asked Miss Morrow sweetly.

'The idea seems to be to keep me in the dark,' Flannery went on. 'What do you think I am? A mind-reader? I've just been talking with Inspector Duff about Colonel Beetham, and I discover you two know a lot more about the Colonel than you've ever told me.'

'Please understand — I haven't been tale-bearing,' smiled Duff. 'I mentioned these things thinking of course the Captain knew them.'

'Of course you thought I knew them,' Flannery exploded. 'Why shouldn't I know them? I'm supposed to be in charge of this case, ain't I? Yet you two have been digging up stuff right along and keeping it to yourselves. I tell you, it makes me sore — '

'Oh, I'm so sorry,' cried Miss Morrow.

'That helps a lot. What's all this about a servant of the Colonel's — a Chinaman named Li Gung? Are you willing to talk now, Sergeant Chan, or are you still playing button, button, who's got the — '

'I'm the guilty one,' the girl cut in. 'I should have told you myself. Naturally, Mr. Chan must have thought I had.'

'Oh, no,' Chan protested. 'Please shift all guilt from those pretty shoulders to my extensive ones. I have made mistake. It is true I have pondered certain facts in silence, but I was hoping some great light would break — '

'All right, all right,' Flannery interrupted. 'But will you talk now, that's what I want to know? When did you first hear about Li Gung?'

'At noon of the day Sir Frederic was killed, I have great honour to lunch with him. After lunch he takes me apart and talks of this Li Gung, a stranger, visiting relatives in Jackson Street. He suggests I might make cunning inquiries of the man, but I am forced to refuse the task. On morning after murder I am in stateroom of *Maui* boat, foolishly believing I am going to Honolulu, when I hear Colonel Beetham in next cabin saying farewell to one he calls Li Gung. The Colonel directs that Gung lie low in Honolulu, and answer no questions.'

'And all that was so unimportant I never heard of it,' stormed Flannery. 'How about the fact that Beetham was one of the guests at the picnic near Peshawar?'

'We did not learn that until Tuesday night,'

306

Miss Morrow informed him.

'Only had about thirty-six hours to tell me, eh? On May fourth, nineteen hundred and thirteen, Colonel Beetham left Peshawar by way of the — er — the Khyber Pass to go to — to — to make a trip — '

'To Teheran by way of Afghanistan and the Kevir Desert of northern Persia,' Duff helped him out.

'Yes. You told the Inspector that, Sergeant. But you never told me.'

Charlie shrugged. 'Why should I trouble you? The matter appears to mean nothing. True enough, I might make a surmise — a most picturesque surmise. But I see you, Captain, floundering about in difficult murder case. Should I ask such a man to come with me and gaze upon the bright tapestry of romance?'

'Whatever that means,' Flannery returned. 'If I hadn't got that Barr girl in, I'd still be in the dark. I was too smart for you — I hit on Beetham's trail myself — but that doesn't excuse you. I'm disappointed in the pair of you.'

'Overwhelmed with painful regret,' Chan bowed.

'Oh, forget it.' A man in uniform ushered Colonel Beetham into the room.

The Colonel knew a good tailor, a tailor who no doubt rejoiced in the trim, lithe figure of his client. He was faultlessly attired, with a flower in his buttonhole, a stick in his gloved hand. For a moment he stood, those tired eyes that had looked on so many lonely corners of the world unusually alert and keen.

'Good morning,' he said. He bowed to Miss Morrow and Chan. 'Ah — this, I believe, is Captain Flannery — '

'Morning,' replied Flannery. 'Meet Inspector Duff, of Scotland Yard.'

'Delighted,' Beetham answered. 'I am very happy to see a man from the Yard. No doubt the search for Sir Frederic's murderer will get forward now.'

'I guess it will,' growled Flannery, 'if you answer a few questions for us — and tell the truth — '

The Colonel raised his eyebrows very slightly. 'The truth, of course,' he remarked, with a wan smile. 'I shall do my best. May I sit down?'

'Sure,' replied Flannery, indicating a dusty chair. 'On the night Sir Frederic was killed, you were giving a magic lantern show on the floor above — '

'I should hardly have called it that. Motion pictures, you know, of Tibet — '

'Yes, yes. You did a lecture with these films, but towards the end you dropped out and let the performance run itself. Later Miss Morrow here asked you — what was it you asked him, Miss Morrow?'

'I referred to that moment when he left the machine,' the girl said. 'He assured me that he had not been absent from the room during the interval.'

The Captain looked at Beetham. 'Is that right, Colonel?'

'Yes — I fancy that is what I told her.'

'Why?'

'Why? What do you mean?'

'Why did you tell her that when you knew damn well you had been down on the twentieth floor talking with a Chinaman?'

Beetham laughed softly. 'Have you never done anything that you later regretted, Captain? The matter struck me as of no importance — I had seen nothing of note on my brief jaunt below. I had a sort of inborn diffidence about being involved in the scandal. So I very foolishly made a slight — er — mis-statement.'

'Then you did go down to the twentieth floor?'

'Only for a second. You see, a motion-picture projector and seven reels of film make a rather heavy load. My old boy, Li Gung, had assisted me in bringing the outfit to Mr. Kirk's apartment. I thought I should be

309

finished by ten, and I told him to be back then. When I left the machine at fifteen minutes past ten, I realized that I still had another reel to show. I ran downstairs, found Gung waiting on the lower floor, and told him to go home. I said I would carry the machine away myself.'

'Ah, yes — and he left?'

'He went at once, in the lift. The lift girl can verify my statement — if — '

'If what?'

'If she will.'

'You were going to say — if we can find her.'

'Why should I say that. Isn't she about?'

'She is not. In her absence, maybe Li Gung can back up your story?'

'I'm sure he can — if you care to cable him. He is in Honolulu at the moment.'

'He left the next noon, on the *Maui*?'

'Yes, he did.'

'You saw him off?'

'Naturally. He has been with me more than twenty years. A faithful chap.'

'When you said good-bye, you told him to lie low over in Hawaii.'

'Yes, I — yes, I did. You see, there was some trouble about his passport. I was fearful he might get into difficulties.'

'You also told him to answer no questions.'

'For the same reason, of course.'

'You knew he would have to show his passport on landing. If it wasn't O.K. did you suppose lying low after that would do any good?'

'Show his passport at another American port? Really, you know, I'm frightfully ignorant of your many rules and regulations. Quite confusing, I find them.'

'You must — a man who's travelled as little as you have, Colonel.'

'Ah, yes. Now you're being sarcastic.'

'Oh, don't mind me,' Flannery said. 'We'll drop Li Gung. But I'm not through yet. I understand you were at Peshawar in India, on the night of May third, nineteen hundred and thirteen.'

Beetham nodded slowly. 'That is a matter of record.'

'And can't very well be denied, eh? You went out into the hills on a picnic. One of the party was a woman named Eve Durand.' Beetham stirred slightly. 'That night Eve Durand disappeared and has never been seen since. Have you any idea how she got out of India?'

'If she has never been seen since, how do you know she did get out of India?'

'Never mind. I'm asking you questions. You remember the incident?'

'Naturally. A shocking affair.'

Flannery studied him for a moment. 'Tell me, Colonel — had you ever met Sir Frederic before the other night at Barry Kirk's bungalow?'

'Never. Stop a bit. I believe he said he had been at a dinner of the Royal Geographical Society in London, and had seen me there. But I did not recall the meeting.'

'You didn't know that he had come to San Francisco to find Eve Durand?'

'Had he really? How extraordinary.'

'You didn't know it?'

'Of course not.'

'Could you have given him any help if you had?'

'I could not,' replied Beetham firmly.

'All right, Colonel. You're not thinking of leaving San Francisco soon?'

'In a few days — when I have completed arrangements for my next long expedition.'

'You're not leaving until we find out who killed Sir Frederic. Is that understood?'

'But, my dear fellow — surely you don't think — '

'I think your testimony may prove valuable. I'm asking you — is it understood?'

'Perfectly. I shall hope, however, for your early success.'

'We all hope for it.'

312

'Of course.' Beetham turned to Inspector Duff. 'A frightful thing. Sir Frederic was a charming fellow — '

'And much beloved,' said Duff evenly. 'Please don't worry. Everything possible is being done, Colonel Beetham.'

'I am happy to hear that.' Beetham rose. 'Now — if there's nothing more — '

'Not at present,' said Flannery.

'Thank you so much,' replied the Colonel, and went debonairly out.

Flannery stared after him. 'He lies like a gentleman, don't he?' he remarked.

'Beautifully,' sighed Miss Morrow, her eyes on the door through which the explorer had gone.

'Well, he don't fool me,' Flannery continued. 'He knows more about this than he's telling. If he was anybody but the famous Colonel Beetham, I'd take a chance and lock him up this morning.'

'Oh, but you couldn't,' the girl cried.

'I suppose not. I'd be mobbed by all the club women in the Bay District. However, I don't need to. He's too well known to make a getaway. But I'd better keep him shadowed, at that. Now, let's get to business. If only Li Gung was here, I'd sweat something out of him. What was that Sir Frederic told you, Sergeant? About Li Gung's relatives in

313

Jackson Street? I might look them up.'

'No use,' Chan answered. 'I have already done so.'

'Oh, you have? Without a word to me, of course — '

'Words of no avail. I made most pitiful failure. I am admitted to house, but plans are foiled by kind act of boy scout — '

'A boy scout in the family, eh?'

'Yes — name of Willie Li. The family of Henry Li, Oriental Apartment House.'

Flannery considered. 'Well, the young generation will talk, if the old one won't. Willie ought to have a chance.'

'He has obtained it. He tells me little — save that once on a hard journey Colonel Beetham kills a man.'

'He told you that? Then he knows something about Beetham's journeys?'

'Undubitably he does. He has overheard talk — '

Flannery jumped up. 'That's enough for me. I'll have Manley of the Chinatown Squad bring the kid here to-night. They're all crazy about Manley, these Chink kids. We'll get something.'

The telephone rang. Flannery answered, and then relinquished it to Miss Morrow. As she listened to the news coming over the wire, her eyes brightened with excitement.

She hung up the receiver and turned to the others.

'That was the district attorney,' she announced. 'We've got hold of a letter mailed to Mrs. Tupper-Brock from Santa Barbara. It was written by Grace Lane, and it gives her present address.'

'Fine business,' Flannery cried. 'I told you she couldn't get away from me. I'll get a couple of men off in a car right away.' He looked at Miss Morrow. 'They can stop at your office for the address.'

She nodded. 'I'm going right back. I'll give it to them.'

Flannery rubbed his hands. 'Things are looking up at last! Make it seven to-night — I'll have the kid here then. Sergeant — you're coming. I may want your help. And you can look in if you like, Inspector.'

'Thanks,' Duff said.

'How about me?' asked Miss Morrow.

He frowned at her. 'I'm not so pleased with you. All those secrets — '

'But I'm so sorry.' She smiled at him. 'And I was a little help to you in finding Grace Lane, you know.'

'I guess you were, at that. Sure — come along, if you want to.'

The party scattered, and Charlie Chan went back to Kirk's place where he found

Barry eagerly awaiting news. When he heard the plan for the evening, Kirk insisted on taking Miss Morrow and Chan to dinner. At six-thirty they left the obscure little restaurant he had selected because of its capable chef, and strolled towards the Hall of Justice.

The night was clear and cool, without fog, and the stars were bright as torches overhead. They skirted the fringe of Chinatown and passed on through Portsmouth Square, the old Plaza of romantic history. It was emptied now of its usual derelicts and adventurers; the memorial to R.L.S. stood lonely and serene in the starlight.

Flannery and Duff were waiting in the former's office. The Captain regarded Barry Kirk without enthusiasm.

'We're all here, ain't we?' he inquired.

'I thought you wouldn't mind,' smiled Kirk.

'Oh, well — it's all right. I guess it's pretty late now to bar you out.' He turned to Miss Morrow. 'You saw Petersen, didn't you?'

'Yes. I gave him the address.'

'He had Myers with him. Good men, both of them. They'll be in Santa Barbara this evening, and can start back at sunrise. Barring accidents, they'll bring Grace Lane into this office late to-morrow afternoon. And if she gets away from me again, she'll be going some.'

They sat down. Presently a huge police

officer in plain clothes, with a khaki shirt, came in. He was kindly and smiling, but he had the keen eye of a man who is prepared for any emergency. Flannery introduced him.

'Sergeant Manley,' he explained. 'Head of the Chinatown Squad for seven years — which is a good many years longer than anyone else has lived to hold that job.'

Manley's manner was cordial. 'Glad to meet you,' he said. 'I've got the kid outside, Captain. I picked him up and brought him along without giving him a chance to run home for instructions.'

'Good idea,' Flannery nodded. 'Will he talk?'

'Oh, he'll talk all right. He and I are old friends. I'll bring him in.'

He disappeared into the outer office and returned with Willie Li. The boy scout was in civilian clothes, and looked as though he would have welcomed the moral support of his uniform.

'Here you are, Willie,' Manley said. 'This is Captain Flannery. He's going to ask you to do him a big favour.'

'Sure,' grinned Willie Li.

'All boy scouts,' Manley went on, 'are American citizens, and they stand for law and order. That's right, ain't it, Willie?'

'In the oath,' replied Willie gravely.

'I've explained to him,' Manley continued, 'that none of his family is mixed up in this in any way. They won't be harmed by anything he tells you.'

'That's right,' said Flannery. 'You can take my word for it, son.'

'Sure,' agreed the boy readily.

'Your cousin, Li Gung,' Flannery began, 'has been a servant of Colonel Beetham's for a long time. He's been all over the world with the Colonel?'

Willie nodded. 'Gobi Desert. Kevir Desert. Tibet, India, Afghanistan.'

'You've heard Li Gung tell about his adventures with the Colonel?'

'Yes.'

'Remember 'em?'

'Never going to forget,' replied Willie, his little black eyes shining.

'You told your friend Mr. Chan here that the Colonel once shot a man for some reason or other?'

The boy's eyes narrowed. 'Because it was necessary. There was no crime there.'

'Of course — of course it was necessary,' rejoined Flannery heartily. 'We wouldn't do anything to the Colonel because of that. We have no authority over things that happen outside of San Francisco. We're just curious, that's all. Do you remember what trip it was

318

during which the Colonel shot this man?'

'Sure. It was the journey from Peshawar through Khyber Pass over Afghanistan.'

'It happened in Afghanistan?'

'Yes. A very bad man. Muhamed Ashref Khan, keeper of the camels. He was trying to steal — '

'To steal what?'

'A pearl necklace. Colonel Beetham saw him go into the tent — the tent which no man must enter at cost of his life — '

'What tent was that?'

'The woman's tent.'

There was a moment's tense silence. 'The woman's tent?' Flannery repeated. 'What woman?'

'The woman who was travelling with them to Teheran. The woman from Peshawar.'

'Did your cousin describe her?'

'She was beautiful, with golden hair, and eyes like the blue sky. Very beautiful, my cousin said.'

'And she was travelling with them from Peshawar to Teheran?'

'Yes. Only Li Gung and the Colonel knew it when they went through the Pass, for she was hidden in a car. Then she came out, and she had her own tent, which Colonel Beetham said no man must enter or he would kill him.'

'But this camel man — he disobeyed? And he was shot?'

'Justly so,' observed Willie Li.

'Of course,' agreed Flannery. 'Well, son — that's all. I'm very much obliged to you. Now run along. If I had anything to say in the scouts, you'd get a merit badge for this.'

'I have twenty-two already,' grinned Willie Li. 'I am Eagle Scout.' He and Manley went out.

Flannery got up and paced the floor. 'Well, what do you know?' he cried. 'This is too good to be true. Eve Durand disappears in the night — her poor husband is frantic with grief — the whole of India is turned upside down in the search for her. And all the time she's moving on through Afghanistan in the caravan of Colonel John Beetham — the great explorer everyone is crazy about, the brave fine man no one would dream of suspecting.' Flannery turned to Chan. 'I see now what you meant. Romance, you called it. Well, I've got a different name for it. I call it running away with another man's wife. A pretty scandal in the Colonel's past — a lovely blot on his record — by heaven — wonderful! Do you see what it means?'

Chan shrugged. 'I see you are flying high to-night.'

'I certainly am — high, wide, and handsome. I've got my man, and I've got the motive, too. Sir Frederic comes to San

Francisco hunting Eve Durand. And here is Colonel John Beetham, honoured and respected by all — riding the top of the wave. Beetham learns why Sir Frederic has come — and he wonders. He hears the detective has been in India — has he found out how Eve Durand left that country? If he has, and springs it, the career of John Beetham is smashed. He'll be done for — finished — he won't collect any more money for his big expeditions. Is he the sort to stand by and watch that happen? He is not. What does he do?'

'The question is for mere effect,' suggested Chan.

'First of all, he wants to learn how much Sir Frederic really knows. At dinner he hears that about the safe being open. He's crazy to get down there and look around. At the first opportunity, he creeps downstairs, enters Mr. Kirk's office — '

'Through a locked door?' inquired Chan.

'The elevator girl could get him a key. She's Eve Durand — don't forget that. Or else there's Li Gung — he's on the scene — maybe that's just by accident. But he could be used — the fire-escape — Anyhow, Beetham gets into the office. He hunts like mad, gets hold of the records, sees at a glance that Sir Frederic has discovered everything.

321

At that moment Sir Frederic comes in. The one man in the world who knows how Eve Durand got out of India — and will tell. The man who can wreck Beetham for ever. Beetham sees red. He pulls a gun. It's a simple matter for him — he's done it before. Sir Frederic lies dead on the floor, Beetham escapes with the records — the secret of that old scandal is safe. By the Lord Harry — who'd want a better motive than that!'

'Not to mention,' said Chan gently, 'the velvet slippers. The slippers of Hilary Galt.'

'Oh, hell,' cried Flannery. 'Be reasonable, man! One thing at a time.'

18

Flannery's Big Scene

Greatly pleased with himself, Captain Flannery sat down behind his desk. His summing up of the case against Beetham seemed, to his way of thinking, without a flaw. He beamed at the assembled company.

'Everything is going to work out fine,' he continued. 'To-morrow evening in this room I stage my big scene, and if we don't get something out of it, then I'm no judge of human nature. First, I bring in Major Durand. I tell him Eve Durand has been found and is on her way here, and while we're waiting I go back to the question of how she got out of India. I plant in his mind a suspicion of Beetham. Then I bring the woman into the room — after fifteen years' suffering and anxiety, he sees his wife at last. What's he going to think? What'll he ask himself — and her? Where's she been? Why did she leave? How did she escape from India? At that moment I produce Colonel Beetham, confront him with the husband he wronged, the woman he carried off in his caravan. I tell Durand I have certain knowledge that his wife left with Beetham. Then I sit back and watch the fireworks. How does that strike you, Sergeant Chan?'

'You would chop down the tree to catch the blackbird,' Chan said.

'Well, sometimes we have to do that. It's roundabout, but it ought to work. What do you think, Inspector?'

'Sounds rather good, as drama,' Duff drawled. 'But do you really think it will reveal the murderer of Sir Frederic?'

'It may. Somebody — the woman, or Beetham — will break. Make a damaging admission. They always do. I'll gamble on it, this time. Yes, sir — we're going to take a big stride forward to-morrow night.'

Leaving Captain Flannery to an enthuiastic contemplation of his own cleverness, they departed. At the door Chan went off with Inspector Duff. Kirk and the girl strolled up the hill together.

'Want a taxi?' Kirk asked.

'Thanks. I'd rather walk — and think.'

'We have something to think of, haven't we? How does it strike you? Beetham?'

She shrugged her shoulders. 'Nonsense. I'll never believe it. Not if he makes a full confession himself.'

'Oh, I know. He's the hero of your dreams.

But just the same, my lady, he's not incapable of it. If Sir Frederic was in his way — threatening his plans — and it begins to look as though he was. Unless you don't believe that Eve Durand was in the caravan?'

'I believe that,' she replied.

'Because you want to,' he smiled. 'It's too romantic for words, isn't it? By George, the very thought of it makes me feel young and giddy. The gay picnic party in the hills — the game of hide-and-seek — one breathless moment of meeting behind the tamarisks. 'I'm yours — take me with you when you go.' Everything forgotten — the world well lost for love. The wagon jolting out through the Pass, with all that beauty hidden beneath a worn bit of canvas. Then — the old caravan road — the golden road to Samarkand — the merchants from the north crowding by — camels and swarthy men — and mingled with the dust of the trail the iron nails lost from thousands of shoes that have passed that way since time began.'

'I didn't know you were so romantic.'

'Ah — you've never given me a chance. You and your law books. Eight months along that famous road — nights with the white stars close overhead, dawns hazy with desert mist. Hot sun at times, and then snow, flurries of snow. The man and the woman together — '

'And the poor husband searching frantically throughout India.'

'Yes, they rather forgot Durand, didn't they? But they were in love. You know, it looks to me as though we had stumbled on to a great love story. Do you think — '

'I wonder.'

'You wonder what?'

'I wonder if it's all true — and if it is, does it bring us any closer to a solution of the puzzle? After all, the question remains — who killed Sir Frederic? Captain Flannery hadn't an iota of proof for any of his wild surmises involving Beetham.'

'Oh, forget your worries. Let's pretend. This deserted street is the camel road to Teheran — the old silk road from China to Persia. You and I — '

'You and I have no time for silk roads now. We must find the road that leads to a solution of our mystery.'

Kirk sighed. 'All right. To make a headline of it, Attorney Morrow Slams Door on Romance Probe. But some day I'll catch you off your guard, and then — look out!'

'I'm never off my guard,' she laughed.

On Friday morning, after breakfast, Chan hesitated a moment, and then followed Barry Kirk into his bedroom. 'If you will pardon the imposition, I have bold request to make.'

326

'Certainly, Charlie. What is it?'

'I wish you to take me to Cosmopolitan Club, and introduce me past eagle-eyed door man. After that, I have unlimited yearning to meet old employee of club.'

'An old employee? Well, there's Peter Lee. He's been in charge of the cloak-room for thirty years. Would he do?'

'An excellent choice. I would have you suggest to this Lee that he show me about club-house, roof to cellar. Is that possible?'

'Of course,' Kirk looked at him keenly. 'You're still thinking about that club year book we found beside Sir Frederic?'

'I have never ceased to think of it,' Chan returned. 'Whenever you are ready, please.'

Deeply mystified, Kirk took him to the Cosmopolitan and turned him over to Peter Lee.

'It is not necessary that you loiter on the scene,' Chan remarked, grinning with pleasure. 'I will do some investigating and return to you later.'

'All right,' Kirk replied. 'Just as you wish.'

It was close to the luncheon hour when Chan showed up, his little eyes gleaming.

'What luck?' Kirk inquired.

'Time will reveal,' said Chan. 'I find this mainland climate bracing to an extremity. Very much fear I shall depopulate your kitchen at lunch.'

'Well, don't drink too heartily of the hydrocyanic acid,' Kirk smiled. 'Something tells me it would be a real calamity if we lost you just at present.'

After luncheon Miss Morrow telephoned to say that Grace Lane, accompanied by the two policemen, would reach Flannery's office at four o'clock. She added that they were both invited — on her own initiative.

'Let us go,' Chan remarked. 'Captain Flannery's big scene should have crowded house.'

'What do you think will come of it?' Kirk asked.

'I am curious to learn. If it has big success, then my work here is finished. If not — '

'Yes? Then what?'

'Then I may suddenly act like pompous stager of shows myself,' Chan shrugged.

Flannery, Duff and Miss Morrow were in the Captain's office when Chan and Barry Kirk walked in. 'Hello,' said the Captain. 'Want to be in at the finish, eh?'

'Pleasure would be impossible to deny ourselves,' Chan told him.

'Well, I'm all set,' Flannery went on. 'All my plans made.'

Chan nodded. 'The wise man digs his well before he is thirsty,' he remarked.

'You haven't been doing any too much

328

digging,' Flannery chided. 'I got to admit, Sergeant, you've kept your word. You've let me solve this case without offering very much help. However, I've been equal to it. I haven't needed you, as it turned out. You might as well have been on that boat ten days ago.'

'A sad reflection for me,' said Chan. 'But I am not of mean nature. My hearty congratulations will be ready when desired.'

Colonel Beetham was ushered into the room. His manner was nonchalant, and, as always, rather condescending.

'Ah, Captain,' he remarked, 'I'm here again. According to instructions — '

'I'm very glad to see you,' Flannery broke in.

'And just what can I do for you to-day?' inquired Beetham dropping into a chair.

'I'm anxious to have you meet — a certain lady.'

The Colonel opened a cigarette case, took out a cigarette, and tapped it on the silver side of the case. 'Ah, yes. I'm not precisely a lady's man, but — '

'I think you'll be interested to meet this one,' Flannery told him.

'Really?' He lighted a match.

'You see,' Flannery went on, 'it happens to be a lady who once took a very long journey in your company.'

Beetham's brown, lean hand paused with the lighted match. The flame held steady. 'I do not understand you,' he said.

'An eight months' journey, I believe,' the Captain persisted. 'Through Khyber Pass and across Afghanistan and Eastern Persia to the neighbourhood of Teheran.'

Beetham lighted his cigarette and tossed away the match. 'My dear fellow — what are you talking about?'

'You know what I'm talking about. Eve Durand — the lady you helped out of India fifteen years ago. No one suspected you, did they, Colonel? Too big a man — above suspicion — all those medals on your chest. However, I know you did it — I know you ran away with Durand's wife — and I'll prove it, too. But perhaps I needn't prove it — perhaps you'll admit it — ' He stopped.

Beetham unconcernedly blew a ring of smoke towards the ceiling, and for a moment watched it dissolve. 'All that,' he remarked, 'is so absolutely silly I refuse to answer.'

'Suit yourself,' replied Flannery. 'At any rate, Eve Durand will be here in a few minutes, and I want you to see her again. The sight may refresh your memory. I want you to see her — standing at her husband's side.'

Beetham nodded. 'I shall be most happy. I knew them both, long ago. Yes, I shall be a very pleased witness of the touching reunion you picture.'

A policeman appeared at the door. 'Major Durand is outside,' he announced.

'Good,' said Flannery. 'Pat — this is Colonel Beetham. I want you to take him into the back room — the second one — and stay with him until I send for the both of you.'

Beetham rose. 'I say, am I under arrest?' he inquired.

'You're not under arrest,' returned Flannery. 'But you're going with Pat. Is that clear?'

'Absolutely. Pat — I am at your service.' The two disappeared. Flannery rose and going to the door leading into the anteroom, admitted Major Durand.

The Major entered and stood there, somewhat at a loss. Flannery proffered a chair. 'Sit down, sir. You know everybody here. I've great news for you. We've located the woman we think is your wife, and she'll be along in a few minutes.'

Durand stared at him. 'You've found — Eve? Can that possibly be true?'

'We'll know in a minute,' Flannery said. 'I may tell you I'm certain of it — but we'll let you see for yourself. Before she comes — one or two things I want to ask you about. Among the members of that picnic party was Colonel

331

John Beetham, the explorer?'

'Yes, of course.'

'He left the next morning on a long journey through the Khyber Pass?'

'Yes. I didn't see him go, but they told me he had gone.'

'Has anyone ever suggested that he may have taken your wife with him when he left?'

The question struck Durand with the force of a bullet. He paled. 'No one had ever made that suggestion,' he replied, almost inaudibly.

'All the same, I'm here to tell you that is exactly what happened.'

Durand got up and began to pace the floor. 'Beetham,' he muttered. 'Beetham. No, no — he wouldn't have done it. A fine chap, Beetham — one of the best. A gentleman. He wouldn't have done that to me.'

'He was just in here, and I accused him of it.'

'But he denied it, of course?'

'Yes — he did. But my evidence — '

'Damn your evidence,' cried Durand. 'He's not that kind of man, I tell you. Not Beetham. And my wife — Eve — why, what you are saying is an insult to her. She loved me. I'm sure of it — she loved me. I won't believe — I can't — '

'Ask her when she comes,' suggested Flannery. Durand sank back into the chair and buried his face in his hands.

For a long moment they waited in silence. Miss Morrow's cheeks were flushed with excitement; Duff was puffing quietly on his inevitable pipe; Charlie Chan sat immobile as an idol of stone. Kirk nervously took out a cigarette, and then put it back in the case.

The man named Petersen appeared in the door. He was dusty and travel-stained.

'Hello, Jim,' Flannery cried. 'Have you got her?'

'I've got her this time,' Petersen answered, and stood aside. The woman of so many names entered the room and halted, her eyes anxious and tired. Another long silence.

'Major Durand,' said Flannery. 'Unless I am much mistaken — '

Durand got slowly to his feet, and took a step forward. He studied the woman intently for a moment, and then he made a little gesture of despair.

'It's the old story,' he said brokenly. 'The old story over again. Captain Flannery, you *are* mistaken. This woman is not my wife.'

19

A Vigil in the Dark

For a moment no one spoke. Captain Flannery was gradually deflating like a bright red balloon that had received a fatal puncture. Suddenly his eyes blazed with anger. He turned hotly on Charlie Chan.

'You!' he shouted. 'You got me into this! You and your small-time hunch. The lady is Jennie Jerome. She is also Marie Lantelme. What does that mean? It means she is Eve Durand. A guess — a fat-headed guess — and I listened to you. I believed you. Good lord, what a fool I've been!'

Profound contrition shone in Charlie's eyes. 'I am so sorry. I have made stupid error. Captain — is it possible you will ever forgive me?'

Flannery snorted. 'Will I ever forgive myself? Listening to a Chinaman — me, Tom Flannery. With my experience — my record — bah! I've been crazy — plumb crazy — but that's all over now.' He rose. 'Major Durand, a thousand apologies. I wouldn't have disappointed you again for worlds.'

Durand shrugged his shoulders wearily. 'Why, that doesn't matter. You meant it kindly, I know. For a moment, in spite of all that has happened, I did allow myself to hope — I did think that it might really be Eve. Silly of me — I should have learned my lesson long ago. Well, there is nothing more to be said.' He moved towards the door. 'If that is all, Captain — '

'Yes, that's all. I'm sorry, Major.'

Durand bowed. 'I'm sorry, too. No doubt I shall see you again. Good-bye.'

Near the door, as he went out, he passed the girl who called herself Grace Lane. She had been standing there, drooping with fatigue; now she took a step nearer the desk. Her face was pale, her eyes dull with the strain of a long, hard day. 'What are you going to do with me?' she asked.

'Wait a minute,' growled Flannery.

Miss Morrow rose, and placed a chair for the other woman. She was rewarded by a grateful look.

'I just remembered Beetham,' said Flannery. Again he scowled at Chan. 'I've tipped off my hand to him — for nothing. I can thank you for that, too.'

'My guilty feeling grows by jumps and bounds,' sighed Charlie.

'It ought to,' the Captain replied. He went

to the inner door and called loudly: 'Pat!' Pat appeared at once, followed by the Colonel. For an instant Beetham stood staring curiously about the room.

'But where,' he remarked, 'is the touching reunion? I don't see Durand. No more do I see his wife.'

Flannery's face grew even redder than usual. 'There's been a mistake,' he admitted.

'There have been a number of mistakes, I fancy,' said Beetham carelessly. 'A dangerous habit, that of making mistakes, Captain. You should seek to overcome it.'

'When I want your advice, I'll ask for it,' responded the harassed Flannery. 'You can go along. But I still regard you as an important witness in this case, and I warn you not to strike out for any more deserts until I give you the word.'

'I shall remember what you say,' Beetham nodded, and went out.

'What are you going to do with me?' Grace Lane persisted.

'Well, I guess you've had a pretty rough deal,' Flannery said. 'I apologize to you. You see, I got foolish and listened to a Chinaman, and that's how I came to make a mistake about your identity. I brought you back on a charge of stealing a uniform, but probably Mr. Kirk won't want to go ahead with that.'

336

'I should say not,' cried Barry Kirk. He turned to the woman. 'I hope you won't think it was my idea. You can have a bale of my uniforms, if you like.'

'You're very kind,' she answered.

'Not at all. What is more, your old position is yours if you want it. You know, I'm eager to beautify the Kirk Building, and I lost ground when you left.'

She smiled, without replying. 'I may go then?' she said, rising.

'Sure,' agreed Flannery. 'Run along.'

Miss Morrow looked at her keenly. 'Where are you going?'

'I don't know. I — '

'I do,' said the deputy district attorney. 'You're going home with me. I've got an apartment — there's loads of room. You shall stay with me for this one night, at least.'

'You — you are really too good to me,' replied Grace Lane, and her voice broke slightly.

'Nonsense. We've all been far too unkind to you. Come along.'

The two women went out. Flannery sank down behind his desk. 'Now I'm going at this thing in my own way for a change,' he announced. 'This has been an awful upset, but I had it coming to me. Listening to a Chinaman! If Grace Lane isn't Eve Durand, who is? What do you say, Inspector Duff?'

'I might also warn you,' smiled Duff, 'against the dangers of listening to an Englishman.'

'Oh, but you're from Scotland Yard. I got respect for your opinion. Let's see — Eve Durand is about somewhere — I'm sure of that. Sir Frederic was the kind of man who knows what he's talking about. There's that Lila Barr. She fits the description pretty well. There's Gloria Garland. An assumed name — Australia — might be. There's Eileen Enderby. Rust stains on her dress that night. But I didn't see them. May have been there — probably not. Another guess on Sergeant Chan's part, perhaps.'

'There is also,' added Charlie, 'Mrs. Tupper-Brock. I offer the hint with reluctance.'

'And well you may,' sneered Flannery. 'No — if you fancy Mrs. Tupper-Brock, then right there she's out with me. Which of these women — I'll have to start all over again.'

'I feel humble and contrite,' said Chan. 'In spite of which, suggestions keep crowding to my tongue. Have you heard old Chinese saying, Captain — 'It is always darkest underneath the lamp'?'

'I'm fed up on Chinese sayings,' replied the Captain.

'The one I have named means what? That just above our heads the light is blazing. Such is the fact, Captain Flannery. Take my advice, and worry no more about Eve Durand.'

'Why not?' asked Flannery, in spite of himself.

'Because you are poised on extreme verge of the great triumph of your life. In a few hours at the most your head will be ringing with your own praises.'

'How's that?'

'In a few hours you will arrest the murderer of Sir Frederic Bruce,' Chan told him calmly.

'Say — how do you get that way?' queried Flannery.

'There is one condition. It may be hard one for you,' Chan continued. 'For your own sake, I beseech you to comply with same.'

'One condition? What's that?'

'You must listen once more — and for the last time — to what you call a Chinaman.'

Flannery stirred uneasily. A hot denial rose to his lips, but something in the little man's confident manner disturbed him.

'Listen to you again, eh? As though I'd do that.'

Inspector Duff stood up, and relighted his pipe. 'If it is true that you respect my opinion, Captain — then, quoting our friend, I would make humble suggestion. Do as he asks.'

Flannery did not reply for a moment. 'Well,' he said finally, 'what have you got up your sleeve now? Another hunch?'

Chan shook his head. 'A certainty. I am stupid man from small island, and I am often wrong. This time I am quite correct. Follow me — and I prove it.'

'I wish I knew what you're talking about,' Flannery said.

'An arrest — in a few hours — if you will stoop so far as to do what I require,' Chan told him. 'In Scotland Yard, which Inspector Duff honours by his association, there is in every case of murder what they call essential clue. There was essential clue in this case.'

'The slippers?' asked Flannery.

'No,' Charlie replied. 'The slippers were valuable, but not essential. The essential clue was placed on scene by hand now dead. Hand of a man clever far beyond his fellows — how sad that such a man has passed. When Sir Frederic saw death looking him boldly in the face, he reached to a bookcase and took down — what? The essential clue, which fell from his dying hand to lie at his side on the dusty floor. The year-book of the Cosmopolitan Club.'

A moment of silence followed. There was a ring of conviction in the detective's voice.

'Well — what do you want?' inquired Flannery.

'I want that you must come to the

Cosmopolitan Club in one half-hour. Inspector Duff will of course accompany. You must then display unaccustomed patience and wait like man of stone. Exactly how long I cannot predict now. But in due time I will point out to you the killer of Sir Frederic — and I will produce proof of what I say.'

Flannery rose. 'Well, it's your last chance. You make a monkey of me again and I'll deport you as an undesirable alien. At the Cosmopolitan Club in half an hour. We'll be there.'

'Undesirable alien will greet you at the door,' smiled Charlie, 'hoping to become desirable at any moment. Mr. Kirk — will you be so good as to join my company?' He and Barry Kirk went out.

'Well, Charlie, you're certainly in bad with the Captain,' said Kirk, as they stood in the street waiting for a taxi.

Chan nodded. 'Will be in even worse presently,' he replied.

Kirk stared at him. 'How's that?'

'I shall point him the way to success. He will claim all credit, but sight of me will make him uncomfortable. No man loves the person who has guided his faltering footsteps to high-up rung of the ladder.'

They entered a taxi. 'The Cosmopolitan Club,' Chan ordered. He turned to Kirk.

'And now I must bow low in dust with many humble apologies to you. I have grievously betrayed a trust.'

'How so?' asked Kirk, surprised.

Chan took a letter from his pocket. It was somewhat worn and the handwriting on the envelope was a trifle blurred. 'The other morning you wrote letters in office, giving same to me to mail. I made gesture towards mail chute, but I extracted this missive.'

'Great Scott!' cried Kirk. 'Hasn't that been mailed?'

'It has not. What could be more disgusting? My gracious host, at whose hands I have received every kindness. I have besmirched his confidence.'

'But you had a reason?' suggested Kirk.

'A very good reason, which time will uncurtain. Am I stepping over the bounds when I seek to dig up your forgiveness?'

'Not at all,' Kirk smiled.

'You are most affable man it has yet been my fate to encounter.' The taxi had reached Union Square. Chan called to the driver to halt. 'I alight here to correct my crime,' he explained. 'The long-delayed letter now goes to its destination by special, fleet-footed messenger.'

'I say — you don't mean — ' Kirk cried in amazement.

'What I mean comes gradually into the light,' Chan told him. He got out of the taxi. 'Be so kind as to await my coming at the club door. The guardian angel beyond the threshold is jealous as to who has honour of entering Cosmopolitan Club. It has been just as well for my purpose, but please make sure that I am not left rejected outside the portal.'

'I'll watch for you,' Kirk promised.

He rode on to the club, his head whirling with new speculations and questions. No — no — this couldn't be. But Charlie had an air —

Shortly after he had reached the building Charlie appeared, and Kirk steered him past the gold-laced door-man. Presently Flannery and Duff arrived. The Captain's manner suggested that he was acting against his better judgment.

'I suppose this is another wild-goose chase,' he fretted.

'One during which the goose is apprehended, I think,' Chan assured him. 'But there will be need of Oriental calm. Have you good supply? We may loiter here until midnight hour.'

'That's pleasant,' Flannery replied. 'Well, I'll wait a while. But this is your last chance — remember.'

'Also your great chance,' Chan shrugged.

'You must likewise remember. We do wrong to hang here in spotlight of publicity. Mr. Kirk, I have made selection of nook where we may crouch unobserved, but always observing. I refer to little room behind office, opening at the side on cloakroom.'

'All right — I know where you mean,' Kirk told him. He spoke to the manager, and the four of them were ushered into a little back room, unused at the moment and in semi-darkness. Chairs were brought, and all save Charlie sat down. The little detective bustled about. He arranged that his three companions should have an unobstructed view of the cloak-room, where his friend of the morning, old Peter Lee, sat behind his barrier engrossed in a bright pink newspaper.

'Only one moment,' said Chan. He went out through the door which led behind the counter of the cloak-room. For a brief time he talked in low tones with Lee. Then the three men sitting in the dusk saw him give a quick look towards the club lobby, and dodge abruptly into his hiding-place beside them.

Colonel John Beetham, debonair as usual, appeared at the counter and passed over his hat and coat. Kirk, Flannery and Duff leaned forward eagerly and watched him as he accepted the brass check and turned away. But Chan made no move.

Time passed. Other members came into the club for dinner and checked their belongings, unconscious of the prying eyes in the little room. Flannery began to stir restlessly on his uncomfortable chair.

'What the devil is all this?' he demanded.

'Patience,' Charlie admonished. 'As the Chinese say: 'In time the grass becomes milk.''

'Yeah — but I'd rather hunt up a cow,' Flannery growled.

'Patient waiting,' Chan went on, 'is first requisite of good detective. Is that not correct, Inspector Duff?'

'Sometimes it seems the only requisite,' Duff agreed. 'I fancy I may smoke here?'

'Oh, of course,' Kirk told him. He sighed with relief and took out his pipe.

The minutes dragged on. They heard the shuffle of feet on the tiled floor of the lobby, the voices of members calling greetings, making dinner dates. Flannery was like a fly on a hot griddle.

'If you're making a fool of me again — ' he began.

His recent humiliation had been recalled to his mind by the sight of Major Eric Durand, checking his Burberry and his felt hat with Peter Lee. The Major's manner was one of deep depression.

'Poor devil,' said Flannery softly. 'We

handed him a hard jolt to-day. It wasn't necessary, either — ' His accusing eyes sought Chan. The detective was huddled up on his chair like some fat, oblivious Buddha.

A half-hour passed. Flannery was in constant touch with the figures on the face of his watch. 'Missing my dinner,' he complained. 'And this chair — it's like a barrel top.'

'There was no time to procure a velvet couch,' Chan suggested gently. 'Compose yourself, I beg. The happy man is the calm man. We have only begun to vigil.'

At the end of another half-hour, Flannery was fuming. 'Give us a tip,' he demanded. 'What are we waiting for? I'll know, or by heaven, I'll get out of here so quick — '

'Please,' whispered Charlie. 'We are waiting for the murderer of Sir Frederic Bruce. Is that not enough?'

'No, it isn't,' the Captain snapped. 'I'm sick of you and your confounded mystery. Put your cards on the table like a white man. This chair is killing me, I tell you — '

'Hush!' said Chan. He was leaning forward now, staring through the door into the cloak-room. The others followed his gaze.

Major Eric Durand stood before the counter. He threw down the brass check for his coat and hat, it rang metallically in the silence. Peter Lee brought them for him. He leaned across the barrier and helped Durand on with his coat. The Major was fumbling in his pockets. He produced a small bit of cardboard, which he gave to Peter Lee. The old man studied his treasures for a moment, and then handed over a black leather brief-case.

Chan had seized Flannery's arm, and was dragging the astonished Captain towards the club lobby. Kirk and Duff followed. They lined up before the huge front door. Durand appeared, walking briskly. He stopped as he saw the group barring his way.

'Ah, we meet again,' he said. 'Mr. Kirk, it was thoughtful of you to send me that guest card to your club. I deeply appreciate it. It arrived only a short time ago. I shall enjoy dropping in here frequently — '

Charlie Chan came of a race that likes its drama, and his fat face was shining with joy. He raised his arm with the gesture of a Booth or a Salvini.

'Captain Flannery,' he cried. 'Arrest this man.'

'Why — I — er — I don't — ' sputtered Flannery.

'Arrest this man Durand,' Chan went on. 'Arrest him at same moment while he holds beneath his arm a brief-case containing much useful information. The brief-case Sir Frederic Bruce left in the care of this club on the afternoon of the day he died.'

20

The Truth Arrives

All colour had drained from Durand's face, it was grey as fog as he stood there confronted by the triumphant little Chinese. Flannery reached out and seized the leather case. The Major made no move to resist.

'Sir Frederic's brief-case,' Flannery cried. His air of uncertainty had vanished; he was alert and confident. 'By heaven, if that's true, then our man hunt is over.' He sought to open the case. 'The thing's locked,' he added. 'I don't like to break it open. It will be a mighty important piece of evidence.'

'Mr. Kirk still holds in possession Sir Frederic's keys,' suggested Charlie. 'I would have brought them with me but I did not know where they reposed.'

'They are in my desk,' Kirk told him.

A curious group was gathering about them. Chan turned to Flannery. 'Our standing here has only one result. We offer ourselves as nucleus for a crowd. Humbly state we should go at once to the Kirk Building. There the matter may be threshed out like winter wheat.'

'Good idea,' replied Flannery.

'I also ask that Mr. Kirk visit telephone booth and request Miss Morrow to speed to same place with all haste. It would be amazing unkindness to drop her out of events at this junction.'

'Sure,' agreed Flannery. 'Do that, Mr. Kirk.'

'Likewise,' added Charlie, laying a hand on Kirk's arm, 'advise her to bring with her the elevator operator, Grace Lane.'

'What for?' demanded Flannery.

'Time will reveal,' Chan shrugged. As Kirk sped away, Colonel John Beetham came up. For a moment the explorer stood, taking in the scene before him. His inscrutable expression did not change.

'Colonel Beetham,' Charlie explained, 'we have here the man who killed Sir Frederic Bruce.'

'Really?' returned Beetham calmly.

'Undubitably. It is a matter that concerns you, I think. Will you be so good as to join our little party?'

'Of course,' Beetham replied. He went for his hat and coat. Chan followed him, and retrieved from Peter Lee the pasteboard check on receipt of which the old man had relinquished Sir Frederic's property.

Kirk, Beetham and Chan returned to the group by the door. 'All set,' announced

Flannery. 'Come along, Major Durand.'

Durand hesitated. 'I am not familiar with your law. But shouldn't there be some sort of warrant — '

'You needn't worry about that. I'm taking you on suspicion. I can get a warrant when I want it. Don't be a fool — come on.'

Outside a gentle rain had begun to fall, and the town was wrapped in mist. Duff, Flannery and Durand got into one taxi, and Chan followed with Kirk and the explorer in another. As Charlie was stepping into the car, a breathless figure shot out of the dark.

'Who was that with Flannery?' panted Bill Rankin.

'It has happened as I telephoned from the hotel,' Charlie answered. 'We have our man.'

'Major Durand?'

'The same.'

'Good enough. I'll have a flash on the street in twenty minutes. You certainly kept your promise.'

'Old habit with me,' Chan told him.

'And how about Beetham?'

Chan glanced into the dark cab. 'Nothing to do with the matter. We were on wrong trail there.'

'Too bad,' Rankin said. 'Well, I'm off. I'll be back later for details. Thanks a thousand times.'

Chan inserted his broad bulk into the taxi, and they started for the Kirk Building.

'May I express humble hope,' remarked the little detective to Kirk, 'that I am forgiven for my crime. I refer to my delay in mailing to Major Durand your letter containing guest card for Cosmopolitan Club.'

'Oh, surely,' Kirk told him.

'It chanced I was not yet ready he should walk inside the club,' Chan added.

'Well, I'm knocked cold,' Kirk said. 'You must have had your eye on him for some time.'

'I will explain with all my eloquence later. Just now I content myself with admitting this — Major Durand was one person in all the world who did not want Eve Durand discovered.'

'But in heaven's name — why not?' Kirk asked.

'Alas, I am no miracle man. It is a matter I hope will be apparent later. Perhaps Colonel Beetham can enlighten us.'

The Colonel's voice was cool and even in the darkness. 'I'm a bit weary of lying,' he remarked. 'I could enlighten you. But I won't. You see, I have made a promise. And like yourself, Sergeant, I prefer to keep my promises.'

'We have many commendable points in common.'

Beetham laughed. 'By the way — that was extremely decent of you — telling the reporter I wasn't concerned in this affair.'

'Only hope,' responded Chan, 'that events will justify my very magnanimous act.'

They alighted before the Kirk Building and rode up to the flat. Paradise had admitted Flannery and Duff with their prisoner.

'Here you are,' said Flannery briskly. 'Now, Mr. Kirk — let's have that key.'

Kirk stepped to his desk and produced Sir Frederic's keys. The Captain, with Duff close at his side, hastened to open the case. Charlie dropped down on the edge of a chair, his intent little eyes on Major Durand. The Major was seated in a corner of the room, his head bowed, his gaze fixed on the rug.

'By George,' cried Duff. 'It *is* Sir Frederic's case, right enough. And here — yes — here is what we have been looking for.' He took out a typewritten sheaf of paper. 'Here are his records in the matter of Eve Durand.'

The Inspector began to read eagerly. Flannery turned to Durand.

'Well, Major — this settles your hash. Where did you get the check for this brief-case?'

Durand made no reply. 'I will answer for him,' Charlie said. 'He extracted same from the purse of Sir Frederic the night he killed

352

that splendid gentleman.'

'Then you visited San Francisco once before, Major?' Flannery persisted.

Still Durand did not so much as raise his eyes.

'Naturally he did,' Chan grinned. 'Captain Flannery, at any moment reporters will burst upon you desiring to learn how you captured this dangerous man. Would it not be better if I told you so you will be able to make intelligent reply?' Flannery glared at him. 'The matter will demand your close attention. I search about, wondering where to begin.'

Duff looked up. 'I suggest you start with the moment when you first suspected Durand,' he said, and returned to his perusal of the records.

Chan nodded. 'It was here in this room, same night when Durand arrived. Have you ever heard, Captain — do not fear, it is not old saying this time. Have you ever heard Chinese are psychic people? It is true. A look, a gesture, a tone of voice — something goes click inside. I hear Mr. Kirk say to the Major he will send guest card for club or two. And from the sudden warmth of the Major's reply, I obtain my psychic spasm of warning. At once I ask myself, has the Major special interest in San Francisco clubs? It would seem so. Is he, then, the man we seek? No, he cannot be. Not if he came entire distance from New York with good Inspector Duff.

'But — I advise myself — pause here and ponder. What has Inspector Duff said on this point? He has said that when he got off Twentieth Century in Chicago, he discovered Major had been on same train. I put an inquiry to myself. Has this clever man, Duff, for once in his life been hoodwinked? Inspector does me high honour to invite to dinner. During the feast, I probe about. I politely inquire, did he with his own eyes see Major Durand on board Twentieth Century while train was yet speeding between New York and Chicago? No, he did not. He saw him first in Chicago station. Durand assures him he was on identical train Inspector has just left. He announces he, too, is on way to San Francisco. They take, that same night, train bound for coast.

'The matter, then, is possible. Men have been known to double back on own tracks. Study of time elapsed since murder reveals Major may have been doing this very thing. I begin to think deep about Durand. I recall that at luncheon when Sir Frederic tells us of Eve Durand case, he makes curious omission which I noted at the time. He says that when he is planning to go to Peshawar to look into Eve Durand matter, he calls on Sir George

Mannering, the woman's uncle. Yet husband is living in England, and he would know much more about the affair than uncle would. Why then, did not Sir Frederic interrogate the husband? I find there food for thought.

'All time I am wondering about Cosmopolitan Club year book, which hand of Sir Frederic drops on floor at dying moment. Mr. Kirk kindly takes me to lunch at club, and checks a brief-case. I note check for coat is of metal, but brief-case check is of cardboard, with name of article deposited written on surface by trembling hand of Peter Lee. A bright light flashes in my mind. I will suppose that Sir Frederic checked a brief-case containing records we so hotly seek, and check for same was in pocket when he died. This the killer extracts; he is clever man and knows at last he has located papers he wants so fiercely. But alas for him, clubhouse door is guarded, only members and guests may enter. In despair, he flees, but that check he carries with him spells his doom unless he can return and obtain object it represents. He longs to do so, but danger is great.

'Then fine evidence arrives. The velvet slippers come back to us on tide of events, wrapped in newspaper. On margin of paper, partially torn, are figures — a money addition

— $79 plus $23 equals $103. This refers to dollars only. Cents have been torn off. I visit railroad office. I decide what must have been on that paper before its tearing. Simply this, $79.84 plus $23.63 equals $103.47. What is that? The cost of railroad fare to Chicago with lower berth. Then the person who discarded those slippers was on Oakland ferry Wednesday morning after murder, bound to take train from Oakland terminal to Chicago. Who of all my suspects might have done that? No one but Major Durand.

'I think deep, I cogitate, I weave in and out through my not very brilliant mind. I study time-tables. Presume Major Durand was on that train out of Oakland Wednesday noon. He arrives in Chicago Saturday morning at nine. He is still distressed about check for brief-case, but his best plan seems to be to proceed eastward, and he hastens to La Salle Street station to obtain train for New York. He arrives in time to see Inspector Duff, whom he met once in Paris, disembarking from Twentieth Century. He is smart man, a big idea assails him. First he will give impression he is alighting from same train, and then he will return to California in company of Scotland Yard Inspector. Who would suspect him then? So the innocent Inspector Duff himself escorts the killer back to the scene of the crime.

'All this seems to possess good logic. But it hangs on one thing — has brief-case been checked by Sir Frederic? This morning I visit with Peter Lee, keeper of Cosmopolitan Club cloak-room. I can scarce restrain my joy to learn Sir Frederic did indeed leave such an object the day he died. His dying gesture then, was to call our attention to the fact. He sought to present us with essential clue — what a man he was! I fondle the case lovingly, observing dust. Inside is no doubt very important information. But I do not desire to open it yet. I desire to set a trap. I have unlimited yearning to show Captain Flannery the man we have sought, standing by the cloak-room counter with this brief-case under his arm. Such evidence will be unanswerable.

'So I leave club, very happy. The affair has now pretty well unveiled itself. I have not yet discovered motives, but I am certain it was Major Durand who objected so murderously to the finding of his lost wife. He has not come to this country in answer to a cable from Sir Frederic. That is a lie. Sir Frederic did not want him. But he has learned, probably from the woman's uncle, that Sir Frederic is on point of revealing wife. For a reason still clouded in dark, he determines

357

this must not happen. He arrives in San Francisco same time as Sir Frederic. He locates great detective, learns of the office, watches his chance. To prevent detective from revealing wife, two things are necessary. He must destroy the records, and he must kill Sir Frederic. He decides to begin with records, and so on night of dinner party he forces his way into office, unseen by anybody. He is searching when Sir Frederic creeps in on the velvet slippers and surprises him. His opportunity has come, Sir Frederic is unarmed, he shoots him dead. But his task is only half completed, he hunts frantically for records. He does not find them. But he finds the check for the brief-case. He abstracts same, casts longing thought towards club, but does not dare. On the next train out he flees, the check burning in his pocket. If only he could return. In Chicago his great chance arrives.

'Building on all this, I set to-night my trap. And into it walks the man who killed Sir Frederic Bruce.'

Inspector Duff looked up. He appeared to have been reading and listening at the same time. 'Intelligence, hard work and luck,' he remarked. 'These three things contribute to the solution of a criminal case. And I may add that in my opinion, in this instance, the greatest of the trinity was intelligence.'

Chan bowed. 'A remark I shall treasure with jealous pride all my life.'

'Yes, it's pretty good,' admitted Flannery grudgingly. 'Very good. But it ain't complete. What about the velvet slippers? What about Hilary Galt? How is Galt's murder mixed up in all this?'

Chan grinned. 'I am not so hoggish. I leave a few points for Captain Flannery's keen mind.'

Flannery turned to Duff. 'Maybe it's in those records?'

'I've got only about half-way through,' Duff answered. 'There has been one mention of Hilary Galt. It says here that among the people who called at Galt's office on the day the solicitor was murdered was Eric Durand. Captain Eric Durand — that was his rank at the time. To discover the meaning of that, I shall have to read further.'

'Have you learned,' Chan inquired, 'this thing? Did Sir Frederic know which of the ladies we have suspicioned was Eve Durand?'

'Evidently he didn't. All he knew was that she was in the Kirk Building. He seemed to favour Miss Lila Barr.'

'Ah, yes. Was he aware how Eve Durand escaped from India?'

'He was, beyond question.'

'He knew she went by the caravan?'

'By the caravan, through Khyber Pass. In the company of Colonel John Beetham,' Duff nodded.

They all looked towards the Colonel sitting silent and aloof in the background. 'Is that true, Colonel Beetham?' Flannery asked.

The explorer bowed. 'I will not deny it longer. It is true.'

'Perhaps you know — '

'Whatever I know, I am not at liberty to tell.'

'If I make you — ' Flannery exploded.

'You can, of course, try. You will not succeed.'

The door opened, and Miss Morrow came quickly through the hall. With her came the elevator girl. Jennie Jerome? Marie Lantelme? Grace Lane? Whatever her name, she entered, and stood staring at Eric Durand.

'Eric!' she cried. 'What have you done? Oh — how could you — '

Durand raised his head and looked at her with bloodshot eyes. 'Go away from me,' he said dully. 'Go away. You've brought me nothing but trouble — always. Go away. I hate you.'

The woman backed off, frightened by the venom in his tone. Chan approached her.

'Pardon,' he said gently. 'Perhaps the news

has already reached you? It was this man Durand who killed Sir Frederic. Your husband — is that not true, Madam?'

She dropped into a chair and covered her face. 'Yes,' she sobbed. 'My husband.'

'You are indeed Eve Durand?'

'Y — yes.'

Charlie looked grimly at Flannery. 'Now the truth arrives,' he said. 'That you once listened to a Chinaman is, after all, no lasting disgrace.'

21

What Happened to Eve Durand

Flannery turned fiercely on Eve Durand. 'Then you've known all along?' he cried. 'You knew the Major had been here before — you saw him that night he did for Sir Frederic — '

'No, no,' she protested. 'I didn't see, him — I never dreamed of such a thing. And if he knew I was in the building that night, he took good care to keep out of my way. For if I had seen him — if I had known — it would have been the final straw. I'd have told. I'd have told the whole story at once.'

Flannery grew calmer. 'Well, let's go back. You're Eve Durand — you admit it at last. Fifteen years ago you ran away from your husband in Peshawar. You went with the caravan of Colonel Beetham here — '

The woman looked up, startled, and for the first time saw the explorer. 'That's all true,' she said softly. 'I went with Colonel Beetham.'

'Ran away with another man — deserted your husband? Why? In love with the Colonel — ?'

'No!' Her eyes flashed. 'You mustn't think that. Colonel Beetham did a very kind act — an indiscreet act — and he shall not suffer for it. Long ago, I made up my mind to that.'

'Please, Eve,' said the Colonel. 'I shan't suffer. Don't tell your story on my account.'

'That's like you,' she answered. 'But I insist. I said if I was ever found, I'd tell everything. And after what Eric has done now — it doesn't matter any longer. Oh, I shall be so relieved to tell the whole terrible thing at last.'

She turned to Flannery. 'I shall have to go back. I was brought up in Devonshire by my uncle and aunt — my parents had died. I wasn't very happy. My uncle had old-fashioned ideas. He meant well, he was kind, but somehow we just didn't get along. Then I met Eric — he was a romantic figure — I adored him. I was only seventeen. On my eighteenth birthday we were married. He was assigned to a regiment stationed in Peshawar, and I went with him.

'Even before we reached India, I began to regret what I had done. I was sorry I hadn't listened to my uncle — he never approved of the match. Under his dashing manner I found that Eric was mean and cheap. He was a gambler, he drank too much. His real character appalled me — he was coarse and brutal, and a cheat.

'Soon after our arrival at Peshawar, letters began to come from London — letters in dirty envelopes, the address written in an uncultivated hand. They seemed to enrage my husband; he wasn't fit to associate with after their appearance. I was puzzled and alarmed. On a certain day — the day of the picnic, it was — one of those letters was put in my hand during Eric's absence. By that time I was desperate. I knew only too well the outburst that would come when he saw it. I hesitated for a while. Finally I tore it open and read it.

'What I read wrecked my life for ever. It was from a porter in an office building in London. It said he must have more money — at once. It didn't hint — it spoke openly. Everything was all too plain. Eric — my husband — was being blackmailed by the porter. He was paying money to keep the man quiet. If he didn't, the porter threatened to reveal the fact that he had seen Eric leaving a London office one night a year previously. Leaving an office on the floor of which lay Hilary Galt, the solicitor, with a bullet in his head.'

Eve Durand paused, and continued with an effort. 'My husband, then, was being blackmailed for the murder of Hilary Galt. He came home presently, in rather a genial mood — for him. I said: 'I am leaving you at once.' He wanted to know why, and I gave him the opened letter.

'His face went grey, and he collapsed. Presently he was on his knees, grovelling at my feet, pleading with me. Without my asking for it, he gave me the whole terrible story. Hilary Galt and my uncle, Sir George Mannering, were old friends. On the morning of that awful day, the solicitor had sent for Eric and told him that if he persisted in his intention of marrying me, he — Mr. Galt, I mean — would go to my uncle with the story of certain unsavoury happenings in Eric's past. Eric had listened, and left the office. That night he had gone back and killed Hilary Galt, and the porter had seen him coming away.

'He did it for love of me, he said. Because he must have me — because he was determined nothing should stand in his way. I must forgive him — '

'Pardon,' put in Chan. 'Did he, in that unhappy moment, mention a pair of velvet slippers?'

'He did. After — after he had killed Mr. Galt, he saw the slippers lying on a chair. He knew that Scotland Yard always looks for an essential clue, and he resolved to furnish one. One that meant nothing, one that would point away from him. So he tore off Hilary Galt's shoes and substituted the slippers. He was rather proud of it, I think. Oh, he was always clever, in that mean way of his. He boasted of what he had done, of how he had thrown Scotland Yard off the scent. Then he was pleading again — he had done it for me — I must not tell. I couldn't tell. I was his wife — no one could make me tell. Heaven knows, I had no desire to tell, all I wanted was to get away from him. I said again that I was going. 'I'll kill you first,' he answered, and he meant it.

'So I went on that picnic, with my life all in pieces, frantic, insane with grief and fear. Colonel Beetham was there — I had met him once before — a fine man, a gentleman, all that Eric was not. He was leaving in the morning — it came to me in a flash. He must take me with him. I suggested the game of hide-and-seek — I had already asked the Colonel to meet me in a certain spot. He came — I made him promise never to tell — and I explained to him the horrible position I was in. If I tried to leave openly I was afraid — I was sure — Eric would carry out his threat. Colonel Beetham was wonderful. He arranged everything. I hid in the hills all night. He came with Li Gung in the wagon at dawn — he had added it to his caravan, intending to abandon it when we got through the Pass. I rode out hidden in that, and beyond the Khyber there began for me the most wonderful adventure a woman ever had. Eight months through that wild country on a camel — the stars at night, the dust storms, the desert stretching empty but mysterious as far as the eye could see. Outside Teheran I left the caravan and got to Baku alone. From there I went to Italy. Eight months had passed, as I say, and the hue and cry had died down.

'But now I realized what I had done. Colonel Beetham was a hero, he was honoured everywhere. What if it became known how I had left India? No journey could ever have been more innocent, but this is a cynical world. Doing a kind act, a gallant act, Colonel Beetham had put himself in the position, in the world's eyes, of running away with another man's wife. If it became known, the Colonel's splendid career would be wrecked. It must never become known. I made up my mind I would see to that.'

'And you have,' remarked Beetham softly. 'Gentlemen, you have just heard what I did referred to as a gallant act. But it was as nothing compared with Eve Durand's gallantry ever since.'

'First of all,' the woman went on, 'I wrote a

letter to Eric. I told him he must never try to find me — for his own sake. I said that if I was found, if the story came out of how I had left India, I would not hesitate a moment. I would clear Colonel Beetham's name at once by a clear account of why I had gone. I would say I left because I discovered my husband was a murderer. Eric didn't answer, but he must have received the letter. He never tried to find me after that. He did not want anyone else to find me — as he has recently proved to you.'

She paused. 'That is about all. I — I have had rather a hard struggle of it. I sold my jewellery and lived on the proceeds for a time. Then I went to Nice, and under the name of Marie Lantelme, I got a place in the opera company. There, for the first time, I realized that another man was on my trail — a man who would never give up. Sir Frederic Bruce of Scotland Yard, in charge of the Hilary Galt case. He knew that Eric had visited Galt's office the day of the murder, and when he read of my disappearance in India, he must have sensed a connexion. One night when I came from the theatre in Nice, an Inspector from Scotland Yard stopped me on the Promenade des Anglais. 'You are Eve Durand,' he said. I denied it, got away from him, managed to reach Marseilles.

From there I went to New York. I changed my appearance as much as I could — the colour of my hair — and under the name of Jennie Jerome, secured a position as a model. Again Scotland Yard was on my track. I had to disappear in the night. Eventually I arrived in San Francisco, desperate, penniless. On a ferry I met Helen Tupper-Brock, who had lived near us in Devonshire. She has been so kind — she got me my position here. I was happy again, until Sir Frederic Bruce came, still following that old trail.'

Durand got slowly to his feet. 'I hope you're satisfied,' he said thickly.

'Oh, Eric — '

'You've done for me. You ought to be satisfied now.' His eyes flamed red. 'You've saved the spotless reputation of your damned Sir Galahad — '

'You're going to confess?' cried Flannery.

Durand shrugged his shoulders hopelessly. 'Why not? What else is left?' He turned his blazing eyes on Charlie Chan. 'Everything this devil said was true. I admire him for it. I thought I was clever. But he's beat me — ' His voice rose hysterically. 'I killed Sir Frederic. Why shouldn't I? It was the only way. He stood there grinning at me. My God — what a man! He wouldn't give up. He wouldn't call quits. Sixteen years, and he was

369

still at my heels. Sixteen years, and he wouldn't forget. Yes, I killed him — '

'And the velvet slippers?' Chan inquired softly.

'On his feet. The same old velvet slippers I'd left in that office, long ago. I saw them just after I fired, and then my nerve went. It was like a judgment — my trade-mark — on the feet of Sir Frederic — pointing to me. I snatched them off — took them with me. I — I didn't know what to do with them. My nerve was gone — but I'd killed him first. Yes — I killed him. And I'm ready to pay. But not in the way you think.'

Suddenly he wheeled about and crashed through the french window into the garden of Kirk's roof-flat.

'The fire-escape,' Flannery shouted. 'Head him off — '

The Captain, Duff and Chan were close behind. Charlie ran to the fire-escape at the left. But it was not that for which Eric Durand was headed to-night. He leaped to the rail that enclosed the garden; for an instant his big figure poised, a dark silhouette against the misty sky. Then silently it disappeared.

They ran to the rail and looked down. Far below, in the dim light of a street lamp, they saw a black, huddled heap. A crowd was gathering around it.

22

Hawaii Bound

Their pursuit so tragically ended, the three men came slowly back into the living-room.

'Well,' said Flannery, 'that's the end of him.'

'Escaped?' Miss Morrow cried.

'From this world,' nodded the Captain. Eve Durand gave a little cry. Miss Morrow put an arm about her. 'There's work for me below,' added Flannery, and went quickly out.

'We'd better go home, my dear,' said Miss Morrow gently. She and Eve Durand went to the hall. Kirk followed and opened the door for them. There was much he wanted to say, but under the circumstances silence seemed the only possible course.

'I can get my car,' he suggested.

'No, thanks,' answered Miss Morrow. 'We'll find a taxi.'

'Good night,' he said gravely. 'I shall hope to see you soon.'

When he returned to the living-room, Colonel Beetham was speaking. 'Nothing in his life became him like the leaving it. What a washout that life was! Poor Major.'

Duff was calmly filling his pipe, unperturbed as a Chinese. 'By the way,' he drawled, 'I had a cable about him this morning. He was dishonourably discharged from the British Army ten years ago. So his right to the title may be questioned. But no doubt you knew that, Colonel Beetham?'

'I did,' Beetham replied.

'You knew so much,' Duff continued. 'So much you weren't telling. What were you doing on the floor below that Tuesday night?'

'Precisely what I told Flannery I was doing. I ran down to inform Li Gung that he needn't wait.'

'I didn't know but what you'd gone down for a chat with Eve Durand?'

The Colonel shook his head. 'No — I'd had my chat with Eve. You see, I'd located her several days before the dinner party. After losing track of her for ten years, I came to San Francisco on a rumour she was here. My errand on the floor below was with Li Gung, as I said it was.'

'And the next day you shipped him off to Honolulu?'

'I did, yes. At Eve's request. I'd arranged that two days before. She heard Sir Frederic was interested in him, and she was afraid something might happen to wreck my next expedition. The thing was unnecessary, Li

Gung would never have told, but to set her mind at rest, I did as she asked.'

Duff looked at him with open disapproval. 'You knew that Durand had committed one murder. Yet you said nothing to the police. Was that playing the game, Colonel Beetham?'

Beetham shrugged. 'Yes, I think it was. I'm sure of it. I did not dream that Durand had been in San Francisco the night of Sir Frederic's murder. Even if I had known he was here — well — you see — '

'I'm afraid I don't,' snapped Duff.

'There is really no reason why I need explain to you,' Beetham went on. 'However, I will. Something happened on that long trek across Afghanistan and the Kevir Desert. Eve was so brave, so uncomplaining. I — I fell in love. For the first and last time. What she has done since — for me — damn it, man, I worship her. But I have never told her so — I do not know whether she cares for me or not. While Durand lived, he was my rival, in a way. If I had given him up — what would my motive have been? I couldn't have been quite sure myself. I did suggest that Eve tell her story, but I didn't press the point. I couldn't, you see. I had to leave the decision to her. When she escaped that night from Flannery's men, I helped her. If that was what she wanted, I was forced to agree. Yes, Inspector

— I was playing the game, according to my lights.'

Duff shrugged. 'A nice sense of honour,' he remarked. 'However, I will go so far as to wish you luck.'

'Thanks,' returned Beetham. He took up his coat. 'I may say that, no doubt from selfish motives, I was keen to have you get him. And Sergeant Chan here saw to it that I was not disappointed. Sergeant, my hearty congratulations. But I know your people — and I am not surprised.'

Chan bowed. 'For ever with me your words will remain, lasting and beautiful as flowers of jade.'

'I will go along,' said Beetham, and departed.

Duff took up Sir Frederic's brief-case. 'Perhaps you would like to look at these records, Sergeant,' he remarked.

Chan came to with a start. 'Pardon my stupidity.'

'I said — maybe you want to glance at Sir Frederic's records?'

Charlie shook his head. 'Curiosity is all quenched, like fire in pouring rain. We have looked at last behind that curtain Sir Frederic pictured, and I am content. At the moment I was indulging in bitter thought. There is no boat to Honolulu until next Wednesday. Five terrible days.'

Duff laughed. 'Well, I've been through the records hastily,' he went on. 'Sir Frederic had talked with certain friends of that porter in London. But the man himself had died before the Yard heard about him, and the evidence of his associates was hazy — hardly the sort to stand up in the courts. It needed the corroboration of Eve Durand, and that was what Sir Frederic was determined to get at any cost.'

'How did Sir Frederic know that Eve Durand was in San Francisco?' Barry Kirk inquired.

'He got that information from a letter written by Mrs. Tupper-Brock to an aunt in Shanghai. There is a copy of the letter here. In it, Mrs. Tupper-Brock mentioned that Eve Durand was in this city, employed in the Kirk Building. All of which explains his eagerness to make his headquarters with you, Mr. Kirk. But he hadn't located her — he died without that satisfaction, poor chap. His choice was Miss Lila Barr. He didn't dare say anything to Mrs. Tupper-Brock, for fear Eve Durand would slip through his fingers again. On the night of the dinner he was setting a trap — the desk unlocked, the safe open. He rather hoped someone would creep in for a look around. That and the chance of identifying Jennie Jerome, or Marie Lantelme

— on these things he placed his reliance.'

'He would have won, if he had lived,' Chan remarked.

'No doubt of it. In Peshawar he established to his own satisfaction the manner in which Eve had left India. When he found her, he would have told her what he knew, and she would have related her story, just as she did here to-night. His long search for the murderer of Hilary Galt would have ended then and there. Poor Sir Frederic.' Duff picked up his coat, and Kirk helped him. 'I'll take the brief-case,' the Inspector continued. 'It will be useful at the Yard.' He held out his hand. 'Sergeant Chan, meeting you would alone have repaid me for my long journey. Come to London some day. I'll show you how we work over there.'

Chan smiled. 'You are too kind. But the postman on his holiday has walked until feet are aching. Free to remark that if he ever takes another vacation, same will be forced on him at point of plenty big gun.'

'I don't wonder,' replied Duff. 'Mr. Kirk — a pleasure to know you, too. Good-bye and good luck to you both.'

Kirk let him out. When he returned, Charlie was standing at the window, staring down on the roofs of the city. He swung about. 'Now I go and pack.'

'But you've five days for that,' Kirk protested.

Charlie shook his head. 'The guest who lingers too long deteriorates like unused fish. You have been so good — more would make me uncomfortable. I remove my presence at once.'

'Oh, no,' Kirk cried. 'Good old Paradise will serve dinner in a few minutes.'

'Please,' Chan said, 'permit me the luxury of at last beginning to mean what I say.'

He went into his bedroom and in a surprisingly brief time returned. 'Luggage was pretty much ready,' he explained. He glanced towards the window. 'Bright moon shines tonight in Honolulu. I am thinking of those home nights — long ones with long talks, long sipping of tea, long sleep and long peaceful dreams.' He went to the hall, where he had left his coat and hat. 'I am wondering how to make words of the deep thanks I feel,' he said, returning. 'Faced with kindness such as yours — '

The door-bell rang, a sharp, insistent peal. Charlie stepped into the bedroom. Kirk opened the door, and Bill Rankin, the reporter, rushed in.

'Where's Charlie Chan?' he demanded breathlessly.

'He's gone into his room,' Kirk answered. 'He'll be out in a minute.'

'I want to thank him,' Rankin continued loudly. 'He sure treated me like a prince. I beat the town. And I've news for him — a woman has just been murdered over in Oakland under the most peculiar circumstances. There are all sorts of bully clues — and since he can't leave until next week — ' Kirk laughed. 'You tell him,' he suggested.

They waited a moment, then Kirk went into the bedroom. He cried out in surprise. The room was empty. A door leading to the passage stood open. He stepped through it, and discovered that the door at the top of the stairs leading to the offices was also ajar.

'Rankin,' he called. 'Come here, please.'

Rankin came. 'Why — where is he — '

Kirk preceded the reporter downstairs. The offices were in darkness. In the middle room, Kirk switched on the light. After a hurried glance around, he pointed to the window that opened on to the fire-escape. It had been pushed up as far as it would go.

'The postman,' Kirk remarked, 'absolutely refuses to take another walk.'

'Done an Eve Durand on us!' Rankin cried. 'Well, I'll be doggoned.'

Kirk laughed. 'It's all right,' he said. 'I'll know where to find him — next Wednesday noon.'

Intent on verifying this prediction, Barry

Kirk appeared in Miss Morrow's dusty office the following Wednesday morning at eleven. He had stopped at a florist's and bought an extravagant cluster of orchids. These he handed to the deputy district attorney.

'What's the idea?' she asked.

'Come on,' he said. 'The morning's as bright as a new gold piece, and down at the docks there's a ship about to set out for the loveliest fleet of islands in any ocean. The flowers are my *bon voyage* offering to you.'

'But I'm not sailing,' she protested.

'We'll pretend you are. You're going as far as the pier, anyhow. Get your hat.'

'Of course.' She got it, and they went down the dark stairs.

'Have you heard anything from Charlie Chan?' she asked.

'Not a word,' Kirk told her. 'Charlie isn't taking any chances. But we'll find him aboard the boat. I'd gamble all I've got on that.'

They entered his car, and Kirk stepped on the gas. 'What a morning,' he remarked. 'Cooped up in that dark office of yours, you've no idea the things that are going on outside. Lady — Spring is here!'

'So it seems. By the way — you know that Colonel Beetham sailed last night for China?'

'Yes. What about Eve Durand?'

'She's starting to-morrow for England. Her

uncle has cabled her to come and stop with him. The Colonel is to be in the Gobi Desert for a year, and then he's going to England too. It will be Spring in Devonshire when he arrives. A very lovely Spring, they seem to think.'

Kirk nodded. 'But a year away. Too bad — so long to wait. Enjoy the Spring you've got. That would be my advice.'

He steered his car on to the pier. Another sailing day — excitement and farewells. Tourists and travelling salesmen, bored stewards waiting patiently in line.

Miss Morrow and Kirk ran up the gangplank on to the deck of the big white ship. 'Just stand here by the rail, please,' said Kirk. 'With the orchids — '

'What in the world for?'

'I want to see how you'll look in the role. Back in a minute.'

When he returned, Charlie Chan was walking lightly at his side. The detective's face was beaming with a satisfaction he could not conceal.

'Overwhelmed by your attention,' he said to the girl.

'Where have you been?' she cried. 'We've missed you terribly.'

He grinned. 'Hiding from temptation,' he explained.

'But Captain Flannery has taken all the credit for your wonderful success. It isn't fair.'

Chan shrugged. 'From the first, I knew my work on this case was like bowing in the dark. Why should I care? May I add that you present charming picture of loveliness this morning?'

'What does she look like to you, Charlie?' Kirk inquired. 'Standing there by the rail with those flowers?'

'A bride,' answered Chan promptly, as one who had been coached. 'A bride who sails for honeymoon in pleasant company of newly-captured husband.'

'Precisely,' Kirk agreed. 'She's rehearsing the part, you know.'

'The first I've heard of it,' objected Miss Morrow.

'Wise man has said: 'The beautiful bird gets caged,'' Chan told her. 'You could not hope to escape.'

The girl handed him a little package. 'This is for — the other Barry — with my love.'

'My warmest thanks. He will be proud boy. But you will not give him all your love. You will not overlook original of same name. Chinese are psychic people, and I have sensed it. Am I right? My precious reputation hangs shaking on your answer.'

Miss Morrow smiled. 'I'm very much

afraid — you're always right.'

'Now this is truly my happiest day,' Chan told her.

'Mine too,' cried Kirk. He took an envelope from his pocket. 'That being arranged, I also have something for little Barry. Give it to him with my warm regards.'

Chan accepted the envelope, heavy with gold pieces. 'My heart flows over,' he said. 'Small son will express thanks in person when you arrive in Honolulu thrilled with the high delight of honeymoon.'

'Then he'll have to learn to talk mighty soon,' Kirk answered. 'But with a father like you — '

The final call of 'visitors ashore' was sounding. They shook hands with Charlie and ran. At the top of the gangplank they were engulfed in a very frenzy of farewell. Mad embraces, hasty kisses, final promises and admonitions. Kirk leaned quickly over and kissed Miss Morrow.

'Oh — how could you!' she cried.

'Pardon me. I was still pretending you were going too.'

'But I'm not. Neither are you.'

'No one will notice in this mêlée. Come on.'

They descended to the pier, and ran along it until they stood opposite Charlie Chan.

The detective had procured a roll of bright pink paper, and holding fast to one end, he tossed it to the girl.

Kirk smiled happily. 'If anyone had told me two weeks ago I was going to kiss a lawyer — and like it — ' He was interrupted by the hoarse cry of the ship's siren.

Slowly the vessel drew away from the pier. The pink streamer broke, its ends trailing in the water. Charlie leaned far over the rail.

'Aloha,' he called. 'Until we meet again.' His fat face shone with joy. The big ship paused, trembled, and set out for Hawaii.

We do hope that you have enjoyed reading this large print book.

Did you know that all of our titles are available for purchase?

We publish a wide range of high quality large print books including:
**Romances, Mysteries, Classics
General Fiction
Non Fiction and Westerns**

Special interest titles available in large print are:
**The Little Oxford Dictionary
Music Book
Song Book
Hymn Book
Service Book**

Also available from us courtesy of Oxford University Press:
**Young Readers' Dictionary
(large print edition)
Young Readers' Thesaurus
(large print edition)**

For further information or a free brochure, please contact us at:
**Ulverscroft Large Print Books Ltd.,
The Green, Bradgate Road, Anstey,
Leicester, LE7 7FU, England.
Tel:** (00 44) 0116 236 4325
Fax: (00 44) 0116 234 0205